The Road to Wanting

Wendy Law-Yone

Chatto & Windus
LONDON

Published by Chatto & Windus 2010

2 4 6 8 10 9 7 5 3 1

First published in Great Britain in 2010 by
Chatto & Windus
Random House, 20 Vauxhall Bridge Road,
London SW1V 2SA

www.rbooks.co.uk

Addresses for companies within The Random House Group Limited
can be found at: www.randomhouse.co.uk/offices.htm

The Random House Group Limited Reg. No. 954009

A CIP catalogue record for this book
is available from the British Library

ISBN 9780701184087

The Random House Group Limited supports The Forest Stewardship
Council (FSC), the leading international forest certification organisation.
All our titles that are printed on Greenpeace approved FSC certified
paper carry the FSC logo. Our paper procurement policy can be found at
www.rbooks.co.uk/environment

Mixed Sources
Product group from well-managed
forests and other controlled sources
www.fsc.org Cert no. TT-COC-2139
© 1996 Forest Stewardship Council

Typeset in AGaramond by Palimpsest Book Production Limited,
Grangemouth, Stirlingshire
Printed and bound in Great Britain by
CPI Mackays, Chatham ME5 8TD

CENTRAL LIBRARY

ALSO BY WENDY LAW-YONE

The Coffin Tree
Irrawaddy Tango

For Tinker, Sean, Chad & Bess

one

Ready at last. I am not afraid. My hands are steady. My breath is even. My hair is clean after the wash in the salon, and smells of overripe melon. Everything is in order; nothing stands in the way. Nothing, except—

I'm not as prepared as I should be. For example, I don't have a rope. I blame this entirely on Mr Jiang. If he hadn't been all over me like a fly on dung, I would have bought myself one by now. A good, sturdy length of nylon or jute. Never mind, I'll make do somehow.

On the floor by the bathroom door lies my open suitcase. Nearly a week in this godforsaken place and I still haven't unpacked. Straight away I find the *longyi* I need, the cheap Thai cotton that will tear without much resistance.

The *longyi* is a wonderful garment. A simple tube of fabric, you tie it around your waist to wear it as a skirt – or around your chest, like a towel after bathing. You can shower in it, swim in it, change in it discreetly while out in the open, as behind a dressing-room screen. Something else you can do with a *longyi*: if you grip it by the seam right under your chin, and fling your arms out to rip it open, what you have is a strip of cloth, two yards long, forty-five inches wide. If you keep on ripping – lengthwise now, from end to end – you'll soon have half a dozen strips. Plait these strips together, knotting them at intervals for extra strength . . .

I

And that's how I come by a good long rope. Colourful too, as it happens.

I can just about reach the grille on that absurdly high window, but I see it isn't going to be easy. The ledge is some seven feet from the floor, and I am five feet four.

I've never seen such an oddly placed window before, but then I've never been in a Chinese hotel before, let alone a Chinese hotel in a frontier town. It's the way of the frontier, for all I know, to model guest-houses on prison plans: bare walls, blotchy ceilings, high windows with bars. On these bars I pin all my hopes.

The inspiration comes to me from the window itself, from watching the sunset through the pane. If I stare long enough, I can erase the sky with its reddish-gold tints and conjure in its place a reddish-gold sea. Soon the clouds start to form a whole new seascape: of large and small islands, breakers and beaches. A golden archipelago is what I see now, afloat on a fiery ocean.

Marvellous! Breathtaking! If only I could keep up the trick! But everything fades soon enough – the sky, the sea, the sorcery at the window. And I am back in my true position, behind bars so to speak.

But it's from staring at the sunset that I've come to see the window in a different way. I see those bars now as a means of escape. If only they were a foot or so lower, though! In trying to secure my rope to them, I keep having to stop and rest. My uplifted arms are soon overtaxed, leaving me light-headed and queasy. Again and again I palm the wall, butting my head against it for balance. The cool plaster is instantly soothing.

I reach for the high window grille once more, keeping my head down while feeling my way through the looping and tying. It would help if I had something to stand on – a chair, a box, anything. But the only solid piece of furniture, apart from the bed, is the sofa by the corner; and it's much too heavy to drag across the carpet. The bamboo bedside table is of no use either. It sags under the weight of a puny brown lamp, a ceramic jar with a plastic shade in which the light-bulb is slowly burning a hole.

Success. I finally have the knot where I want it. Now I must fiddle with the dangling end, and this part is tricky as well. The rope must be long enough, while I'm on my feet, to wind round my neck – but short enough to hang from, once my knees are lifted.

There. I think I've done it. Looped the loop at just the right position. It remains only to stand on tiptoe for the lasso to fall into place. But the minute the noose cinches my wind-pipe, the unexpected happens. I'm seized by a cramp – a charley horse, I think they call it – the kind that attacks the calf muscles and paralyses a leg. This charley horse has me by the neck. I can't move. I can't see. And I'm about to fall into the deepest, blackest pit.

So this is what it's like. This is it – the dreaded and desired end. But it's not what I desire, not at all what I planned. I want to stop. Step back from the pit. Walk away. But how to walk when every muscle in every limb has lost all sen-sation? Then something stirs and trembles in the lower regions. Something starts to convulse down deep. My cunt, what do you know, is protesting.

I can think of only one way to break a spell of this nature, and that is to let out a war-cry. *Do it!* I yell. *Do it!* For the feet to leave the floor, the knees must co-operate. But the knees are simply refusing. *Do it!* I insist, in a tantrum. With a surge of will I never knew I possessed, I get them to rise in obedience.

In that moment of conquest there's a banging at the door.

Down come these legs by eager reflex: I'm back on my feet with the rope still round my neck. Who on earth can be needing me so urgently? The banging continues, feeble but desperate, like a child wanting in. Then there's a cry. 'Mr Jiang . . . Mr Jiang . . .'

It's the girl from the reception desk. She sounds as if she's having an asthma attack.

Frantic to free myself of this insufferable noose, I manage to call out: 'No Mr Jiang! Mr Jiang not here!'

'Open the door! I must tell you! Mr Jiang . . .'

'What is it?' I shout.

'Mr Jiang . . . he kill himself!'

two

I waited too long. I knew from the start that I would never be able to make it across the border, never want even to try. Still I waited. I knew it back in Bangkok, on the day Will came to tell me it was all over.

From under the flap of his new leather briefcase he brought out a note pad. In the ten years we'd been together, I'd seldom seen him leave the house without stuffing a couple of three-by-five cards into his shirt pocket. At night when I emptied his pockets those cards would be filled with lists, phone numbers, diagrams or just doodles. But the note pad was something new – like the leather briefcase, like the way his eyes avoided mine.

'So here's the game-plan,' he said, leaning forward in his seat and flipping the pad to a fresh page. He set it on the coffee-table to sketch, and for a moment I hoped that what lay ahead was just a game. But then I saw what he was drawing and my heart sank. His outline of northern Burma was quick and sure and, to my mind, accurate. I recognised the jagged borders, so like the edges of a flame: one flame licking India to the north-west, another blowing north-east, into China. On the top right-hand quarter, well over on the Chinese side, he drew a small circle. 'You'll fly here, to Kunming,' he said.

'Kunming?'

'Yes, Kunming. That's the capital of Yunnan.'

As if I didn't know where Kunming was. It was all he'd talked about for the past year: Kunming – an old Chinese city modernised overnight in the new economic boom. Yunnan – the rough and remote south-west, now open to tourism and trade. Kunming this, Yunnan that. I'd heard it all.

'In Kunming, someone will meet you and put you on the bus,' he was saying. 'You'll take the old road.'

The old road. I'd had an earful of that too. The old Burma Road had been closed for half a century, but now it was humming with trucks bearing Chinese arms and illegal immigrants in one direction, Burmese teak and heroin in the other. This great Smugglers' Highway, as Will called it, began in Kunming and cut across the mountains of Yunnan, all the way to the Burmese frontier. And Yunnan Province, as it happened, was the untapped frontier of China's south-west, rich in natural resources, ripe for development. The old road served many purposes.

In the past, whenever Will had mentioned the Burma Road I had put it down to his fascination with forbidden or un-explored places – like the blank swathes on his old army intelligence maps, marked 'RELIEF TERRITORY INCOMPLETE', or 'BOUNDARY ONLY APPROXIMATE'. I never could understand his yearning for unmapped regions; surely they remained blank for good reasons. He once showed me a book of ancient charts with illustrations of dragons over certain landmasses. 'Here be dragons,' he said, explaining that this was the way map-makers of old marked unknown regions. I used to think the Burma Road represented one of those dragons for him, but I could see now that his interest had lain elsewhere: he'd been thinking of putting me on it.

'Three days on the bus along the old road,' he went on, 'and you'll be at the border. On the Chinese side. The town

6

is called Wanting, the end of the line.' He drew another dot and next to it wrote, 'WANTING', in his lanky script. 'Damn, I wish I had a felt-tip,' he said. 'But wait a minute. Mole has one here, I've seen it.'

Mole was the friend who had agreed to have me to stay. A nice man, English, and kind to a fault. He must have known what Will had in store for me. When he left the house that morning, saying he'd be gone all weekend (so as not to be in the way), I'd thought he might cry.

Will went inside to look for the pen, leaving me in the glass room that Mole called the conservatory. His was the only house boasting a conservatory in that neighbourhood reserved for diplomats and rich foreign residents. 'It's not a conservatory,' Will had insisted, in one of his many mock-arguments with Mole. 'It's a folly.' A room so exposed was an open invitation to prowlers and burglars. All the other houses, boxy brick buildings with air-conditioning units plugging up the small windows, were sensibly gated and walled off from the world outside. But Mole had charmed his British-educated Thai landlady into adding the impractical glass extension, and even into furnishing it stylishly. The low wicker chairs had high backs, round and ornate like peacocks' tails, with thick cotton cushions in a peacock blue print.

The conservatory was Mole's favourite room now: he liked to smoke his Cuban cigars there, even though all that glass made it a furnace, impossible to sit in without the windows cranked open and the ceiling fan going at top speed. When it rained and the windows needed shutting, the noisy air-conditioner had to be turned to high. It was raining hard that evening. The air-conditioner was chugging like a run-down locomotive.

So it was finally happening. Will was sending me away.

Maybe not, though. Maybe the pen was just an excuse to go inside and pour himself a drink. Anything was possible once Will had a drink in his hand. His mood could change. My fate could change.

But there was no glass in his hand when he came back. Only the pen. He returned to his map and drew a line west, then south, from Kunming to the border of Burma. 'That's your route, right there.' He went on adding all kinds of unnecessary finishing touches: darkening lines, shading in areas. Then he printed 'MYANMAR' in parentheses next to 'BURMA' – as if I didn't know my country's new name. In smaller print he filled in the names of the ethnic regions to the east – 'CHIN, KACHIN, SHAN' – and, in tiny letters, 'LU'. 'Your homeland . . .' He kept tapping that last spot until it was heavily pocked. '. . . begin to imagine what you'll find there . . .'

I couldn't think any more with the ruckus around me. The rain was hammering on the roof, the air-conditioner was roaring, the bucket by my side kept up a steady plink from the leak in the ceiling. The map was a chicken scrawl, mere scratchings in the dirt. I snapped out of my daze when I heard Will say, 'You mustn't worry, Na Ga. My old buddy Yan Ding is setting it all up.'

I couldn't believe it. Yan Ding, the Yunnanese billionaire with homes in Bangkok, Hong Kong, New York and Kunming; the man to whom just about anyone interested in the drug trade went for help or advice – students, journalists, government agents, the leading drug lords, even. Will was actually calling on a powerhouse like Yan Ding to help remove me.

'He's known as the Prince of Yunnan.' Will was chuckling now, diverted by a fond recollection. 'His family *owned* Yunnan province before the Communists took over. But the guy has friends *everywhere*, in every government and opposition group in the region. If anyone can get you back home without a hitch, it's him. He'll have someone meet you in Kunming and put you on the bus. In Wanting, a guy called Jiang, his right-hand man at the border, will get you all the papers you need. He'll make sure you have protection all the way.' Will leaned back in his chair and looked me in the eye at last – in that haughty way he had of tilting his head back to look down his nose. 'Any questions?'

You're afraid of me, I thought. And I'm so afraid of you, my teeth are chattering.

'You cold?' He jumped up to turn off the air-conditioner. It gave him something to do now that he'd finished with the map. 'I know what you're thinking,' he said, still standing. 'You're thinking, "Why don't I just fly?"'

The thought had crossed my mind. Why such a round-about route, when I had a passport, after all – a valid Thai passport, thanks to Will.

'Things aren't that simple!' With the air-conditioner switched off he sounded loud and threatening. 'You'd have to fly to Rangoon. And with a foreign passport you'd never be allowed up-country – especially not to a problem area like Special Zone B.'

He was packing his things. He was leaving. The notebook was back in the briefcase. He'd ripped the map out and laid it on the coffee-table. All the while he was pretending not to be in any great hurry. I was eye-level with his belt-buckle. I'd bought that belt for him just weeks ago, at the Jatujak weekend market: good leather, black on one side, brown on the other. You changed the colour simply by twisting the buckle. Maybe it meant he wasn't throwing out everything I'd given him, that he had found a few things worth keeping.

'Nooo,' he said, making himself sound playful. 'Nooo, you want to go through China. Through Wanting. It's the closest border point to the Lu state. They're not as strict at the checkpoints there. A day's walk, once you're across, and you're home safe.'

Will's hand was on the door. I had a mind to throw myself against it, knock him out of the way, and lock it until we'd settled things properly – not in this false-casual fashion. But surely there was still a chance he'd turn around and say, 'Boo! Fooled ya! Didn't think I'd let you go like this, did you? What do you take me for, a jerk?' I had to keep reminding myself that this man who'd saved my life and put me on my feet – this man whose bed I'd shared for some ten years, whose rigid back I was now facing – was not a jerk. Just a stranger. A stranger I'd made a life with.

I watched him step out onto the portico and take a deep breath of air, like a prisoner just released who drinks in his freedom. The filthy rain was still going strong, but you would have thought he was basking in sunshine.

I did throw myself against the door – but only after he'd shut it behind him and driven away in his Toyota Camry, the opaque windows sliding up immediately. I pounded on that front door as though he'd locked me in, till my fists were numb and swollen.

Then I sank to the floor, defeated. *You want to go through China . . . That's the way you want to go . . . that's the way you want to go . . .* I mocked him between clenched teeth, in a sobbing fury.

But, in the end, that was the way I went.

three

The girl from the front desk has asked me to stay.

Did she mean I shouldn't worry about the hotel bill? But I'm paid up till the end of the week: Jiang saw to that, as he saw to everything else – duty-bound to the last, poor man. Or was she saying I should stay even longer, now that my escort to the border has gone and shot himself?

Still rubbing the noose-burn on my neck, I unlocked the door – and there she was, a little rag doll in her funny patchwork capris, hugging herself in the dim light of the hallway.

'Mr Jiang?' I was having trouble taking it all in. 'Killed himself? But how?' What I meant, of course, was not *how* but *why*.

The girl shocked me by crooking a forefinger at her temple, squeezing her eyes and lips shut, and holding it there for a long moment. Then she pulled the imaginary trigger. The blast sent her staggering. 'Blood!' she wailed, waving her hand to indicate the walls, the ceiling, the floor. 'Blood – and – and – what-what . . .'

She covered her face and was sobbing into her palms when the man downstairs, the one who works with her on Reception, began yelling out a complicated demand. Taking a deep breath, she let go of her face and shot back a longish question of her own. I couldn't understand a word they were screaming at each other, but it sounded as if the guy was now threatening violence. Of course, he might have been asking the girl where she had left the salt, or the keys to the front door. When the Chinese shout at each other, you have no way of knowing whether it's a life-or-death contest or a ho-hum discussion.

The girl's eyes were puffy from crying; her tiny nostrils were still streaming. She pulled herself together, wiping the tip of her nylon sleeve across her nose, and gave me a wincing smile. 'No worry to stay,' she said, with a pat on my shoulder. She speaks a little Burmese but it's sketchy.

'No need to leave right away,' she was trying to say. 'Stay. Please stay . . .' She waved me down like a traffic cop, as though I were speeding, as she searched for the right words to tell me to take my time, to relax. 'Stay . . . nicely.'

'Thank you, thank you.' I couldn't wait for the wretched girl to get back to her station downstairs so I could *think*. I was practically pushing her out of the door. She went away at long last. At the sound of her retreating footsteps I collapsed onto the bed.

Mr Jiang! Mr Jiang, of all people! How could he and I have been thinking along the same lines and *at the same time*? What were the chances? Impossible. Impossible but true, apparently. He beat me to it, the bastard. And showed me up as a fake. Because of course I was only *playing* at killing myself. If I'd been serious, I would have succeeded. How horribly, stupidly incompetent.

I grabbed my hair by the roots and tugged till it hurt. I wanted to cry – it was all so hopeless – but the sight of that absurd rope still hanging from the grille struck me as pathetically comic. Thank God the girl was too distraught to notice my makeshift, make-believe noose.

*

But now what? I must do something – must move from this bed, for a start. I can't go on lying here, flattened as though under layers of earthquake debris. The sun is up, highlighting the barred window, casting a jail-house pall. But I'm not in jail, not really. I'm in a Chinese hotel, free to get up and go about my business.

With Jiang gone, however, I must rethink my business. Stay? I have no option but to stay.

Money, fortunately, is not a problem; not yet. In the zippered slit of my money-belt – the first thing I put on each morning, under everything else; the last thing I take off at night – are five brand-new one-hundred-dollar bills, folded lengthwise to fit the hidden pocket. When I take out these crisp notes and set them on a hard surface, they make a neat little five-layered tent.

Five is a lucky number, a rounded, a necessary number. The hand requires five fingers for completion, the foot five toes, and five is half of ten, the basis of all counting. I've kept these lucky notes intact as a safety net, and a good thing I have too. I'll be needing them now that I'm on my own.

But there is another reason, besides superstition and thrift, why I am loath to reach into my little nest egg. (Now there's a term that's never made sense. How is it that the same word can mean 'savings' as well as 'tricking', for doesn't a *nest* egg, in English, also mean a *trick* egg, a lure for a hen to come and lay more eggs in that selfsame nest?) This particular nest egg was Will's parting gift to me. A parting shot, I should say. He stuck the whole wad into the back pocket of my jeans, like a tip for a haircut, as I started to climb into the car that was waiting, with engine running, to take me to the airport (alone, needless to say, for Will did not like airport farewells). 'Mad money' he called it, when I turned around, startled. I caught the look on his face as I took it out and counted it. The look of a man who seeks atonement by over-tipping.

Five hundred dollars is not bad for mad money, especially when everything else has been accounted for – every ticket, bribe, tip and pay-off – up to the border and beyond. And I still have the savings account Will opened for me, with funds I can draw on once I'm back 'home'. Will is nothing if not generous, I am the first to admit. But I don't know which is more offensive: the stealthy nature of the tip, or the calling it 'mad money' – as if I was off on a shopping spree.

Right, I thought, getting into the back seat of the car and immediately unzipping my bag to slip the dollars into the innermost pocket. I'll keep this for now, I may need every penny of it. But one day . . . I didn't bother to wave goodbye as Will's driver, Nid, pulled out from the driveway, swerving as usual to avoid the ruts in the road just beyond the gate.

. . . One day you'll be sitting down to breakfast – to your toast and fresh orange juice and multi-vitamins. You'll be sipping your coffee while opening your mail. You'll slit open the flap of an unfamiliar envelope with your fake silver dagger (the Mexican letter-opener with the gecko on the handle, a gift from your fiancée) . . . and in it will be five brand-new hundred-dollar bills.

It will take you a while to figure out who the sender is; then you'll shake your head as your wife looks on, curious. She'll be your wife by then. She'll be sitting across the table in the chair I once sat in. But just as you're about to put the money into your wallet, you'll see the piece of paper tucked between the bills, and your expression will change.

Up yours, my little note will say.

Time to put away the dollars and strap on the money-belt. Time to get dressed and face the day. To breakfast, then. First things first. Breakfast – my stomach rumbles at the thought – in the Wanting market. Not one of those all-you-can-eat buffets that Jiang, may he rest, was so determined to shove down my gullet day after day.

The lobby is empty, thank God, allowing me to leave the hotel unnoticed. The last thing I want is to bump into the grieving girl or her loudmouth colleague. I brace myself for the early-morning chill, wishing I'd dressed more warmly. But in a half hour or so I'll be sitting in bright sunshine, sipping hot tea. The snap in the air recalls a mood, a season, that escapes me for a moment. Then I have it. Christmas! It's the day after Christmas – the day I was supposed to leave – and here I am still . . . in Wanting, on Boxing Day.

It's quiet on the streets, even though it's late morning. The shop-houses are still shut: chains and locks on the expanded metal store-fronts, darkness in the rooms upstairs. This is the frontier, after all, a world of night life, night trade. But a few early birds are out on the sidewalks: a red-cheeked toddler curled over his slate board, frowning in concentration; a cobbler studying the sole of an old shoe over his morning cigarette; a young woman and her daughter swabbing the tin table and setting out the sauces and pickles in their noodle stall.

By the time I reach the tea-shop in the market – the Burmese tea-shop, under the enormous banyan – my mouth is watering. I spot a free table, pull up a stool and sit. The proprietor's son, a fly-swat under one arm, a dish-rag draped like a prayer shawl over one shoulder, comes to take my order.

I've been waiting days for this treat, this breakfast staple from my Rangoon period. But when the boy brings out my tray and I've sipped the scalding, bittersweet brew of tea and condensed milk; when I've torn off a piece of flat bread (still plump and warm from the oven, still blistered on top, lightly charred and crisp underneath); when I've scooped up a handful of brown peas (stewed to a soft putty, with a drizzle of sesame) in readiness for that first bite, that first taste . . . I find myself saying, of all things, grace. Not out loud, of course, not mouthing the words even, but in secret supplication. *Bless us, O Lord, and these thy gifts which we are about to receive from thy bounty, through Christ our Lord, amen.*

Without warning my nose fills; my eyes start to leak. Not that this prevents me from shovelling it in as I keep my head down, hoping no one will notice the tears and snot sliding through my lips, changing the taste of things, but not stopping me, oh no, not for a beat.

I saw a movie once, about a famine in India. A young couple, a schoolteacher and his wife, are struggling to eke out a living in a village where food has become scarcer and scarcer. One day the young wife joins a group of women who go foraging for old root vegetables in some scrubby fields. They fan out in all directions, and start digging. The schoolteacher's wife ends up near a bombed-out building where a disfigured leper has taken shelter in the rubble. He watches her for a long time, unseen, while she digs and digs, finally unearthing an old potato. Then, under cover of the roar of jet fighters flying overhead, the leper rushes out and rapes her.

When the planes and the leper have disappeared and the other women discover what has happened, they gather round to help the schoolteacher's wife to her feet. She takes her first shaky steps, supported on either side, when she remembers something. She turns to the women behind her. 'Bring the potato!' she cries.

No, one must never forget the potato. One must never let tears get in the way of feeding one's face.

four

'You'll love the frontier market,' Will predicted brightly. 'It's crazy. It's the Wild West.' The Wild West put me in mind of Cowboys and Indians, but he was speaking, of course, of a different west – the Wild West of China.

What is so wild about this West? I ask myself now. Or so crazy about this frontier market? I've seen dozens like it in my time. I've seen rice merchants and spice merchants like these before. I've known such tea-shops and cloth-shops, known the likes of those skinny whores, dressed in shorts like panties and high heels like weapons, laughing and arguing with their pimp. I've walked the same muddy, bloody pathways between just such butchers and fish-mongers, smelt these very combinations of smells. Rotting fruit and charred meat. Turmeric and salt fish. I've peered into pink plastic bags just like the ones spread out on the ground over there, all rolled open to display their home cures and remedies: their seeds, powders, dried plants, dried ants, roots, rock crystals, animal parts, and pickled foetuses.

And those nomad-traders swarming through the aisles in their embroidered skirts and silver-coin jackets, their tasselled hats and sombre turbans, must be distant relatives of mine. The trouble is, I don't know any of their names. But why bother with names any more? We're all of a piece, at the end of the day: like a segment of this small forest under which I sit. This dusty jungle of a banyan tree, with its aerial roots, braided limbs and fractured trunks, all intertwined and unsortable each from each.

It was over there, by the public bulletin board, that I first waited for Jiang – just last Saturday, less than a week ago. I didn't have a clue as to what the man looked like, but I left it to him to find me.

The postings on the board, in Chinese and Burmese, concerned a recent execution. Before-and-after photographs showed a total of twenty-two men and women, each holding at chest level a placard marked with a large X. Beneath this line-up there was a single snapshot of bodies sprawled on the ground, leaking dark stains in the dirt.

'Miss Na Ga? Sorry to keep you waiting!' The slight, grey-haired figure who came up from behind spoke English with a choppy accent, like a Hong Kong Chinese. But he didn't look Chinese. His skin was dark – the ashy dark of a lowland Burman or Thai, not the rosy tan of a Han Chinese.

'Mr Jiang?'

'Jiang,' he said. 'Just Jiang.' He positioned himself in front of the bulletin board to face me, but ended up gazing shyly at my crotch.

I motioned to the pictures behind him. 'When did this happen?' I asked.

'Last month.' He didn't turn to look. 'They put on the show last month.'

'Show?'

'*Pya-zat*,' said Jiang, switching to the Burmese word for theatre.

Ah, he spoke Burmese. I asked him if he was from Burma.

He just smiled and offered me a cigarette. No? I didn't smoke? Good, he nodded, a very good thing. 'Filthy habit,' he said; then, in English, 'Coffin nails.'

'Coffin nails,' he repeated, chuckling at the phrase as he lit up, took a deep drag, and turned his head to exhale, exposing a long scar at the base of his neck.

Oh, great, I thought. I'm in the hands of a thug – the kind who gets his throat slit. And this was the man arranging my safe passage.

Couldn't I tell? he said, returning to my question about whether he was Burmese with an upward tilt of his chin. He was inviting me to examine his face. Didn't I know a fellow countryman when I saw one?

No, I said. I didn't. It was a long time since I'd lived in Burma and, anyway, the people of Burma had such a variety of faces, didn't he think? Chinese faces, Indian faces, Anglo faces, Malay faces . . .

Yes, yes, all those and so many native ones too, he said, taking up the rote . . . Shan faces, Karen faces, Kachin faces . . . But what he meant, if he could explain, was a certain look, a bearing, that distinguished a Burmese person from, say, a Thai, or a Cambodian, or a Vietnamese. Couldn't I recognise that at least?

No, I repeated. I couldn't. I didn't like the way this two-bit fixer was trying to rope me into kinship. I changed the subject by drawing his attention to the bulletin board again. So it wasn't real? I asked. This – execution?

Oh, it was real all right. Again that woebegone smile. Only – those bodies in the picture were not all drug-dealers, as it said in the news clips.

Then who *were* they? I asked. Not that I gave a damn.

'Just bodies.' He shrugged. Clearly he didn't give a damn

either. 'Bodies of no account. Robbers, petty thieves, unlucky crooks who happened to be sitting in jail.'

'Yes, executions are the thing now,' he said mildly. 'To show that the Chinese authorities are getting tough on drug-dealers. You heard about it, right?' he asked, switching to English. I'd heard nothing; I knew nothing. My orders from Will were to wait at the hotel to be contacted by one of Yan Ding's men. Now here he was: my minder and fixer in Wanting. A fellow Burmese at that. All well and good. But what next?

Jiang seemed in no hurry to enlighten me. 'Take a good look, aha!' he said, moving aside to give me a better view while he finished his cigarette. I wasn't sure whether he meant I should take my time, there was no hurry – or whether I was supposed to find some hidden meaning in the grisly notices. It was difficult to get the measure of a man who flaunted his sliced throat one minute, touted a public execution the next. A harmless-looking man for all that, with his hangdog eyes and a mouth that went on smiling through every kind of setback.

I stepped up to the glass for one last look. The reflection of my face landed squarely on one of the Xs marking the condemned. Another omen, I thought. I was beginning to see omens and portents everywhere – all pointing to the only path I could imagine myself taking.

five

Americans, I have noticed, are fools for homelands – especially the homelands of others. To determine a person's provenance is as important to them as it is to the Chinese to determine a person's worth. And to Americans like Will, who have escaped their own homelands, proudly calling themselves 'expats', it seems even more important to repatriate everyone else. Will's mother was American, his father was Swiss, but Asia was his adopted home. He'd been to almost every city, every province in the region, and knew a great deal about the clans and customs of each. I could only be thankful for his interest. I wouldn't have been with him otherwise: he would never have noticed me. What set me apart was my particular rarity: I belonged to one of the smallest ethnic minorities on the South East Asian mainland.

I once overheard an Australian journalist make a comment about me. We were attending a lecture at the Bangkok Foreign Correspondents' Club. During the intermission, Will must have been telling him where I came from, because the Australian said, 'Why she's one of the abos, then.'

When I asked Will later what 'abo' meant, he explained that my people were thought to be the earliest settlers of the region, the ones that arrived before even the Mon and the Khmer. That they were to their area what American Indians were to America, or the aborigines to Australia. It was a compliment, he said of the Australian journalist's remark.

Will seemed proud of the fact that I was an abo. It disappointed him that I didn't share his pride, that I remembered so little about my childhood. But trying to recall those days was like piecing together a dream. Just as I caught hold of one bit, the rest slipped away. Will refused to let things be, however. He thought up countless methods for jogging my memory. One method was to hand me a book or a magazine, and say, 'Here, read this. Tell me if it's true.'

'"In general,"' I read out loud, '"the Wild Lu are far too busy taking it easy to waste much time in farm work." Untrue!' Taking it easy was not how I would have described our way of life, had I known how to describe it at all.

Will laughed. 'A little defensive, are we? But go on, keep reading.'

'"A Wild Lu selling bananas at so much for six cannot sell fifteen of them because of the odd number; and if three were left over he would eat them or carry them home."'

'I don't know what that means, so I can't say if it's true,' I said.

'Obviously true. You can't add two and two.'

'"Hygiene is unknown, washing done by nobody . . ." True, I suppose.'

Hygiene. Poverty. What did I understand about those conditions when I was living them? The horseflies that clung to the sores on our noses and lips. The rats that burrowed through the beds of garlic bulbs on which we slept. The stink of vomit in old blankets. There had been no one word for it all then, no word like 'hygiene'. Or 'poverty'.

'"Victims,"' I went on reading, '"prisoners in most cases,

23

were bought for sacrifice like cattle on the hoof . . ." Will, I don't want to read any more.'

'"The aquiline Red Indian nose,"' he read over my shoulder, before taking the mouldy book out of my hands. Turning my head to one side, he said, '"The flat back of the head . . ."'

'I do not have a flat head!'

'Of course not. A *hard* head, maybe . . .'

Later, free from his scrutiny, I studied those books and journals more closely. But try as I might I couldn't connect the photographs (neither the glossy new ones nor the grainy old ones), less so their confident captions, with the patchy dream-memories I retained. The images of my childhood that came readily to mind were of frailty, of impermanence. I remembered trees on fire, fields of ash, thatch sheets sailing off in the wind. I remembered holes and gaps: in a roof that let in the rain, in the floor that let in the draught, in the hearth at the centre of our living space – the source of endless smoke but never enough heat. Especially I remembered smoke – from cooking-fires, bonfires, burning fields – and the way it blackened the floor, the ceiling, the walls, the bedding.

But every so often, all that smoke and haze hanging over my childhood would part of its own accord to bring back a scene, or a sensation, or a face. Then, for a vivid instant I would catch sight of our shaman staggering about drunkenly in a storm, the rain streaking his sooty cheeks. Or my skin would tingle, taking me back to a time before speech (before I could remember speaking, anyway), when I stuck my arm through a gap in the bamboo floor, letting it hang into the space below where our cow and mule lived – and felt the lick of a thick warm tongue on my hand. Or a smell would return to me: the sour-bamboo tang of my mother's lap, for instance. Even her face might appear at such moments, in a liquid flash

– though soon enough a stone would drop from somewhere on high, and splinter the watery image.

But these memories were not willed: they flared up unbidden, sparked by a stray ember in a bed of ash. And how true they were was hard to say. I couldn't swear that the thick hedge of thorn and bramble enclosing our village was as high and forbidding as I remembered it. Or that the tunnel I saw in my mind's eye – the long dark tunnel of barbed twigs that served as the entrance – wasn't shaped by a story I came to know later, the story of Briar Rose. The hedge around the castle of that sleeping princess grew higher and higher, the thorns holding fast 'as if they had hands', until whoever tried getting through them ended up impaled on the spikes.

That the tunnel and hedge existed I had no doubt. It said so, after all, in one of the books Will kept thrusting at me. 'To gain entry into a Lu village you must either be invited or fight.'

True or false, I was not prepared to put these memories into words for Will's benefit. I was ashamed of my past, and suspicious of his probing. I couldn't see why it should make such a difference to him whether or not I kept alive my childhood home – a home so far away now, in memory and in fact, that it might as well not have existed.

six

A girl I met at a refugee camp (another fugitive from Burma who had grown up, as I did, not far from the Chinese border) once told me how, as a child, she would run and hide at the sight of a giant caterpillar crawling across the valley and up the hill towards her village. The caterpillar was a Chinese opium caravan, a mile-long mule-train led by soldiers in green uniforms with machine-guns and walkie-talkies.

The girl described how she would freeze in her dark corner underneath her hut, scarcely daring to breathe, while she waited for the soldiers to finish their business. When at last the mules had been watered and the men had made off with the harvest they'd come to collect – the sticky black lumps of opium the size of elephant turds that the village had kept at the ready – she would come out of hiding. Then she would run and throw herself at her mother's knees, crying with relief, because her mother, when angry, often threatened to sell her to the Chinese.

I had no such memory of Chinese invasions, but my own secret fear took another shape. In my school in Rangoon I once failed a geography test for spoiling an otherwise passable map of Burma. All along the jagged edges that bordered China, I had drawn a line-up of little block figures that resembled chess pawns. I was trying to illustrate an image that had lodged in my mind since I witnessed a scene in a tea-shop:

a very angry Chinese man being hustled out by an anxious friend. The angry man was shaking his fist at someone over his shoulder, shouting, 'We don't need armies! We don't need guns! If we want to take over, all we have to do is line up along your borders, and start pissing. You'd drown in our piss, every last one of you!'

Landing at Kunming airport, I remembered the Chinaman's tirade and an old fear came over me. I was in the real China now – not in the Chinatown of cities like Rangoon or Bangkok, but in China proper, in an actual Chinese city – home of millions upon millions of mighty Chinese who could drown a neighbouring country with one simultaneous piss.

But then, at Immigration, I saw something too strange to credit. An officer in army fatigues was trying to speed things up for the tourists in line by *waltzing* through the queues, plucking passports out of random hands, and flourishing them overhead. He pranced and pirouetted, counting heads with a playful *eeny-meeny-miny-mo* to see which lucky person's passport he should snatch next. His smile was wide and freakish, like the grins on the faces of heroic peasants in old Communist posters.

Later, in the grand marble lobby of the Kunming Hotel, I watched a stocky young man in a long blue coat with 'ASSISTANT MANAGER' embroidered on his breast pocket, talking into a cordless phone. Walking in circles, he kept his eyes on the floor, repeating the same apology – in English. He was sorry. Yes, they were working on the electricity. No, there was no other room; not one other room could he offer, unfortunately. He was sorry, he was very, very sorry. He went on apologising for a full five minutes.

I didn't trust such jolliness, such meekness in uniformed men – especially uniformed *Chinese* men.

Out in the airport arrivals hall, I had spotted my name in the sea of hand-held placards, and introduced myself to the bearer, a Mr Wei. Cutting crisply through the crowds, Mr Wei led me to the car park with a series of turns and half-turns, as in a solo foxtrot, to his midnight blue Mercedes. He had a cell phone, a car phone, and a pager, all buzzing, beeping and trilling as he drove. No sooner had he shouted orders into one, pressing buttons on another, than the third would summon him insistently.

Pulling into the driveway of a hotel where the doormen were dressed like tribal chieftains from a region that probably didn't exist, he asked if I would wait in the lobby while he took care of some business. So I sat and waited, listening all the while to the assistant manager's lengthy apology for the electricity problem.

At last I noticed Mr Wei approaching me, sizing me up for the first time. I knew what he was thinking: a lady friend of Mr Will's, and so little to show for it. So ordinary! Not beautiful, not stylish, not worth a second glance if passed on the street. I could see him taking in my faded blue T-shirt and drab black jeans; my sturdy sandals with the two wide straps; my blunt-cut hair without a touch of what they called styling . . . and thinking, Peasant. I, meanwhile, was taking in Mr Wei's pigeon-grey silk shirt with jade cuff links, his black linen trousers with crisp front pleats, and thinking, Chinaman.

Still at the mercy of his assorted telephones, Mr Wei drove me to the bus station, where he bought me my ticket, and handed me over to the bus driver, making the man laugh by waving a pen in front of his nose. 'It's a bribe.' He turned to explain to me in English. 'You cannot get these pens in China, but everyone wants them.'

The pen was green, veined like jade, and obviously expensive. 'I told this driver: take care of this passenger. If she is still alive when you reach Wanting, she will give you this beautiful pen. But if you drive too fast and you kill her, she will not give you the pen.'

The driver guffawed, pointing to a photograph clipped to his rear-view mirror. That was himself in the helmet, he boasted. That daredevil at the finish line of the motorcycle rally – in Tokyo, no less. Yes, yes, he was a motorcycle racer. He bared his teeth at me, then adjusted his reflector sunglasses in the mirror. Sure he'd make it to the frontier! He stuffed his gums with tobacco pellets as he bragged, fat-lipped and confident.

Mr Wei glanced at his gold Rolex, eager to be off. 'Good luck!' he said to me, after translating the driver's boasts. 'Good luck, okay?' – as if my good luck were up to me. He pressed the pen into my hand, lifted my suitcase, and pretended to be thrown off balance by its lightness. Then he gave me a look that said, 'What sort of loser returns home to the hills without luggage bursting at the seams?'

I took a window seat at the back of the bus. By the time I settled in I could spot Mr Wei in the distance, phone to ear. Not once had he asked me anything about myself; not once had I asked about him, for that matter. It wasn't my place to question Will's contacts, or to second-guess his decisions – especially since I no longer cared.

We pulled out of the bus station into the centre of Kunming – into streets choked with phalanxes of pedestrians, with bicycles by the battalion. Everything seemed built either for hordes or giants. Billboards and signposts were twenty storeys high. On the rooftop of a hotel there was a single running-shoe the size of a large sampan. Dragon balloons sailed above banks and gas stations, writhing in the wind (like the snake, in the old fable, forever cursed with a warring head and tail).

Out in the steaming, seething suburbs, plumes of soot and smoke hung like proud banners over coalyards, silos, cement factories. And emblazoned across every last bridge and construction site, in red and white lettering, was the selfsame slogan: 'MAN AND NATURE, MARCHING TOGETHER INTO THE 21ST CENTURY'.

The man seated one row ahead and across the aisle – a yellow-haired foreigner in sandals and khaki shorts – had struck up a conversation with the young Chinese man directly in front of me. On the floor of the bus, beside the foreigner's seat, was a canvas bag stuffed with maps. The foreigner – an engineer from Denmark, as he introduced himself – was full of questions. He wanted to know all about Chinese computers and keyboards, and something called the five-stroke method. He wanted to know what the Chinese man did for a living. (A student, said the prim young man in wire-rimmed glasses; 'a student of national minorities'.) He wanted to know about methods of road construction, systems of irrigation, traditions of farming. There was no end to what this European wanted to know.

The bus driver interrupted with a sudden yell as he pointed out of the window. '*Lao lu! Lao lu!*'

'What is he saying?' asked the engineer.

'He is showing the old road,' said the student. 'The old way. We call it here the Yunnan–Burma highway.'

Out came a map from the engineer's bag. Now, with his pen poised, his thumb against the push-button like a syringe at the ready, he demanded to know about *elevations*.

Running parallel to the highway, at the foot of a slope, was a little black road that could have passed for a stream.

Along its banks were uniform rows of tall, pointed trees, all painted white at the base. Cypresses, I guessed. Or cedars. I never could remember the names of trees. But if I waited long enough the man with the maps was bound to enlighten me. He would enquire, no doubt, about every tree, every bush, every rock along the way. Now he was asking the young man whether he thought Marco Polo had really come to China. Some scholars seemed to be saying that he hadn't.

'Oh, Marco?' said the student, as though speaking of an old classmate. 'Marco came for sure. There are many proofs. For example, he wrote that the Yi people, a minority in this area, never marry. And that is fact. How would he know something like that? He came here himself. Therefore. You can check in the history books.' The young man was starting to sound testy; perhaps he wished, as I did, that the engineer would shut up and poke his long nose elsewhere – into the folds of his maps, maybe, instead of into everyone else's business.

The old road teased like a mirage, disappearing beneath the bus, reappearing first on one side, then on the other.

Then we turned a corner, and all peace was at an end. Dust-storms were raging over quarries so vast that the bulldozers, trucks and cranes poised around their rims looked no bigger than Matchbox models. Convoys of trucks bearing gravel, sand and cement pipes crawled up and down hillsides shaved to a raw red, along riverbanks trashed with boulders and trees. Mile after mile, for a hundred miles or more, colonies of workers lined the roadside, washing and cooking under lean-tos with tin roofs and striped plastic sheets. A brand new highway was under construction.

I couldn't have nodded off; I had been unable to sleep since leaving Bangkok. But now my mind must have blinked like a tired eye, because again a page had turned while I wasn't looking. Hills like surf – pale green, dark green, blue-black – billowed out and out into haze. Paddy terraces, tiny and obstinate, climbed like dwarf staircases to a fastness for ever beyond reach. A lone farmer stood at the edge of a field, waiting for his buffalo to finish its mud wallow. Along hillsides and ditches, women trudged in groups and pairs, heads held high, baskets strapped to their foreheads and slung on their backs.

And although I hadn't thought about them in a long, long time, all at once I was reminded of them by the faces at the roadside – my old master and mistress, the tattooed headman and his eel-loving wife.

seven

It was the Daru headman who taught me how to catch – or rather how *not* to catch – eel. He took me down to the creek in the early mornings, to watch while he fished. He used blood worms for bait, sometimes shrimp or raw chicken; but no sooner did he pull in a loach or a barb than he would throw the thing back into the stream. It was eel he was after, not just any edible fish, and between catches he chanted *ka-zon, ka-zon* (the Daru word for eel) like a prayer – or perhaps a tease. He seemed to think I was lying when I said I didn't know what an eel was.

I was a child of seven, but I came from a Wild Lu village. And the Daru, it seemed, were never sure whether the Wild Lu were really stupid or just lazy and *pretending* to be stupid. But whatever an eel was, it was required by my new mistress, the headman's wife, who was sickly and weak. Not too weak, however, to make me hop in pain for the fun of it.

Her cane had a way of stinging the backs of my legs when I least expected it. 'Just playing.' She would grin when I leaped and sucked in my breath. I was wary of approaching her with a load of firewood balanced on my head because she couldn't resist extending her leg in my path to send me sprawling. 'Watch where you're going!' she'd scold. Then, pleased with her joke, 'Just teasing.' If she held one hand behind her back and said, 'Open your mouth, I have something for you,' I knew better than to open. She had once fed me the snout of a dead rat.

It was only at night, in the safety of her snores, that I could let down my guard a little; but even then I was afraid to fall asleep. I worried about crying noisily without knowing it. Awake, I knew how to swallow my tears without making a sound. Asleep, I couldn't control them. In my corner of the floor, where the thatch wall buckled in a heavy wind, I learned to lie still, forcing the tears back, down my nose and throat, longing for sleep but unable to stop myself fighting against it.

I prayed to wake and discover I had only been dreaming, that I was back in my own corner of my real home, shaking my mother awake to tell her about my strange dream of the big Daru village.

But suppose I did sleep, only to wake and discover I hadn't been dreaming at all, that the day ahead of me was just like the one before? Suppose this was my home now, this house, this village? Better, then, to keep myself awake, waiting as long as I could for the owl's whistle and screech, the *chigga-chigga-chigga-chigga, toktè, toktè* of the giant lizards in the rafters. Because as long as I could put off sleep I could hope.

At the edge of sleep I began to imagine things. The bats swooping through the eaves were really the swallows that had followed me from home, and the shape in the thick blanket a few yards away was not the headman's wife but my sleeping mother. I didn't dare try to wake her. Every time I made to reach out with a trembling hand I stopped myself. For what if it turned out that I couldn't wake her? Better to believe my mother was still alive and breathing, just fast asleep under that heavy blanket.

*

Years passed before it was explained to me why the headman's wife was so full of spleen. It was simple, really. She had wanted a child-servant, and I was delivered to her village for that purpose, but she hadn't bargained for the bad luck I would bring. The very day I arrived on her doorstep, she took to her bed moaning and clutching her belly. When the midwife was called in the next day, it was to deliver a dead baby – a boy, to cap the shame. I didn't understand, then, that I would be blamed for the miscarriage, that my mistress would see me ever after as a malign spirit.

She kept me on, nevertheless, for I had my uses. I could fetch water and firewood, I could sweep the mud floors and the dirt yard. I could fan and blow on the fire to boil rice. I could massage her back by stepping lightly astride her spine as she lay flat on her belly, groaning and farting. And I could be trained to catch eel.

So I waited with her husband in the changing light of dawn, watching the mist curl and skitter over the creek while he fished. It cheered me to see how the wet weeds glistened as the sun came up, reminding me of the bits of broken glass I used to collect and admire, and bury like treasure in the soft earth underneath our hut.

As the sky grew brighter and the air warmed up, the headman rucked his *longyi* into a loincloth, exposing the blue tattoos on his thighs. And when the sun struck his eyes they seemed to melt into a kinder, softer brown. I sensed we had something between us, the headman and I, and it gave me comfort: we were both afraid of his wife.

We had packed up and were heading home one morning, empty-handed once more, when we passed another fisherman who stopped to show us the contents of his bucket. 'That,' said the headman, gripping the back of my head and making me look closely at the long snake coiled at the bottom, 'is an eel.'

One full-moon night the whole village crowded by the river to watch the children float their candle boats as offerings to the spirits. I had no boat of my own, but one in particular caught my eye, veering off by itself on a wobbly course downstream. I followed the stray craft, dodging the rocks and tree roots at my feet, my shadow in tow like a faithful sidekick. I saw the boat disappear under the small footbridge and was about to turn back when I spied it grounded along the bank, its candle still alight and twinkling. And there, by the foot of the bamboo bridge where leaves, twigs and dead wood formed nests in the shallows, I could see the eels, a whole school of them playing tag and hide-and-seek.

Catching eel would be easy, I somehow knew then. I would need no hook or bait. I would need only a net of some sort, a long basket. Oh, wouldn't my mistress's face light up! Maybe she'd get well, become strong and benevolent. Maybe she'd let me go home.

But although she granted me a nod of satisfaction whenever I returned with an eel or two in the basket I'd learned to use as a trap; although she seemed proud of me at times, boasting that 'stolen cats make the best rat catchers', she showed no sign of softening. Now it was not just the chickens I fed but the pigs as well; not just the yard that needed sweeping, but the paddy that needed pounding at dawn, and the rice that needed washing and boiling in time for the men's early-morning meal. All day long I was at her beck and call – and, when the moon was bright, into the late hours as well.

It was at night that I went eel-catching, at night that the shallow pools by the bridge became their playground.

36

They let me watch while they burrowed in and out through the mud, and slithered through the reeds, and showed off by swimming backwards out into the stream. They nosed the surface, nudging aside floating leaves and seedpods; they raised their heads to catch the spill of a cascade from a rock as though playing in the rain. Then they let me trap them. I had only to bend forward with my long creel (a basket not really meant for fishing, but it worked all the same) and follow their movements with the mouth of the creel pointed in the right direction. I had only to sway when they swayed, hold still when they retreated, *dance* to their rhythm till one (at times even two) slid or flipped into my basket.

I never saw a single eel by daylight. That same spot by the river was without distinction by day – a scattering of rocks and stones that splintered the water's flow into a dozen eddies and mini-currents. A spot like countless others upstream and down.

In the mornings I waited for the look of greed on my mistress's face. I watched her bite her tongue as she grabbed the eel's head and pulled the skin back in one long sheath. I watched her eyes glitter as she gutted and cleaned, then diced and fried the meat. I watched her lick her lips before the first bite.

'Take some,' she said, between mouthfuls. But when I reached for the tin plate she slapped my hand away. Who had told me to take the flesh? The nerve, the disrespect! What she meant for me to taste was the *flavour*. 'Like this . . .' She formed a handful of rice, patted it on to the skin of the cooked eel, then fed herself a mouthful. 'Only the flavour, not the flesh . . .'

One night I went down as usual to the creek. The eels were there, as I'd known they would be, they almost never let me down, but I'd lost heart for the sport. I was tired of standing by for their dance and play. As soon as they began swishing about in the water I lowered my basket – and almost immediately there was a flurry. Not just one, or two but *three* eels shot in.

Three eels for my mistress would be a waste: no one else in the house liked eel. But wasn't every one I caught a waste, since she was never going to let me go, anyway? I tipped the creel into the stream and swirled it about to make sure it was empty. Then I skipped home, feeling a weight had been lifted off me, and not just the weight of the eel.

But the next morning, when I offered no excuse or apology for the empty basin in which the eels were kept alive overnight, my mistress shook me and shook me till my teeth felt loose in my head. We were out in the yard, and I noticed out of the corner of my eye that Daw Daw Seng was passing by. To attract her attention, I cried noisily.

Daw Daw Seng, like me, was not a native of the Daru village – her people were from the southern Shan state – but she came often to visit the Daru, among whom she had blood relatives. Everyone recognised her as a *lu gyi*, a big person. Not big in the physical sense, though she was that too, but big in importance. For Daw Daw Seng had a job in the city: in Rangoon, the biggest city of all. And she was a Christian. Christians had books and were keen to teach children how to read them. I had never been given a book or a lesson by Daw Daw Seng, but I could tell from the way she smiled at me, and patted my head in passing, that she was not someone I needed to fear.

My cries stirred Daw Daw Seng to action. She took hold of my shoulders, pushed me behind her and faced my mistress squarely. 'You are wasting your time,' she said, batting the air behind her to show that I was of no consequence, 'dirtying your hands for nothing. A child like this . . . a Wild Lu savage. How can you teach it anything? I'll find you a good child. A child you can love and trust. Let me take this one away.'

My mistress's eyes darted about in defiance. Her cheeks reddened. Then she brought her thin nose up close to Daw Daw Seng's flat one, and bared her teeth in a false-friendly grin. 'I know what this is,' she whined. 'You are trying to shame me. You are saying I don't treat the child right. How have I not treated her right? How have I hurt her? Show me how I've hurt her. Show me the cuts and bruises, then.' She tried to reach behind my protector to reclaim me, but Daw Daw Seng put out an arm.

'No, no, Mrs Headman's Wife! Not so! I am thinking only of your well-being. This child is not good for you. She is causing trouble. She is causing distress. She is making you unwell. Leave her to me. Let me take her away.'

The headman's wife lunged without warning to deliver a loud clap right next to my ear, as though smashing once and for all a bothersome bug. 'Done!' she crowed. 'Settled and done! Take her! Take her *far* away!'

Daw Daw Seng pushed me ahead of her, away from the headman's hut. But I wasn't going fast enough for her liking. 'Walk!' she said, pulling me along by the hand. I was running to keep up. 'Walk, and don't look back.'

eight

Two days on the bus – five hundred miles from Kunming to Wanting – and all I seemed to catch in the way of sleep were catnaps. But I must have slept soundly enough from time to time for I managed to dream in my seat. In one dream I was trapped in a high-speed vehicle, a cross between a speedboat and a tank. I went shooting down roads criss-crossed by teeming intersections, whizzing through red lights, squeezing through narrow paths between tall cypresses – always avoiding collision by impossibly narrow margins. And that was the worst of it, in a peculiar way: that somehow I never did crash.

In another dream, I was back to my search through the pages of a book. (I know this book well from many a previous dream. Sometimes it's thick, a telephone directory; sometimes it's a ledger with handwritten entries. But whatever its size or shape, I never manage to find what I'm seeking – for the simple reason that I don't *know* what I'm seeking.)

My dream on the bus took an unpleasant twist: I'm searching as usual through the cryptic pages when my heart starts thumping in dread. It dawns on me that the book in my hands is the Big Book itself – *The Book of Records*, written by Lu Sa, creator of the Wild Lu. (When a person is born, the Lu believe, the Great Creator records in this book the exact day on which he or she will die.)

But I don't even believe in Lu Sa! I thought, cracking my

knuckles to make sure I was fully awake. It was all myth and superstition. And yet . . . there I was, eyes open and scared witless.

I stood up to stretch, looking down on the heads of my fellow passengers with envy. They seemed to have no problem sleeping. They slept in their seats, in the aisle, in the luggage racks overhead. Families snored together, in pairs, in threes. Single men were sprawled like gangsters shot dead in mid-sentence. Clutching a leather jacket that stank of onion and sheep, a very old man in a Muslim cap dozed with his head hung low, as if in shame. Even the engineer and the student were out cold at long last, the student with his back to the talkative engineer, to make clear perhaps his need for a bit of silence and rest.

How they slept and slept, like the drugged, like the hexed, through the dust and the fumes and the jerky stopping and starting. Through the one-two punch of the driver's horn. Night and day his horn blared, at every turn on the road, now to greet another bus, now to give an old peasant the fright of his life. Or maybe just to keep *him* awake, that mad motorcycle racer with the tobacco pellets in his teeth.

'Wanting!' he yelled suddenly, loud enough to wake the dead, as he swerved into the bus station. 'Wanting! Wanting!' It sounded like a threat, a warning.

I was the last to get off, and found the driver waiting to help me down the steps. I handed him the cash tip I'd set aside, and turned to leave. He seemed dissatisfied. Mr Wei had told me exactly how much to tip the man, and it was rather a generous amount. He had no reason to grumble that I could see. But it was late, I was exhausted, and I wasn't going to trouble myself over his gripe.

I was walking away when I heard him shout something

41

vile in my direction. I wanted to shout back something equally insulting, but didn't have the strength for anything other than a mild 'Fucking *tayok!*' muttered under my breath. Tired as I was, the meaning of '*tayok*', the Burmese word for a Chinese person, struck me as fitting. For *tayok* can also mean 'one-face'. They were all alike, these Chinese bullies. All *same-same*, as they say in Thailand.

Half past midnight, according to the clock tower of the Yunnan Development Bank – and the town was wide awake. Naked bulbs burned brightly, and neon lights flashed round and round their elements, like dogs doomed to chase their tails. Up and down the main street mopeds were sputtering, bicycle bells ringing, car horns blaring. Three hotels, lit up like night ferries, were docked in the mist. I made for the smallest, at the far end of the street – the one with winking letters that spelled FRIENDSHIP HOTEL.

The girl at the front desk was expecting me. She was small and lively and, despite the late hour, seemed eager to please. She handed me an envelope with my name on it. The handwritten note – unsigned – told me where to wait the next morning.

'From Mr Jiang?' I asked her, just to make sure – although who else would be contacting me? The girl nodded, smiling. Mr Jiang . . . She clasped her hands, then tapped her heart, indicating they were friends.

Was there nothing for me to sign, no deposit to pay? I enquired in sign language.

No, it was all taken care of, she signed back. Behind her, tacked on to the wall, was a mysterious message. LEAVE WITH VALUABLE BODY.

The lift was locked for the night, the girl indicated. She didn't have the key; she was sorry. She tried to wrest my suitcase from me, but I waved her ahead and followed her upstairs.

I wondered why she had her trousers rolled up, all the way to her knees. Then I saw they were made that way: she was wearing a pair of jaunty capris.

We had reached the third-floor landing when I was stopped by the sight of a shadowy figure trailing the girl down the corridor. Then I shook my head to clear it, and saw who it was: myself – none other than my ghostly self. It was only a phantom, a trick of fatigue, and I caught up with my shadow, so to speak, at the door to the last room.

The girl went in first, to turn on the light. There was a bed, a bamboo bedside stand with a lamp on it, a sofa with a plastic covering, and that was it. But there was a private bathroom, at least: a toilet with a shower cubicle. And there was a high window, with iron bars for a grille. The girl showed me how to open it by means of a long handle with a crank at the end. She switched on the television set to see if it worked (it didn't), shook her head in apology and turned to leave. Was everything else all right, she wanted to know. Yes, fine, I nodded, handing her a tip. She thanked me with a bow and a giggle.

Now, a week later, I'm still here, in this room. And still unable to sleep. If only I could get one good night's rest. I can't make any sensible decisions, I can't *think* in this foggy state, when I keep blacking out for stretches without actually passing out, losing track of where I was only a moment ago. It doesn't help, of course, that I've ended up in a town like Wanting, a town that never sleeps either. What with round-the-clock karaoke and drunken street brawls, the generators humming and the air-conditioners droning, I have yet to know a moment of utter silence.

I switch on the bedside lamp, and pick up a tourist pamphlet

43

someone has left on the bedside stand. *Wanting, the City of Sun*, it says in English, above the blurred photographs of Chinese temples, Burmese pagodas, and tall buildings still under construction.

Wanting, the City of Sun, is saying goodbye to the past fields and gardens on the way to the glory of Prosperity!
 In Wanting of the new millennium will be gardens of nature with artificial flavour!
 In Wanting it has been planned to build a city of hotels and casinos with the style of local feature and modern setting. Building materials will include glitter tile, which looks so nice and neat!

The print is swimming; my eyelids are leaden. *Killing me softly,* I hear again and again, from the karaoke stalls thrumming in the street. *Wanting,* I read, before the pamphlet drops from my hand, *is far away from the urban noise, full of quiet and noble sentiment.*

In that instant I am jerked awake.

It's no good. Lying here hour after hour is neither useful nor restful. I might as well get up and go downstairs.

The girl is alone, behind the desk in the lobby, her pretty head propped on one hand. She is reading magazines. I watch her for a while with something like disgust. Her good friend Mr Jiang has just blown his brains out – and she's engrossed in cartoons. Or horoscopes, for all I know. Or movie-star gossip. So quick to grieve, so quick to forget. Of course, she's still young. She'll learn. She'll change.

Before she can see me, I creep back upstairs – to wait out my as yet undefined sentence.

But now, all of sudden, it comes back: the reason the bus

driver was so annoyed with me. Of course. I forgot to give him the pen!

I go through my bag to find Mr Wei's bribe. Studying its gold nib and marbled jade shell, I am reminded of his words. 'Take care of this passenger. If she is still alive when you reach Wanting, she will give you this beautiful pen.'

Maybe, I think now, the pen is still with me for a reason. The reason is that I haven't in fact made it to Wanting alive. Maybe I'm already dead, simply unaware of it. Maybe that's why I've been unable to take my life: it's already been taken. Maybe I am nothing more than the severed tail of a lizard, a useless piece of flesh thrashing about in the dirt well after the creature has darted off elsewhere.

nine

This morning it's back to the Burmese tea-shop for another breakfast – my new routine in this limbo of indecision.

I've just about cleaned my plate, and drunk my tea to the dregs, when a beggar tugs at my sleeve. *Nothing to eat, no rice, no salt* . . . A girl, I am guessing, without turning to look. Or a stunted woman. I will not look. Whatever she is, she will not get a penny out of me. Not a single Chinese *yuan*, not a *jiao*, not a *fen*. Not one worthless Burmese *kyat*, even. I'm not stupid enough, either, to buy her a plate of boiled peas. Beggars never want only the food on your plate . . . *Have mercy, hunger, sickness, God bless* . . .

I could give the pest a jolt by wheeling around and yelling at her to GET LOST, INSECT! I could stay as I am, turned away, and slyly mimic her misery, reciting my woes like an old nursery rhyme. Maybe then she might *hear* how it sounds, that singsong of perpetual self-pity. Why does it never occur to beggars that they might have better luck if they just kept their mouths shut and held out their hands?

Then I hear her say in Burmese, I swear, 'Go home, go home . . . Jiang said go home . . .'

I swivel around, knocking over my teacup. 'What was that?'

The girl's eyes are hooded, almost slammed shut. Her face is a fright. Raw sores have eaten into her forehead, chin and cheek. She arches her back, defiant in her repulsiveness.

46

'What was that about Jiang? You know Jiang?'

A flicker of puzzlement passes over those slit eyes.

'You said something! About Jiang! I heard you say *Jiang*!' I'd shake the wretch if I could bring myself to touch her.

'Get away! Leave the customers alone!' The proprietor's son is aiming the flyswat at her head. 'Get away, didn't I say?' The girl takes a step backwards and spits on the ground, narrowly missing my foot. 'Filthy disease carrier!' The boy takes a whack at her. She stamps her foot and turns her back on us in a showy huff, like a lover scorned in a comic play. Then off she darts across the square, disappearing into the market.

'Disgusting!' mutters the tea-shop boy. 'A-I-D. Too disgusting for words.' It's been a while since I heard the Burmese term for Aids, always spelled out that way. B/C was what they are calling it now in Bangkok – the new HIV strain.

'Scared,' the boy is saying. 'We're all scared these days, everyone's scared, even the government. That's why they're putting up those pictures. You've seen those pictures?' He nods towards the bulletin board.

The boy offers to bring me a fresh cup of tea, but I pay up in a hurry, still shaken by the beggar's warning. Now I am not only seeing things; I am hearing things, I am losing my grip. I have an urge to rush back to my hotel room and hide; it's the only hiding-place I know. What I want to hide from I can't say precisely – maybe only from my new-found freedom. Freedom! As if being free of Jiang is the same thing as freedom. As if his disappearance changes anything.

They're setting up the stalls with the same old tat – and I'm thoroughly sick of it all. Sick of the peacock-feather fans, the glass bangles and beads, the painted stone eggs in water-filled basins, the jujube-coloured shoes and the Hello Kitty mittens . . .

But things are no better back at the Friendship Hotel. The minute I open the door to my room, I curse myself. I forgot to close the window, and now the place is full of flies. Flies on the ceiling, on the floor, on the mirror, on the bed. Flies dimming the glass globe on the bathroom light. Flies circling their targets, on a dive-bombing mission.

I whack left and right, first with the tourist pamphlets, then, more effectively, with the sole of my shoe. My aim is good and my score is high, but the more flies I bring down the more they seem to multiply. I give up finally, and crouch to study the carnage.

Whirring on the floor are wind-up propellers, silvery wings spinning first in one direction, then in the other, as the bodies rotate on their backs. 'Dropping like flies', I am only now seeing, means something other than instant death upon dropping. They drop, they play dead, but they spring back to life if you so much as nudge them with the tip of your toe. Then they dart off suddenly for one final tease before you get lucky and *smash* them.

Enough of this grisly entertainment; I'm going downstairs to complain.

The girl – what a nuisance – is not at the front desk. Instead I must deal with a receptionist who speaks no known language – the same man, I'm almost certain, who was yelling for her when she came up to give me the news about Jiang. I try speaking Burmese to him. I try English. I even try Thai. But I get nowhere in my enquiries about when the girl is expected back. Meanwhile, he is becoming increasingly ill-tempered, and difficult to understand.

'Are you cowed?' he sneers, in what sounds like English.

Cowed? I frown. I am making every effort to understand.

'Are you *cowed*?' he repeats.

'Cold?' Is he asking if I am *cold*?

'Are you cowed? Are you cowed?'

Is it necessary for him to *shout*, the oaf? I glower back at him, then shrug. What's the point anyway?

'Pez,' he says darkly.

'Pez?'

'Pez!' He's raising his voice again.

I raise mine even louder. 'Pez? What Pez? What are you saying?' I want to smack his sullen face with its over-large Chinese pimples.

'Pez! Pez!' he hisses, waving me away, and giving his full attention to a newspaper he's pulled out from under the counter.

So this is what I face from now on, with Jiang gone: no one to rely on, no one to speak to in a language I fully understand.

I'm halfway up the stairs when the girl emerges from one of the back rooms. The Pez man has vanished. 'Ma Ma!' she cries, like a child calling for its mother; but she is simply addressing me as 'Big Sister' in Burmese. 'Ma Ma! Where you go? I worry. I bring you tea . . . you not there,' she says.

What business is it of hers where I go, or when I leave the room? Ignoring the accusation, I get to the point. 'Flies,' I say, pointing up towards my room. 'Many, many, *many* flies.' I make little buzzing sounds to help her understand, but not only does she understand perfectly, she seems to have been *expecting* them.

'Ah, flies,' she says, and holds up a finger asking me to wait. Then she fetches something from underneath the front desk and leads the way upstairs. Today her capris are tomato red and freshly ironed. Her mismatched camisole is pink, in a rubbery fabric that glitters with tiny mirrors and sequins. I wonder how old she is: sixteen or so, I would guess. Her hair is tied back in a wide velvet bow with a two-tone sheen. Only her black slippers – flat canvas slip-ons – are plain. But they give her the air of a dancer as she bounces up the stairs ahead of me.

She pretends to be taken aback by the flies that await us. She claps a hand to her mouth and widens her eyes. Then she giggles and goes into action. Fly-swat in one hand, insect spray in the other, she leaps about, clowning. She catches the toe of her slipper on the carpet, stumbles and dives for the wall, bonking her head on it. Then she looks up at me cross-eyed, rubbing her forehead.

I signal her to get on with it. I'm not about to encourage her silly high-jinks. But she won't be dissuaded. Now the fly-swat and spray can become part of her act, the stupid dance with the swirls and pirouettes, the mincing steps on tiptoe, the absurd poses with one arm flung forwards and one leg kicked back.

She dances to the beat of the scratchy martial music coming from the karaoke strip, a dance with no charm or skill. But all the while she hasn't stopped working: she has kept up the swatting and spraying. Now the air is thick with insect spray. In the columns of sunshine slanting in through the window, it looks almost like rain.

She calms down at last, the little idiot. Coughing and sneezing from the noxious spray, she scoops up the dead flies in a dustpan (the same colour as her capris, I can't help notice), then blows kisses and bows to me, her stony-faced audience. Stepping forwards theatrically, as in a curtain call, she taps her chest and says, 'Minzu.' When she sees I am uncomprehending, she says it again. 'My name.' She giggles. 'Minzu is my name.'

*

'All clean now, Ma Ma,' says Minzu, sobering up when she sees I'm holding the door open, impatient for her to leave. And indeed she has cleared the place of every visible fly. She has knotted the top of the plastic bin liner containing the litter and is taking it with her, along with the fly-swat, the dustpan and the spray.

As much out of relief to be rid of her as to reward her efforts, I try to hand her a tip. She leaps back, as though I were offering her a fistful of maggots, and shakes her head in refusal. 'I don't want!' she says – or, rather, means to say.

For the first time I am tempted to laugh. In her funny Burmese accent, what she has actually said is, 'I don't want to fuck.'

ten

To think that once, long ago, I used to be able, like Minzu, to play while cleaning. It was early days in Rangoon, where Daw Daw Seng took me to help in the household she managed. The American family she worked for treated her like a friend, she boasted; a friend, not a servant. I heard all about them on our overnight train journey: their names, their likes and dislikes, their funny habits.

When Daw Daw Seng dozed off I leaned out the window, into the wind's rush and roar, watching the train's tail whip this way and that, breathing in the fumes of its sooty belches, trembling in the blasts of its whistles and shrieks. By morning we were in different country: flat and scrubby, with low-lying skies. The air, too, was foreign: heavy and hot and dusty. Over the wide, wide plains the paddies went dashing by, now gold, now green.

At a station in the lowlands Daw Daw Seng bought me a bottle of Vimto that made my teeth ache and my bladder close to bursting. 'Here,' she said, producing a plastic cup from the inside of her bag. 'Pull your pants down and sit.' We were out in the corridor, with a window to ourselves, away from the crowded compartment. She stood with her back to me while I squatted over the cup. She turned just as I got up and emptied it out the window, spattering her face with the blown-back spray.

Daw Daw Seng yelped and raised her arm – to strike me, I thought, and flinched. But she was only wiping her face. Then she laughed with her head thrown back and her mouth wide open. It was a long time since someone had laughed over a mistake I'd made.

She laughed again on our drive from the Rangoon railway station to my new home in the city when I kept pointing at the immense white buildings all along the river – grand palaces with turrets and towers – asking, 'Is *this* where you live?'

No, she said. Those were government offices. Her American family was different from the other white people in the city. They chose not to live in a big house like other foreigners of their kind. Theirs was a simple house, in a simple quarter.

Simple or not, I wasn't let into the main house without supervision. I slept in Daw Daw Seng's room, in the shack by the outdoor kitchen, and spent my days helping her clean and cook. But little by little I was allowed to dust the furniture on my own, to sweep the wooden floors, hose down and mop the bathroom and toilet, hang out the laundry to dry. I took to my chores eagerly: they were a lot easier than fetching firewood, or winnowing rice in a bamboo tray twice my size.

When Daw Daw Seng wasn't watching I skated over the floor, a duster under each foot, or pushed off on my belly as I polished with the bristles of a halved coconut husk, clutching the dome under my chin. But it was the laundry I loved most, the sorting, washing, wringing, hanging out, bringing in and folding of laundry. I loved the warm, earthy smell of clothes – even the soiled ones, waiting in piles to be sorted. I loved sniffing the sun in the sheets and pillowcases hung out to dry, and folding the soft cotton panties and pyjamas belonging to Pia, the child of my new master and mistress.

She was only seven, a year younger than I, but being much taller, looked older to me.

Pia and I made friends between the laundry lines. For a long time I had watched her from behind the sheets as she wandered about the garden, grabbing handfuls of star-shaped blossoms from a flowering hedge, then stringing the red stars together with needle and thread. Every time she looked up, I shrank back into hiding.

One afternoon she crept up behind me and parted the curtain between. After we had both jumped, she seized me by the arm and led me to a bush underneath the almond tree. Caught in it was a tiny egg, of the palest shade of blue. We looked up into the canopy of the almond, but there was no sign of a nest anywhere. Pia insisted I be the one to retrieve the egg. Then, gripping my elbow as though bearing a platter, she led me into the house for her mother to see what we'd found.

In time I was excused from my chores to play with Pia. Daw Daw Seng had taught me to eat with a fork and spoon, to say *Thank you*, and *Please*. And to call my master and mistress 'Far' and 'Mor' as she herself did. Far and Mor meant 'father' and 'mother' in the language of Mor's ancestors, who had lived in a country called Sweden, long before they moved to America and became Americans.

I was cleaned up, more or less. Daw Daw Seng had washed my hair with kerosene, in case I had lice, and cut it as short as a boy's. She had swabbed every scab and sore on my body with 'red medicine', a stinging liquid that left scarlet pock-marks on my skin. She'd fed me castor oil to rid my stomach of worms. (Although, as it turned out, Pia was the one with the worms. 'Oh, my God, Oh, my God, something's tickling my butt and I can't get it out!' she cried, shuddering.

'Let me look,' I offered. When she bent over I could see the inch-long protrusion, limp as a rubber band. I pulled out a good twelve inches, bit by bit, careful not to snap it. Then I flicked the thing on the ground. Pia couldn't stop shaking, even though I kept saying, 'It's just a worm, Pia. A worm is all it is.' But this happened much later, after we'd become sisters.)

In the beginning I was careful to know my place. My place was in the servants' quarters, with Daw Daw Seng. I liked sleeping with her, liked her clean smell and her old-maid habits. Absent-minded as she was about where she had left things, or when she had put the rice on to boil, she remembered to light a match each morning, blowing it out almost immediately, then screwing the blackened tip into her chin, to leave a beauty mole.

She was faithful about plucking her eyebrows, too, though not the three lucky hairs that grew out of her chin. Her underarm hairs she left to me. At rest on her pallet in the room we shared, one arm raised over her head, she presented me with a fleshy underarm whose creases were dry riverbeds of talcum. While I plucked with her rusty tweezers, taking care not to pinch any skin along with the black stubs of hair, she told me stories about her life as a girl in the northern hills, about working in the mission for Father Roberto, the kind priest from Italy who had taught her prayers and hymns and how to be a good Christian.

From Daw Daw Seng I learned the Lord's Prayer, the Hail Mary, the Glory Be. I learned about the saints: about St Thérèse, 'the Little Flower', St Francis and the almond tree.

It puzzled me no end as to why these martyrs and miracle-workers were made to suffer so. The same was true, it seemed, of the *nats*, those spirits to whom all Buddhists made offerings.

So many of them had died from broken hearts, as the stories went; from the shock of some terrible grief.

'You ask too many questions,' was Daw Daw Seng's answer. 'Don't question. Just pray.'

She wanted to make sure that I prayed to the right god, the Christian god. She had no quarrel with other religions, she said. She herself had never come face-to-face with murderers among other religions – except Buddhism, of course. Because everyone knew there were murderers among the Buddhist soldiers and politicians. These Buddhists were mostly Burmans, it was true, the lowland Burmans who ruled the country and bullied the rest of the Burmese population, who would stop at nothing to wipe out the non-Burmans – people like her, like me. Yes, you had to be careful of those Buddhists with their so-called respect for every living being! With their gaudy temples that took twenty years to build – pagodas thick with gold leaf and studded with gems. Temples funded by generals anxious to make up for all the innocent lives they'd taken so they wouldn't be reincarnated as earth-worms – as their karma would dictate, and quite rightly.

But why? I asked. What had we done to make the Burman Buddhists so full of hate?

'Hate doesn't always have a reason. Did *you* do something to make your old mistress hate you the way she did?'

'I understand,' I said.

Daw Daw Seng snorted. 'You understand nothing.' It was then that she explained the behaviour of the headman's wife to me, how she couldn't help blaming me for the birth of her stillborn boy.

'But why?'

'You see? You don't understand anything. But you will. That's why I'm giving you lots of fish to eat. Fish is good for the brain. The bigger your brain is, the more worthy a sister you will be to Pia.' Sister! Me, a Wild Lu, a sister to Pia? How was that possible, I asked.

'You can be very stupid, you. If Pia's *mor* and *far* are your *mor* and *far*, what do you think that makes you and Pia?'

But then why did Daw Daw Seng call *them* 'Mor' and 'Far', when she was old enough to be *their* 'mor'? I was beginning to doubt if she knew as much as she claimed to. She had to be wrong about the Buddhists. Not all Buddhists were bad; they couldn't be. Mor would certainly not be studying to be a Buddhist, if that were the case. One day I heard her say something to Daw Daw Seng that was even more puzzling. Buddhism taught the most important lesson for a human being, said Mor. It taught the way out of suffering.

A way out of suffering! What did that mean, I asked Daw Daw Seng.

'The only way out of suffering is the way Jesus tells us.' She sniffed. 'Suffer the little children to come unto me.'

When I did reach the point where I was bold enough to ask Mor what she meant by a way out of suffering, she said it would take a lifetime to learn, but I could start by reciting the *dhamma*. So I did. *Aneiksa-doukha-anatta*, I recited. All things are impermanent, all things bring suffering, all things are no-thing, no-self.

From Mor, too, I learned the oddest of prayers: *thabbe thatta bhawuntu thukhitatta.* May all beings find happiness.

To ask God the Father to give us this day our daily bread; to beg the Mother of God to pray for us now and at the hour of death; these were fair enough requests, it seemed to me. But to pray for the happiness of all beings – mosquito and worm and man alike – was this not the most hopeless plea?

I prayed to them all, nevertheless: to Daw Daw Seng's gods

and saints, to the *nats* and spirits, to the Buddha not least. I tried to pray properly, without begging outright. Surely the gods were sick and tired of begging. The first time I was taken to the Rangoon zoo, I came upon a noisy mob in front of the orang-utan's cage. The dispirited old beast was staring into the distance above their heads, doing its best to ignore the hecklers jumping up and down, shouting, clapping and whooping. Then it saw me. It came to the corner where I was standing quietly, and stuck out its rusty arm in greeting; in gratitude for my silence, I was certain.

So I prayed to the gods, all the gods alike, as I paid my respects to the ape – by trying to keep still and on the good side of each. Best not to make demands, to utter too many wishes. Best to keep quiet as a church mouse, as Daw Daw Seng liked to say.

eleven

Since yesterday's fly episode, the girl called Minzu seems to think I've given her licence to dawdle and chat when she comes up to clean my room. I keep my distance, or try to, but it's awkward when she carries in, for instance, a complimentary tray of tea and sweet pork dumplings, setting it on a wooden stool right next to the sofa.

'Where you learn your English, Ma Ma?' she chirps in Burmese, needlessly pushing a rag over the door frame. 'You speak so fast, so well. I hear you speak with Jiang.' The mention of his name is like a small shock, but she recovers quickly. 'You learn from a cat?'

Her accent is a joke. 'School' is what she means; but it comes out 'cat'.

'Yes, school.' I say. 'That's where I learned English.' The usual answer. The American family is too long a story.

In fact it was Daw Daw Seng who first taught me English. In the beginning we spoke to each other in Daru, our common language. Many Daru words were the same in Lu, my mother tongue. I couldn't remember any more which words belonged to which language, and adding to the muddle were the bits of Chinese and Burmese I had learned as a small child. The Chinese I remembered from horse talk, from the orders given to mules and ponies, which responded only to Chinese commands. The buffalo and ox we directed in Burmese, the main language spoken in the lowlands.

'What is your name?' Daw Daw Seng's drill would begin.

'My name is Na Ga.'

'Not "neigh", "name". Shut your lips at the end.'

'My naima is Na Ga.'

'Don't say "Nah Gah" like that, unless you want everyone in Rangoon to think someone nicknamed you "Ears-that-stick-out". You want to say N'*gah*. N'*gah*, like the serpent-dragon.'

I cleared my throat to try again. 'My naima is Nah Gah.'

Daw Daw Seng sighed. 'Well, at least you're closing your lips.'

I complained to her often about the many meanings of my name, none of them particularly pleasing.

'Don't worry, Na Ga is not your real name anyway,' she told me one day. 'You left home before you were given your real name.'

'My real name?' This was news to me.

'It's a custom with your people,' she explained. 'The Lu keep a child's name secret until it's old enough to ask. Then the mother whispers the name into a dried poppy seed. She dips the seed in a kind of hard glue and winds string round it, like a top for spinning. That's your real name, and you wear it round your neck. It's what protects you, your *name seed*.'

A memory comes back to me, too unfocused to grasp.

'So . . . I'll never know my real name?'

'Don't think about things like that. Things you can't change.'

'Why can't I change them? Why can't I find out my real name? Go quickly back to my village, for a little while, just to find out, then leave.'

'Your village is not where it used to be. I've told you that a hundred times,' Daw Daw Seng said, not unkindly. 'They've built that great dam so they've moved your people to another province.'

'Who is "they"?' I asked.

Seng tapped her shoulder with two fingers to indicate stripes on a uniform – her shorthand for an army officer. 'Don't worry, I'm trying to find out where they've gone, your folk. It will take time, but you'll see them again. The government has moved them to another province.'

I knew she was lying. I didn't think she wanted to deceive me, just that she was never going to succeed in finding my home. But we went on with our lesson. 'Once again now. Say "name" with your lips shut at the end.'

I came to understand that knowing when to open my mouth and when to keep it shut was important for other reasons. I learned by reading the faces of Mor and Far. From their smallest expressions of approval or displeasure I learned to tell when they were inviting me into their world, when they were keeping me at a distance.

I learned so quickly that by the end of my first year I was moved into the main house, promoted from Pia's playmate to roommate. I slept in the spare bed next to hers. I even had my own shelf in the clothes cupboard; my own hairbrush, toothbrush and towel. And Santa at Christmas brought me my own silver-haired, long-lashed, long-legged Barbie doll.

'I know something you don't know,' Pia confided, when it was nearing Christmas. 'Santa Claus doesn't exist.'

Really? It was news to me that he did.

*

They had their doubts about me, nevertheless, and who could have blamed them? They were never sure if I knew right from wrong. Mor took me with her once to a lacquer factory where a spindly old monk was squatting under a tree, working his bellows on an open flame. In the blackened pot hanging over the fire, a molten liquid was seething. One of the factory workers, a woman having a smoke outside, explained to me that the monk was a *zawgyi* – the Burmese word for 'wizard', a word I didn't understand in any language, so couldn't translate for Mor's benefit. But when the woman mentioned magic – turning lead into silver and copper into gold – Mor nodded knowingly. 'Ah, alchemy!' said she.

The factory worker dropped her voice. She'd heard it said that if you buried a *zawgyi* for seven days, his flesh turned sweet enough to eat and, eaten, brought all sorts of super-human powers.

On the way home I asked Mor why, if the monk's flesh was so sweet to eat, someone hadn't killed and eaten him already. She seized my shoulders and bent low to face me. 'Because it is wrong! Na Ga, you do know that it's wrong, don't you, to eat human meat?' She seemed to think I might sneak off for a bite of the *zawgyi*'s thigh the minute her back was turned.

Far had his own way of testing me on some truth or other. He lowered his voice to sound soothing, the way you would coax a shy beast. It didn't sound soothing to me; instead it put me on my guard, afraid of saying the wrong thing.

'Look at me, Na Ga, look at me!'

I gazed at the curling mustache that gave him a smile when he was not really smiling. I couldn't bear to look into such searching eyes. I couldn't give what they were asking of me.

'What was it like in your village? What songs did you sing? What games did you play?'

He wanted to know all about my native village, not the Daru village. Life in the Daru village I could describe quite easily. But what was there to tell about my childhood home? I rose with my mother just before dawn. I watched her pound paddy. I helped her carry water from the bamboo pipe at the foot of the hill. I fanned the fire when she put on the rice to boil. At harvest time, when the men were in the field, I carried rice bundled in thick leaves for their midday meal. When it was dark I ran around with the other children. Sometimes I watched the women stitch and weave by the light of torches. Sometimes I fell asleep in my father's lap while he sat in the men's circle, puffing a huge cheroot that left ash in my hair.

Ordinary days. What was there to tell? Nothing.

'Na Ga? Look at me. You don't remember *anything*?'

'I don't remember.' It was only when I looked up and met his beseeching gaze that Far would stop.

Yet he never lost his patience – not when he taught me my letters and numbers in English; not when he taught me to swim. He took me to the old tank reservoir, where a ladder made from pipes hung down one side, into cloudy water too deep for me to stand in. I clung to his neck, leaving nail marks on his skin. But slowly, firmly, he moved me away from him as I lay on my belly, kicking. I clutched and clawed at his big hairy arms, refusing to let go. Still, he held me steady and safe from the crowds, from the rowdy boys who shrieked and splashed and pulled at the hairs on his chest.

Far used to be a schoolteacher in Pennsylvania before he came to Burma. Now he was called a technical adviser, but his job was to teach English to government workers in

Rangoon. Being a teacher gave him the patience, I supposed, for the complicated cardboard models he built in his spare time: the miniature pagodas and palaces with drawbridges and weather-vanes, with windows and doors that could be shut and opened. The same meaty hands holding me afloat in the tank fumbled for hours over the tiniest paper chips, the thinnest razor blades, to craft those paper models.

Patient and solid among the noisy bathers, Far kept up his encouragement. I could trust him, he wouldn't let go; he would teach me to swim.

But what should I believe? If he let go of me, I would stop trusting him even though I might manage to swim. If he *didn't* let go, I would trust him, of course. But then how would I ever learn to swim?

Far taught me to swim, Mor taught me to pray, and Pia taught me the importance of silence. Whenever she became excited about something, she chattered non-stop, hardly pausing to breathe, making me wonder if she was possessed.

'Pia! Calm down!' Mor would say. 'Take a deep breath!' But with the next breath she was babbling again. Sometimes she turned wild, stamping on the ground and shrieking. Yet she liked to call *me* a Wild Thing.

'"*And when he came to the place where the wild things are,*"' she said, pretending to be the boy from one of her favourite books, '"*they roared their terrible roars . . .*"'

'Rowr rowr', I said lamely, just to make her happy.

'"And gnashed their terrible teeth . . ."'

I bared my teeth, and made them chomp noisily, like the joke plastic teeth that chattered when you wound a key.

'"And rolled their terrible eyes . . ."'

I rolled my terrible eyes.

64

Then abruptly she ordered, '"Be still!"'

In an instant I was a statue, not breathing, not blinking, to show that Pia, like the boy in the book, had tamed me with her magic trick.

She herself could not be tamed. When out of sorts she landed powerful kicks on anyone who came near. The only thing that seemed to soothe her was playing with my hair. It had been allowed to grow out now. Plaiting and unplaiting it, tying it, pinning it, threading it with jasmine or hibiscus blossoms from the garden, she muttered, 'I love your hair, Na Ga. I love-love-love your black hair.'

And I loved her smell – especially after our bath, when she put on her nightie with the frills on the panties, climbed into bed, lifted her hair before lying on the pillow, and picked up her book to read. If gold had a smell, that was how I imagined it would be.

'Whose hair is thicker? Feel!' she'd say.

Pia was full of comparisons. Who do you like more? Which doll do you want? Which is better, this colour or that? Choices were a burden to me. I often did not know which of two things I preferred, and was only too willing to let her decide. This was taken as generosity by Mor and Far. 'Can't you be generous like Na Ga?' they said.

How easy it was to wake up one day with a mask on your face. More than one mask, even. One for generosity, one for indifference, one for atonement.

Wearing the mask of courage, I was the first to expose my arm for our vaccinations, while Pia whimpered and fussed. I was the first to turn my head and offer my ear when both of us were taken to have them pierced. And when one of my new earrings got caught in Pia's blouse as we wrestled in play, causing it to rip through my lobe when she pulled away, I wore the mask that told her not to cry, not to worry about the blood, because it didn't really hurt anyway.

I learned not only how to hold back tears, but when scolded or blamed I understood that atonement was expected of me, and I learned to oblige by crying. But tears of that sort weren't the real thing. The real thing came only in sleep, when I'd wake up sobbing, unable to remember anything except a colour, nothing more – an indigo of deepest longing. Or a spreading grey dread that filled the horizon. Or a black, black tide that sucked me out into a hopeless ocean.

Sometimes I'd wake to find Mor in my bed, shaking me. 'Na Ga, you're dreaming, honey. You're having a bad dream.' She'd press my head into her chest, into the freckled flesh of her nightgown's V. 'Oh, my baby! Mor's here! Mor will always take care of you!'

Her smell made me doubt it. Mor's smell was ever-changing. Early in the mornings, her breath was a quenched fire, smoky and stale. When she came in from the outside, sweating, she smelt of engine grease. Evenings, she smelt of gardenias; then later at night, of cigarettes and whisky.

But there was another smell I picked up when she lay next to me. It came from her thighs, from the place in between. Sharp and metallic, it was the smell of a just-opened tin of Kraft cheese. That very same place in my own mother's body gave off a different odour entirely. Just this difference told me that Mor wasn't my mother and would never be. Then I could hear myself saying – although she couldn't hear, *No, you will not. You will not always take care of me.*

Minzu shows me a book she is hoping to study: a book of tests for English-language learners. She finds it difficult. Can I help her with it? I glance at a page – and my mind seizes up.

1) 'I'm sorry. I had something to say, but that siren outside made me lose my........of thought,' Larry said to Karen.

(a) source
(b) train
(c) chain
(d) course

How I hate these games of choice. Really, how is one to know whether it's his source, his chain, his train or his course of thought that Larry has lost? Perhaps he has lost them all. Or none of them.

I remember how Pia used to torment me with choices.

Mor and Far had an air mattress that they inflated for us on rainy days when it was too wet outside to play. On nights when they were out, we would turn it into the bouncy surface of the moon.

In the dark of the living room, we'd push back the chairs and tables to clear a space, and step onto the wobbly mattress, bouncing lightly to imitate the astronauts Pia had seen on television in America. She showed me how they had walked when they landed on the moon, and I followed along.

On full-moon nights we went lolloping across our mattress, pointing out of the window, singing, 'The earth! The earth! The beautiful earth!' We waved and blew kisses and sent our love to the big yellow earth, now that we were walking on the moon.

Then Pia would spoil the adventure with one of her tiresome tests. 'Where would you rather live, Na Ga? On the earth or the moon?'

'I don't know.'

'Choose!' she would insist. 'You *must* choose. Just pick one. Earth or moon? Which?'

'The earth,' I'd say, because I knew she wanted the moon.

'You're sure now? The moon, you know, is a heavenly body.'

'The moon, then.'

I skim through more tests in Minzu's book, but they're all more of the same.

> (3) Soldiers are forbidden to visit the red ....
> districts in other countries. Not only does it
> tarnish the reputation of the army, but those
> places are also dangerous for foreigners.

> (a) door
> (b) welcome
> (c) light
> (d) traffic

I hand the book back to Minzu. 'Too difficult for me too. Sorry.'

Minzu looks crushed, but she pulls herself together with a smile, refusing to give up. What strange dimples she has: they're in the wrong place for dimples – not on her cheeks, but lower down, on the sides of her chin. And they are more pronounced when she is trying to speak English.

'Excuse me, madam,' she dimples, 'will you please teach me anguish?'

twelve

The days pass in a delirium of fatigue. The sleepless nights are long and bring no rest, no peace, no clarity of purpose. This is my pattern at the Friendship Hotel. If it weren't for the different mat I find by the lift door each morning, the jute mat with the day of the week printed on it, I'd be hard pressed to distinguish day from day.

When the blessed dawn ushers in a new morning with a pale wash of light on the high window-panes, I go downstairs and ask Minzu for some tea. Then I step out for my breakfast at the market.

For reasons that escape me, Jiang's death has left me racked by appetite. Hunger cramps tug at my gut at odd hours; and whenever I stop to think about the meals we shared – those rich, all-you-can-eat buffets I could scarcely stomach at the time – I salivate and feel faint.

What I craved most, those first mornings in Wanting, was a soggy, greasy chunk of deep-fried Chinese dough, and a cup of sweet tea to dunk it in. But Jiang's routine wouldn't allow it. There he'd be in the lobby, at seven thirty every morning, waiting for me to come downstairs, to escort me to a proper feast. I'd find him chatting with Minzu in Yunnanese. At least, I assumed it was Yunnanese they were speaking, but a few days in China was not long enough for me to distinguish one language or dialect from the next.

We'd walk to the south side of town for breakfast, Jiang and I – to the New Prosperity Bridge Hotel. There, faced with the giant horseshoe of buffet tables laden with Chinese, Japanese and Western dishes, I would promptly lose my appetite. Plate in hand, I shuffled past the smoking kettles, steaming bowls and platters, sweating plastic jugs and glass decanters, up and down the length of that cavernous, foggy, mostly empty dining hall, with the pianist already churning out a seamless loop of Chinese, Japanese and Western tunes – and couldn't find anything I wanted to eat.

Congee – a bowl of congee would do me. But the big black cauldron of rice gruel was surrounded by bowls and cups brimming with minced chicken, pork and beef; with fish balls, fish cakes, crab sticks and raw shrimp; with eggs – boiled eggs, tea eggs, 'hundred-year-old' eggs; with sauces and condiments, spring onions, red onions, fried onions, fried garlic, green chilli.

Next came the noodles: fat noodles, thin noodles, fried noodles, crisp noodles, noodles in broths and sauces – to say nothing of the dumplings, bite-sized *shu-mai* and loaf-sized *bao*, stuffed with greens and sweet bean, with shrimp and pork and sausage and beef. After that came the cakes: turnip cakes, sponge cakes, rice cakes, iced cakes, and moon cakes with red letters stamped into the thick pastry, even though Chinese New Year was still two months away.

Soon the pianist was joined by a singer in a folk dress – embroidered skirt, beaded vest, red and white pompoms jiggling on her hat. I recognised snatches of tunes, 'Moon River', 'Shall We Dance?', 'Plum Blossoms In The Twilight', but just when I thought she was singing in English, the words seemed to switch into Chinese, maybe even into Burmese.

The language was uncertain, and so was the voice: throaty one minute, nasal the next.

The Chinese table turned a corner at last . . . and now here was the Western spread, with its metal trays on stands, heated by blue flames from beneath: trays heaped with scrambled eggs, fried eggs, boiled eggs, egg pies and omelettes; with sausages the size of cat turds and glassy bacon strips steeped in grease; with pancakes as stiff as plates, and waffles the size of egg cartons; with potatoes sliced, diced, mashed and shredded.

Why was it all so unappetising? Jiang's presence had something to do with it, perhaps. He would follow close behind, so close I'd get a whiff of his nicotine-stained fingers that reeked of stale cigarettes. The place was deserted, no one ahead and no one behind us, but I could feel his impatience as I hesitated, moved on, hesitated, from dish to dish, table to table, unable to settle on anything . . . not even when we turned the corner once more to proceed down the Japanese breakfast spread.

Now I had only to make it past this end of the horseshoe to get through the ordeal, past the islands of pickles and preserves, the platters of sushi and sashimi decorated with fruits and vegetables all fashioned to appear fake; past carrots carved into roses, and edible leaves trimmed to imitate plastic ones, and radishes shredded like the paper stuffing used to line the boxes in which fragile objects are shipped.

We had our pick of tables, but Jiang always led the way to one by the entrance. The hordes for which this vast dining hall was prepared had yet to arrive, if they ever would. Outside, in the lobby, no more than a half-dozen bodies were seated at the bar, hunched on their high stools and watching the front entrance with grim expectation.

Jiang would stare aghast at my plate, at the spoonful or two of fried noodles and scrambled eggs, the inch-high cut of a sushi roll. He would pretend to be aghast, anyway. It was more of the old hospitality ritual: shock and dismay over a guest's modest appetite – *Woh! Wah! Bah!* – expressed with bulging eyes. What's wrong? he'd ask. Was I sick? Allergies? Stomach problems?

No, it was just – too much choice, I'd reply. *Too much! Too kind!*

But, look, what about you? I'd point out in return, tut-tutting my concern over *his* appetite. His plate always had even less on it than mine: a small dumpling, a crescent roll, a fishcake. He'd shrug off his leather jacket, hang it on the back of his chair, light up and take a long drag before sitting. He would extend the cigarette in my direction, indicating that this was all the breakfast he needed.

'Then why don't you *eat* it?' I wanted to say, as long as we were both in the spirit of force-feeding.

It was more than food that Jiang needed, however: he needed sleep. He yawned while I ate, fidgeting to keep himself awake. He twisted his watch back and forth across his wrist. He tapped his foot under the table. He kept leaning so far in his chair that just one more inch and he'd be flat on the marble floor, still wet from the morning mop.

Jiang waited till I was finished before cleaning his own plate. A stuffed mouthful or two, a quick wipe of his finger-tips on the roll of pink toilet paper that sat in its holder side-by-side with the toothpicks, and he, too, was done. He couldn't be bothered even to tear off a piece, only left a greasy imprint on the edge of the roll.

'Shall we?' he'd say, gathering up his packet of Marlboro and his leather jacket. I'd follow him to the cashier, and from the back he looked like an old man, with his grey hair and slight shuffle. With breakfast behind us, however, Jiang came alive, turning into an over-eager tour guide. He couldn't wait to show me the wonders of the region. Temples – 'famous temples' – seemed to be at the top of his list. Temples, famous or not, were the last thing I wished to see.

I tried to sound curious. 'Famous for what?' I asked.

'For escaping destruction,' was his curious reply.

Escaping destruction, it appeared, was a hallmark of the region. Here was a monument the Red Army had spared; there was a temple the Red Guards had missed. In that very plot of land precious musical instruments had been buried for decades, thus escaping destruction when others had been smashed to pieces and thrown on bonfires during the Cultural Revolution.

'Miracle!' was Jiang's glum conclusion to every tale of survival or endurance.

Never were miracles so uninviting. I followed him from shrine to shrine, landmark to landmark, listless and restless – and guilty. I was leading him on, leading him to think his efforts on my behalf were being gratefully received, when all the while I was biding my time, plotting my exit.

By the third day, when we arrived at the most famous of all the temples that had escaped destruction, the Buddhist temple about two miles from town, I was in the grip of a new foreboding. I wondered whether it wasn't Jiang who was stringing me along. He was talking non-stop, in a jumble of English and Burmese. It wasn't easy to follow much of what he was saying, but then much of it didn't seem worth trying to follow. By mid-morning, Jiang's commentaries on every-thing from Buddhism to heroin, from temples to TV programmes, from stomach ailments to aphrodisiacs, were positively *frantic*. What was he trying to cover up with all that gabble, I wondered.

The temple grounds were deserted in the glaring sun – not a monk, not a dog in sight. Inside the main hall I tried to show interest in what there was to see: the smirking Chinese-faced Buddha cross-legged on the throne, the gilded pillars and lacquered beams, the toothy demons on the ceiling. But I kept stealing glances at Jiang's watch.

He finally stopped talking long enough to light some joss-sticks. I went outside to wait. But when I looked back over my shoulder, I could see he'd resumed his chatter. Even while kneeling and kowtowing, he kept his lips moving. He kowtowed four times, I noticed, three for the gods, one for the ancestors, which made him, I supposed, a Chinese Buddhist.

I watched his devotions with a twinge of envy. If only *I* could pray. About a hundred yards from where I was standing, a dusty almond tree cast a patch of shade. I thought of St Francis who, according to Daw Daw Seng, had only to stand before an almond tree and say, 'Speak to me of God!' for the tree to break out in blossoms. I stared at the tree for a long time, willing it to speak to me: of God, of hope, of *anything*. I can't say I was surprised that not a branch bestirred itself – not a twig, not a leaf.

Jiang came out to join me, refreshed by piety and full of new things to say. What had I been doing, he wanted to know.

Praying, I said, which gave him the wrong impression. The man wouldn't know a joke if it bit him on the neck. Taking me for a fellow Buddhist, he now wanted to expand on the *bodhisattva*.

I thought about how, in the house where I lived until not

so very long ago, Will's house in Bangkok, a silk scroll painting hung on the wall of my room: a glittering image of a *bodhisattva* in garments of scarlet, turquoise and gold. It was already there when I moved in, greeting me with a smile of benevolent boredom, and I grew to think of this 'Buddha of Compassion' as my guardian spirit, neither Chinese nor Indian, male nor female, earthly nor heavenly.

Was it still there, I wondered, on the wall of the room I had so recently called my own, or had it been replaced by another deity, as I had been replaced by another woman? Was the house once mine now rid of every trace of me?

'Just imagine!' said Jiang. 'A *bodhisattva* gains enlightenment, gains release from the cycle of living and dying, but throws itself back into the world of suffering. All out of compassion for those still caught there.'

Difficult to imagine but, 'Yes,' I said. 'Just imagine!'

It was only over lunch on the fourth day, in the courtyard restaurant a mile out of town, that Jiang admitted he was tired, so tired. He collapsed in his chair, abruptly drained. He had selected the menu from the display in the glass cabinet near the front entrance: Yunnan ham slices, diced pork with pea shoots, yellow tofu cakes steeped in red chilli oil. But when they brought out the steaming dishes neither of us wanted much to eat. Jiang picked at his plate between cigarettes and sips from a Pabst beer can, not bothering any more to comment on my own lack of appetite.

By the time the main course arrived we weren't able to manage another mouthful: Jiang because he was filled to bursting (he patted his skinny ribs as evidence); and I because the dark, gelatinous mass in the clay pot contained, to my horror, 'turtle meat'.

I shuddered, and Jiang laughed, misunderstanding my revulsion.

I couldn't expect him to know that in my Rangoon days my real mother was a turtle I could visit only in secret.

thirteen

There was a pagoda in Rangoon, not far from our house, where an important relic was held. It was said that one of the Buddha's hairs was enclosed in a strong-box above the main shrine. I loved going there – not for the sacred hair but for the sacred turtle pond outside. In the scummy waters of the pond or along its weedy rims, I could hope to meet my mother once in a while.

She was the largest of the turtles, my mother – a queen among commoners. She towered above the scrappy little scavengers that bickered and snapped, ignoring the popcorn treats showered on them by pilgrims and picnickers. But she was not always to be seen. At times, though I waited and waited, she preferred to stay hidden among the tall mustard and watercress along the pond's edges. When luck was on my side, however, I could spot her just below the water's surface, a slight disturbance beneath the popcorn islands – a sign that she would soon reveal herself to me. Then the dome of her shell would burst into view, through the pond's litter, like the sunrise itself. Everything stopped – my thoughts, my heart, my breath – as I waited for the beautiful, beaky head to turn in my direction. It never did, of course. But I knew why. We had to be careful. There was no telling who might be watching –

who, seeing us greet each other, might conspire to keep us apart.

So I kept very quiet, and my mother looked away.

It was Mor who read us the turtle story from a book of Burmese folktales.

A poor fisherman and his wife went out on a lake, waiting for their luck to turn. Heavy storms had kept them land-locked for days, and they were hungry and desperate. But their first catch brought discord when it should have brought relief. It was only a small fish, hardly worth selling, and the man was for grilling and devouring it there and then. But his wife was thinking of their only child who, like the parents, had gone hungry for days. 'No, no! We have to save that for Little Daughter!' she insisted, and put the fish away. The fisher-man found this stupid and unfair. Surely, as head of the household, his needs should come first. Surely he deserved a little nourishment for the long day ahead. But he gave in and carried on fishing. After a long while he caught another fish. 'Oh, save that for Little Daughter, too!' cried the wife. 'The other one's so small.' Again the fisherman bit his tongue. But when he pulled in his third, a nice fat specimen, and his wife had the nerve to say, 'That one's to salt and preserve for Little Daughter,' he lost his temper and hit her with the oar, knocking her into the water.

He rowed home alone, and back in his village was greeted with sympathy as he related the sad story of how his wife had tried to stand up in the boat, tripped, fallen into the lake and been swept away.

When, after a time, the fisherman took a new wife, everyone wished him well, believing it would be good for the grieving young daughter to have a mother. The new wife, however, turned out to be a jealous shrew with an equally jealous daughter of her own. They soon put the fisherman's girl to work as their servant, treating her with cruel contempt.

One afternoon the unhappy child slipped out of the house and went for a walk by the lake. Missing her mother, she sat and wept. She was sobbing her heart out when she spotted a great turtle swimming towards her through the waves. To her astonishment, the turtle was crying too. Right away the girl knew it was her mother and stretched out her arms in welcome. The melancholy creature climbed into her lap – and there it stayed nestled till dusk, when it was time for the girl to go home.

From then on the fisherman's daughter took every chance to slip away to the lake, where her mother the turtle would be waiting. The girl's life was transformed: there was nothing that could not be endured, now that her mother had returned to her. But the stepmother and her daughter had noticed the girl's absences, and one day they followed her secretly to the shore. What they saw defied belief – the fisherman's daughter, snuggled up with a huge turtle, of all things. They couldn't wait to put an end to such nonsense.

First the stepmother pretended to fall ill. Then she bribed a village doctor to pronounce her illness a rare disease curable only with turtle meat.

'I know just where we can find a turtle,' said her daughter to the fisherman. That afternoon, when she knew her step-sister had stolen away to the shore, she led the fisherman to that secret spot where, sure enough, the girl had her arms around the large reptile.

The fisherman pounced, attacking the turtle with one of his oars.

How the girl screamed and pleaded for mercy. But while

her stepsister wrestled her to the ground and kept her pinned, her father clubbed the turtle to death.

No sooner had the girl been dragged home, senseless with horror and grief, than she was ordered to put the pot on to boil, to stew the butchered chunks of her mother's carcass.

I must never let on, I thought ever after, must never betray any recognition of my mother in the turtle pond. And so it was that we never exchanged glances except in the stealthiest way. We certainly never dared embrace.

fourteen

So now, with Jiang gone, I am finally a free agent. Free to spend the day as I wish. To sit here in this tea-shop under the banyan tree for as long as I please. To watch the parade of hill folk and town folk, farmers and merchants, from both sides of the frontier divide.

Without Jiang to distract me however, I find I am seeing things. My mother, for instance. Not the one with the hard shell and the wizened face, but the mother I knew as a child. I keep seeing her ghost among the women of the poorer, drabber clans before me – the ones in black tunics and black turbans, with their long baskets of chestnuts and twigs.

I remember my mother's black tunic – the one she wore to the New Year festival in the Daru village. It was decorated with a row of safety pins. She had no jewellery to display. No silver coins, no pompoms, no shiny bangles and necklaces to match those of the Daru women. But her breasts were covered for a change. And coloured yarns trailed from the topknot on her head.

It was my first big outing – an overnight journey to attend a festival on the other side of the hills. I was six years old, almost seven. The Daru, our neighbours in the valley, were celebrating their New Year with a temple fair, and word came that we were invited.

We went in a group: my mother, myself and a few of our

relatives. We left by the back gate to the village, the one I had never been allowed through before. Like the main entrance on the opposite side, this gate opened on to a tunnel hollowed out in a hedge of dead branches, bramble, and thorn. But while the other, main, tunnel was arrow-straight, and high enough for the grown-ups to pass through without crouching, this one zigzagged in pitch darkness, with a ceiling so low that even I had to duck my head in places.

By the light of a lantern we picked our way through that jagged black passage, the grown-ups bent double, side-stepping the wooden pegs and sharp sticks planted in the ground to keep out strangers and ghosts.

Then someone put out the lantern because it was bright enough to see. We could suddenly stand upright: we were out in the open. It was still very early, still half-night, and when I looked back towards the village, all I could make out was the black wall of a hedge.

We walked all day, from the dark of dawn to the dark of night, stopping only for the grown-ups to squat by the road-side to have an occasional smoke and a rest. We walked till my feet began to bleed and I had to be dragged along, half asleep. My mother kept sticking her cigar into my mouth, trying to keep me awake. We came to one downhill footpath, very steep and slick, with no trees or bushes to act as brakes. The grown-ups were forced into awkward sprints, or had to slide down on their backsides.

'Our feet,' I remember someone saying, 'are made for mountains. If we stay in the lowlands too long they'll become misshapen.' Everybody laughed and looked at their feet.

Somewhere in the valley we hitched a ride on a bullock cart. Too tired to sit up and enjoy the luxury, I put my head on my mother's lap and went to sleep. What woke me was a bright light, a clammy chill. A giant moon was by my side, sidling so close I could feel its breath on my skin.

The cart driver was singing in a warbly voice. He sang about a frog, the great frog in the sky that opened its mouth once every few weeks to swallow the moon and darken the sky. The cartwheels made a shrieking music, keeping tune to his song. I searched the skies for signs of the frog, but all I could see was the moon by my side, the round and massive moon. If you looked too long at the sun you went blind, it was said. What would happen, I wondered, if you looked too long at the moon?

Lying on my back, rocked by the cart, I dared to stare down the silvery globe of light . . . and the next thing I knew, my mother was shaking me awake.

I sat up and saw smoke rising from wood fires, and shadows wading through a thick ground cover of mist. I saw men with guns and crossbows leading a long caravan of ponies. I saw haughty women with silver coins on their jackets and bright yarns in their hair, with goods in long baskets, or babies in silk carriers, on their backs.

I jumped down from the cart and went to warm myself at a brazier, where two girls were shaping sticky rice flour into cakes, then toasting them on the flames. The fumes, nutty and thick, made my mouth water. I hovered over the girl flipping the purple cakes and held out my hand. She plucked one off the fire, dropped it onto a banana leaf, sprinkled salt over it and handed it to me. Then she held out *her* hand, expecting payment. When she realised I hadn't understood I'd have to pay, she raised her arm in threat and told me off loudly.

What I thought was salt turned out to be a new taste, dark and lingering: the taste of brown-sugar jaggery. But before

I could take another bite, the cake slipped out of my hand and onto the ground, not far from where a little black pig had just been shitting. My mother appeared at that moment and bent over to pick up the cake. Finding it covered with mud, she turned it over in her hand, looking thoughtful, before slapping me with it.

The dolled-up Daru children found this very funny. 'Wild Lu, Wild Lu!' they sang, pointing at us. Yes, we are the Wild Lu and what of it, I thought. But I was suddenly ashamed of my dirt-covered self, my ragged dress, my tangled hair. I could see now that the Daru were our betters. Their altars were decorated with streamers and paper figures; their slaughtered pig was enormous, and all decked out for sacrifice. It lay grandly on its side, surrounded by saucers of yellowish wine, grinning like a shaman who had drunk himself to death.

We had nothing like that in our own village, nothing like the colour and noise of the Daru fair. Loud guns were fired but nobody seemed frightened. Gongs began tolling in the temple, the big Buddhist temple set way back on the hill. Cymbals clashed in a hectic rhythm. Men blew on their gourd pipes and beat their drums. Women joined hands and danced, stamping their feet around an open fire. Little children threw wooden tops and seed pods onto the ground and ran through the crowds spinning whirligigs.

I couldn't stop thinking about the purple cake, its sweet sticky crispness I'd only just tasted before dropping it. When my mother wasn't looking I made once more for the brazier, but something caught my eye and stopped me.

Underneath the neem tree where the bullock carts were tethered was an extremely tall man, the tallest I'd ever seen. His cloak was made from strips of fur, with feathers and claws and seeds sewn along the edges. A crown of bone sat on his bushy mane. He was guarding the entrance to a stall with a curtain and collecting money from the crowd waiting to get in. I found myself somehow squeezed in among the bodies, pushed forward inch by inch – until the curtain parted and I stumbled in.

A woman. It was only a woman behind the screen, sitting on some kind of crate. On her head was a black turban, on her lap a mound, concealed. What was so unusual, anyway? What were all those people outside lining up to see? Slowly, dreamily, the woman uncovered her lap, exposing a lumpy, scaly thing. It wasn't easy in the half-light to make out the creature: it wasn't a snake, or a lizard, but some incomplete toad with no head, no feet. It clung to her lap calmly, it made no move to leave.

The toad's hide – now I could see better – was as thick as a wild pig's, but raw and festering. The thing was moving slightly. Yes, moving in time to the woman's breathing, which made a wet noise from the long pipe she was sucking. Behind the sweet fumes of the pipe was a stronger smell of rot that made me hold my breath.

But what *was* that creature so at home on the woman's lap? My God. The thing wasn't just sitting *on* the woman: the thing *was* the woman. The beast was none other than the woman's sex; the festering hide was her very own festering skin.

The next thing I knew a large hand had clamped on the back of my neck and sent me hurtling outside.

Everything around me was spinning. The boys had formed circles and were playing wicker-ball, keeping it aloft with their heads, knees and feet. The girls were dancing with paper streamers, making circles in the air. High above the temple, the swaying bamboo poles were paying out their pennants – silver and gold, silver and gold – that wiggled and swam in the wind.

'You! Where did you go?' My mother's voice came from a long distance, even though she was right beside me.

'I want to go home,' I said, still sitting where I had fallen. I wanted to be back in my own village, among the animals I knew and the cousins I played with, in the dirt yard behind the thorn hedges of our village gates.

I wanted to be back on the other side of the booby-trapped tunnel that kept out strangers, tricksters and freaks.

fifteen

Among the many new lessons I learned in Rangoon were rhymes for remembering things. Or sayings, for example, like 'Thirty days hath September, April, June and November'. But there were no tricks, it seemed, for forgetting the things I wanted to forget, now that I had a new family, a new life, a whole new way of reading, writing, speaking, and behaving. Now that a new home awaited me in the States.

The States! I never tired of Pia's stories of the States. Late-night movies shown at home! ('No kidding,' said Pia. 'Cross my heart and hope to die. You can watch TV in the middle of the night!') Cities jammed with buildings as high as mountains! Drugstores selling much more than medicines: books and toys and hair-clips and sweets! Supermarkets the size of football stadiums! Houses as grand as palaces, with bubbling bathtubs for six at a time to bathe in! ('No, not swimming-pools, Jacuzzis!' said Pia. 'Katjoozies?' I repeated. Pia threw herself back on the couch, laughing. 'Mama, guess what Na Ga calls Jacuzzis! Katjoozies!)' And movie theatres selling foot-long hot-dogs, ice-cream cones with triple scoops, and *barrels* of popcorn and potato chips.

When Pia's grandparents sent pictures from California, I studied them so closely that I could smell the flowers in their tidy garden, although they were flowers I'd never seen. I could feel the very sharpness of the grass on their green, green lawn, the softness of the long sofa on which the old couple sat side by side, smiling shyly. From the photos of their kitchen I imagined the cold fumes released when the door to their fridge was open. I could taste the ham on their Christmas table, the sweet brittle crackling.

The grandparents were not *real* grandparents, however. They were Aunt Edith and Uncle Harry, an aunt and uncle who had raised Mor, an orphan. Far called them Uncle Edith and Aunt Harry, making Mor angry. Uncle Edith wore a plaid shirt, had bristling grey hair, and was half a head taller than Aunt Harry, who had wide, high hips, and a timid smile. Far made Mor even angrier by calling them Jesus Freaks, even though Mor didn't seem to like them much either, and spoke more fondly of her other aunts and uncles, the ones who had never left Sweden for America.

Mor had her own way of teasing Far, who came from a place in America 'where people talk funny' – a place called Texas.

'You know how they say, "Hi, how are you?" in Texas?' she'd say. 'They say, "Ha! Hair yew!"' Then she'd spell it out: h-a-i-r, y-e-w.

Far didn't like to show that her teasing annoyed him, but I could tell it did from the way he said, 'You're not as good a mimic as you like to think, honey.'

It was Pia who minded most when Mor and Far went on needling each other. Once, when Mor kept calling Far stupid, Pia shouted her down. 'Hey! Don't call my father stupid!' Mor looked shamefaced but I was on her side, because Far *was* being stupid that time. Still, I admired Pia's courage in standing up for him.

Pia was bold in ways I could never have been – even though Mor often said we were like Siamese twins. It was true that we were together all the time – except during school hours, for we were in different classes (though a year younger, Pia was a year ahead of me). We met for lunch every day at the far end of the playground to share the fried rice and Chinese sausage that Daw Daw Seng had cooked and wrapped in banana leaves, keeping it warm and moist till we unpacked it.

After school we met up again by the gate and raced to the vendors for a snack of preserved mango, salted leathery strips with a thick coating of chilli so sour and fiery that just licking them made us sniffle and wince. Although I had the bigger appetite by far, and the urge to rush through every meal, I tried to let Pia eat her fill before me. Whenever I thought about her getting hurt, I felt my stomach clench. Once, when we were climbing a tamarind tree she fell to the ground with a thump so sickening it knocked the breath out of me, as though I was the one who had fallen.

But the worst scare came when Pia was twelve – on the day she failed to show up for lunch. After waiting longer than usual, I went looking all over the school, in every likely place. I found her at last in the bathroom, trying to hide a pair of blood-stained undies. 'There's no water!' she burst out. 'And I cannot go without undies, I cannot!'

Water shortages were common at the time, and the taps at school were almost always dry. But in a corner of the bathroom there was a watering-can, half filled.

I took the panties from Pia and washed them under the drizzle of the watering-can while she looked on, disgusted and ashamed. Then we found a spot on the grass outside where we left them to dry in the sun.

I tried not to let on how worried I was. Suppose she was dying. Suppose I was somehow to blame.

But when Mor heard what had happened, she startled me by clapping. 'Celebration time!' she said. 'You're a woman now, Pia!' Then she pulled me to her and pressed one of her violent kisses onto the side of my forehead. 'What a doll!' She kept shaking her head, frowning in wonder. 'What an absolute doll! What a sister! Could you wish for a better sister, Pia-bins? Could you?'

When Mor showed us how the Kotex pads worked, I understood the purpose of those loincloths worn by the women in the Daru village – those strips of tree bark, thick as sponges.

'Are you a woman too, Na Ga?' Pia asked that night.

'No, not yet.' I didn't mind. I was used to having Pia ahead of me in everything.

I could never predict Mor's moods, or her reactions to things. She needed at times to suck on a tube attached to a machine that helped her breathe. I didn't understand, then, what asthma was, but I could see why she would need extra air. Her smoking and coughing, her wild solo dancing to music with loud drums, her gasping bouts of laughter, all of this could only leave a person winded. She seemed afraid to sit still, jumping up suddenly for no good reason to pace like a wild cat in a cage. But when she was meditating, seated cross-legged on the floor with her eyes closed and her back straight, she was stone-still, stone-deaf – a garden statue made flesh.

Year by year, the arguments between Mor and Far grew louder and angrier. They challenged each other not only about who was right about a certain small thing – how ripe a piece of fruit was, how heavily it would rain – but about more diffi-cult decisions they had to make: when to leave the country, what to do about me. Maybe they thought I couldn't hear them; maybe in the heat of the quarrel they didn't care.

What was Mor doing with me, Far wanted to know. Had she stopped to think what she was doing? Suppose – just suppose – they couldn't get me my papers: what would happen to me then, after they were gone? She had to start thinking with her *head*, not her heart. Where would I go if things went wrong? Back to a village of head-hunters?

Head-hunters. I'd thought I'd heard the end of that shameful name-calling. They had teased me about it enough in the Daru village. *The Wild Lu chop off heads, the Wild Lu chop off heads; the Burmans chop down coconuts but the Wild Lu chop down heads. Then they drink the blood like coconut juice, slurp slurp slurp . . .*

Why were they saying such horrible things? I never once saw anyone cut off anyone else's head, and what was a coconut, anyway? It was only in Rangoon that I saw my first coconut.

'I *hate* this place!' Mor screamed. 'This goddam police state. I can't take another minute. I'm sick of the heat, the dust, the water shortage, the light shortage, the food shortage. I'm sick of being a have surrounded by have-nots. I want proper plumbing!'

'Plumbing?' Far repeated, in the soft voice he used whenever Mor was furious, making her even more furious. 'You, a Buddhist, bothered about plumbing?'

What Buddhists had to do with plumbing, or what head-hunters had to do with me was not my concern. Let Mor and Far quarrel: it didn't matter so long as I was still part of the family. Best not to worry too much, to listen too carefully. I shut my eyes and stuffed my ears with tissue from the Kleenex box by my bed. But in my sleep I itched and scratched, and woke in the morning with welts on my eyelids, a rash on my face, scratch marks on my arms and legs and dried blood in my finger nails.

Daw Daw Seng was no help when I went to her with questions about whether I was going or staying. She wrung her hands even as she told me not to worry, not to fret. 'Think too much about a thing, and you'll make it come true,' she warned. The worry lines in her forehead had turned into deep gashes. She urged me to light candles and pray. But I was afraid to annoy the gods with my prayers. I pretended, of course, by mouthing the words, for her sake. But they were words without meaning, without faith.

Around this time a new tenant moved into the house next door, a thin, blond man from Holland. The old tenants, a couple, also from Holland, had left some months before, allowing Pia and me to play in their garden to our hearts' content. The new occupant, Mor learned, would be there only for a short while. He'd come to shut down the oil company that employed both him and the man before. The government had given the order: all foreigners must pack up and leave promptly, taking their business with them. This was why my family had to pack up and leave as well – taking me, they hoped, with them.

The man next door drove the same red car that had belonged to the previous tenants. Every morning, having had his breakfast and read his newspaper, he drove off; every afternoon, before dark, he came home.

I waited outside whenever I could, just to wave to him. He always wore a dress shirt rolled up to above his elbow, and rested his forearm on the open window-frame. I liked his thin, serious face, his close-cropped hair the colour of sand, his evenly tanned skin. He never smiled, but waved back at me with a formal nod, holding up his hand as if asking me to wait.

The previous couple had not been as friendly. Their only neighbourly act in three years was a worried enquiry, when they first moved in, about the danger of snakes. 'You have,' said the husband to Far, pointing nervously to the bushes, then forming a cobra head with his fingers, 'serpents?' Perhaps they thought serpents were more likely to find refuge in our backyard because our house, unlike theirs, was built for natives, not Europeans, a big open bungalow of nipa and wood that let in the heat, wind and rain without hindrance, plus spiders, scorpions, bats, lizards, frogs and snails. Mor and Far liked it that way.

The new neighbour kept to himself, but not in an unfriendly way. He didn't honk his horn when he found Pia and me playing hopscotch in front of his driveway. He simply waited till we had finished the round of our game before driving in through his gate.

The bedroom I shared with Pia was on the side of the house facing the dining room of the man from Holland. If I knelt on my bed, I could see part of that room, the side where he sat at a small oval table, under a cone of light. He attended to his meals with care and deliberation, like a monk in a sacred rite. I never could see what he was eating, only how he raised and lowered a spoon or a fork to his mouth, or placed his clenched fists on the table at either side of his plate.

Breakfast between seven thirty and eight; dinner between six and six thirty. At these times I waited at the window by my bed, kneeling. My throat tightened at his appearance: I knew it wasn't right to be spying on him. Still, I couldn't stop myself – and knelt, watching, till he pushed his chair away from the table, out of the circle of light, to vanish into the darkness.

Whether or not he could see me was impossible to tell. I *wanted* him to see me: I grew rigid with the effort of willing him to notice. But whenever he looked up towards my window, I ducked, heart pounding.

Once or twice Pia caught me. When she asked what I was doing, I pretended it was something in the yard that had caught my eye. Once I said I was praying. It wasn't a lie exactly. I *was* praying – for the man next door, in his lonely, friendless state, to *need* me, and needing me, to *adopt* me. Because even as I prepared to leave with my family, I was preparing to be left behind. Somehow I knew all along – even before they explained the new laws that made it impossible for them to take me with them; even before Mor's grieving hugs and fierce kisses; even before Far's heavy hand stroked my shoulders as he ordered me to look at him, listen to him, trust him – I knew I'd be left behind.

Pia knew too – I could tell from the way she'd stopped chattering. There were days when she hardly said a word to me. Especially I could tell by the way she took back the music box she'd given me, a brick-red lacquer box painted with gold cherry blossoms. It played a tune that used to lull me to sleep – until I broke the mechanism with over-winding. But the glossy little box with its velvet lining was still precious to me, a container for keepsakes like the blue bird's egg, and I never expected she would take it back some day.

'It's to have it fixed, back in the States,' Pia said in explanation. 'I'll keep it for you, for when you come there to live.'

I was tired of the promises – of hearing that I wouldn't be abandoned once they were back in America. That I would be sent for, I would be saved. That the music box would

94

be repaired and waiting for me. It was not that I didn't believe *their* belief in those promises. It was that all the time another voice within me was saying, *No, they will not send for you. You will not be saved.*

On the day of their departure, I felt as if I had gone to the dentist and been given an injection that took away all feeling where before there was pain. Mor must have had a similar injection. She busied herself with last-minute items for packing: toothbrushes, pyjamas, books and sweaters. She behaved as if they were leaving only for a week. She yelled at Pia for sulking. She pretended not to see Far wipe his eyes and blow his nose.

At the very last minute, when the taxi was already waiting, Pia took my hand and placed in it the bird's egg we had found together. Hollow from the start, it was a freak of nature: no bird had formed inside it.

Daw Daw Seng stood beside me, and I let go of her hand to wave to them as they drove away. Then I was staring at the empty street, and feeling in my palm the eggshell I'd crushed to grit.

On the train going north, I could see the city being snatched away and cast to the winds, chunk by chunk, shred by shred. Blocks of flats and offices. Laundry lines strung from windows with smashed panes. The Xs of wooden planks over boarded-up gates. The horse carts and sampans and river ferries. The stockades of timber on the wharves and jetties.

Then there were only paddies, and orchards, and parched tracts with nothing growing.

Once again I was on the train with Daw Daw Seng. Seven years had passed since she'd come to take me away, out of the Daru village and down to the capital city. Now we were going north, back to her home in the Shan state, to a town with a permanent market, with pine needles carpeting the footpaths, and wild mint sprouting on the steps to houses – a paradise she had so longingly praised. But she didn't seem the least bit gladdened at the thought of going home. She unwrapped her little packets of banana rice and pressed them on me sadly, as if it might be the last time I was ever fed. For herself she had packed dry biscuits, which she nibbled while gazing out of the window and fighting back tears.

The train was climbing into cloudy air, heavy with eucalyptus and pine. But I knew this air, this land! I recognised those hills – pale green, dark green, blue-black hills. And all those paddy terraces, cut into the hillsides like dwarf staircases that went nowhere.

Daylight was behind us; night lay ahead, behind the choppy hills. Sunset appeared in the gaps between mountains, draping cobwebs of light between the peaks. All over the valleys an ink spill was spreading . . . and then it was too dark to see.

Daw Daw Seng was fast asleep – I could tell by her breathing, even though the train had plunged into blackness. I was tired – I was so tired – but I was not about to give in like her.

Someone had to keep watch always. Someone had to stay awake.

sixteen

'Why won't you sleep, Na Ga?' Will would groan. He could tell I was wide awake, even though I did my best to lie still.

Sleep didn't come so easily for him, either. Will needed drink – more and more of it to make him sleep. Or maybe it was the drink that ruined his sleep. What if he went to bed at an early hour, I wondered, before the drinking began? Would he be different then? Would he expect different things of me? Would he want me to excite him, inflame him, in ways that I hadn't? Would he allow himself something other than the groggy fumble with the condom, followed by the hard, hasty fucking?

But that rare event – to lie abed without drink – would have had to take place during a very brief period: between ten in the morning, when he got up, and noon, when he left for the day. First for lunch at the club (a sandwich, two beers, and a Bloody Mary). Then to the office for an hour or two. Back to the club in the afternoon, for a game of squash or a few laps in the pool, followed by a couple of cocktails. Or home to shower and dress for the evening, and more drinks at clubs, bars, restaurants or the homes of friends.

By the time he came home and fell into bed, it was almost morning.

*

Only when Will was sound asleep could I observe him as closely as he observed me. Eyes narrowing and flaring as though to focus his gaze, he seemed to be looking *through* me, *past* me, down his nose at me, trying to see beyond the obvious, to pick out some hidden detail. But whenever I tried to return his scrutiny, I came up against a stillness, an emptiness, in the glassy depths of his green-blue eyes.

Eyes closed, however, Will's face opened itself to me. Then I could see in the worried frown, in the pouting lips, the fear and petulance of a child. I came to know the patterns of his breathing, and what the different patterns meant – shallow sleep, or restless dreaming, or death-like oblivion. With my ear on his chest, I could tell from his heartbeat how far he was in that other world, or how close to waking.

Once I felt confident that he wouldn't be easily awakened, I turned on the bedside lamp and examined his body from end to end. I lay alongside him, propped on an elbow, or sat up the better to take in the length and breadth of his naked frame. Neck: sun-reddened. Shoulders: wide and pale. Nipples: dark and tough, like the navels of old oranges. Chest: hairy. Arms: likewise. Belly: concave, with the navel sunk in its fur pit. Pubic hair: fine and frizzy, not coarse and straight like the hair on his arms and legs. Cock: quiescent. Balls: without distinction. Thighs: hairy and sinewy. Knees: large and knobby. Calves and shins: hairy, with prominent veins. Feet: long and white. Toes: wide and curled inwards. Nails: battered, with jagged edges.

When I moved to the foot of the bed for a different view, it was my custom to begin by touching my head to his feet, pressing my arms along the sides of his legs. Someone watching from a distance might have thought I was praying.

What a singular beast is the body of a man, a body with

a mind behind it! The bodies of beasts are menaces too, but a beast can only crush you, maul you and devour your flesh; it cannot imagine, and plan, and carry out, and enjoy – not only enjoy but *rejoice* in your degradation.

The body I studied under the light was not one that had ever harmed me. Those big solid ribs had never ground against mine, harshly or otherwise; those legs had never bruised me; those feet had never kicked me; those big broad hands, with the fingernails chewed down to the quick, had never once struck me . . . Yet how could I approach that harmless being, that blameless body, except with utmost caution?

seventeen

Daw Daw Seng's village was up in the blue hills of the eastern Shan state, between Kengtung and the border with Thailand. At one time, when the British ruled Burma, Loi Lun, the nearest big town, had been a popular hill station and even as recently as a few years ago, it seemed there were cherry orchards and jade-green lakes with plenty of waterfowl and fish. Now, as I saw it, it was just a muddy market town, with unfriendly Chinese merchants. And the houses in Daw Daw Seng's village were depressingly similar to the Daru and Lu huts I had known.

We went to live with her aunt and uncle, a deaf old lady and her betel-chewing younger brother who suffered from a weak heart that kept him unemployed. Things had changed quite a bit, apparently, in the years since Daw Daw Seng's last visit. The only cherry trees I saw were in the compound of a rich Chinese merchant, and the famous pine needles covering the footpaths were not nearly as fragrant as she'd said they would be. As for the wild mint growing on the steps to houses, I saw no such phenomenon. But perhaps I was looking at the wrong kind of house.

The floor of Daw Daw Seng's hut was made of wood, not bamboo, and the blankets were thick and clean. Still, I had grown accustomed in Rangoon to sleeping on a mattress, and it took me a while to get used to a bare floor again. I tried not to think of the foam pillows on my bed in Pia's room, and the soft pastel sheets that smelt of Lux soap powder and sun-dried cotton.

Once again I shared a bed with Daw Daw Seng. Or, rather, a mat and a mosquito net. The last time we had slept side by side was in her timber shack outside the main house in Rangoon, before I was moved into Pia's room. I would be the first to wake then, in those early days in the city, and while Daw Daw Seng went on sleeping I would marvel at the sounds of the morning.

I soon learned that every roar, every shriek, came from machines and engines, from motor-cars, scooters and buses, not from jungle cats yawning or gibbons hooting, not from hawks in the treetops or mules in the valley. Even the squawking of chickens sounded different in the city: nervous, tuneless and shrill.

It was back in those days, too, that I learned about the monks' morning bell that came from the monastery down the street. Daw Daw Seng once told me that the monk in charge of the prayer bell would time it according to the first light of day. When he could make out the veins on his hands, he would ring it. Waking in the dark, then, with Daw Daw Seng asleep beside me, I took to holding up my hands and waiting. Sure enough, as soon as I could trace my veins, there it was – the tuneless rattle of the wooden bell. She would groan and stir. Still half asleep, she'd utter one of her strange complaints: 'No one listens to the cry of the poor or the sound of a wooden bell!' Every dog and cock in the district seemed to listen, however, and answered back with a racket of barking and crowing.

Lying next to Daw Daw Seng now and reliving those days,

I missed the clacking of that rude, urgent bell, that reminder of duty and purpose. So long as I was under the same roof as Mor and Far, I had known my duty and purpose. Now that I could see them only in my dreams, I no longer knew what I was good for, or meant for.

I tried to forget them, my American family. I wanted to think of them as dead and buried. But I could hear their voices in my sleep: I could *smell* them still. Sometimes I woke with the scent of Pia's hair on my pillow. Then I buried my nose in it, sniffing like a bloodhound, not caring if I woke Daw Daw Seng.

At other times Daw Daw Seng would be the one to wake me, to stop me flailing at the mosquito net. 'What are you doing? What's happening?' Then she would roll over with a moan, annoyed that she'd worked herself up over a stupid dream and not a real drama.

For the first year and a half I attended the local school, but with two extra mouths to feed, Daw Daw Seng's aunt and uncle began to mope and complain. In the end it was decided that I should leave school to work at the local paper factory.

The job was not difficult. It was the routine I minded. Strip the mulberry bark. Build the wood fires to heat the kettle. Stew the bark. Pound the stew with the pestle into a thick pulp. Plug up the drain in the holding tank. Spoon the pulp onto the square wooden frame. Set the frame at the bottom of the tank and let the water fill. Then drain the tank slowly. Then sift the frame, leaving a thin layer of pulp. Then lift out the tray and set it in the sun to dry. Peel off at last the sheet of raggy paper to add to the stacks made ready for shipping. Then start the whole business all over again.

It could have been worse, of course. I could have been stuck in the hut where the glue was extracted, forced to stand ankle deep all day in glue-apples, in the slime of the peelings that left a rash on your skin. Or stuck with a task requiring absolute precision: carving, for example – and from a single inch of cane – the tricky little catch in every paper umbrella that allowed it to shut and open.

I could have been trapped – God forbid – in the cigar factory further down the street, where girls my age sat cross-legged on the floor, ten rows deep, for ten hours straight, stuffing, rolling and licking a supply of leaves without end. By comparison I had it easy.

Still, the sameness of my days wore me down. After the routine at the factory came the routine of housework, mornings and evenings: the cooking, sweeping, washing. Then the routine of bathing with the evening's ration of three buckets of water, drawn from the slimy earthenware jar. Then the routine of knotting my hair in the same old-maid twist before lying down on the pallet as quietly as possible so as not to wake Daw Daw Seng.

'Who's that?' the old fatty would exclaim – as though anyone else would be stealing into her bed. She never failed to moan, disappointed, turning to give me her backside.

Months passed. Then a year. Then two. My dreams of Pia faded to be replaced by strange nightmares. One night I dreamed of a dragonfly. It looked beautiful at first, suspended in mid-air with its azure wings shimmering. Then it started to rise horizontally, and the higher it rose the bigger it grew, until the shadow it cast turned day into night. When I looked up, alarmed, I couldn't see anything – not the sun, not the sky – through the thick mesh of its wings.

The very next day, I'll never forget, another sort of dragonfly dropped from the sky.

Helicopters were not uncommon in that region, in the foothills of eastern Shan state. A Burma Army garrison occupied the next valley, and from time to time we could hear the buzz of those killer engines, out on a spraying mission. They were supposed to be dousing the poppy fields with their poison, but we knew it was some hapless village or other that ended up getting hit.

Over the treetops this big insect came, chop-chop-chopping, beating the air, doing violence to the trees. It wobbled into position, listed heavily, then lowered itself onto the empty field at the foot of the Loi Lun market.

Out of the door stepped a broad-shouldered lady, all decked in white and gold. Her bright white trouser suit had gold braid on the shoulders, down the front of the jacket, and along the sides of the crisp legs. Her high platform shoes were made of gold crocodile, likewise her large shoulder-bag. Hands over her head, she charged through the dust and the thwacking wind, while the villagers stood by and gaped.

The factory had let us out earlier than usual, and I was tagging along with some vendors on their way home after the morning's trade when the helicopter landed. A *nat gadaw*, I thought, as the lady in white and gold touched her way through the crowd, like some powerful healer, patting heads and cheeks.

Nat gadaw – often males in female dress – were spirit mediums who drew large crowds at temple fairs. They were wives for a day, wed to one of the *nats,* the local spirits, and on that one day they carried on as they pleased, guzzling palm toddy, eating like swine, singing and dancing without shame. They were allowed, even encouraged, to behave that way because, after all, they had been possessed – by a demanding *nat* husband.

But *nat gadaw* were usually paid by the public, and now the public was getting paid – and handsomely. The Patroness, call her, was giving out money left and right – and the children, adoring, rushed up with hands outstretched: one for begging, the other for presenting wilted wildflower posies and garlands of jasmine.

The Chinaman who stepped forward to greet the Patroness was reverent in the extreme. He stood with head bowed and knees slightly bent, ready to drop to them in an instant. I recognised him; he was a mechanic, a fixer of motor-boat engines. He owned a shop at the lake an hour away. I remembered his nickname: Phyekanik, a play on *mekanik*, for *mechanic*. A *mekanik* fixed things; a *phyekanik* broke them.

The Fixer was leading a troupe of dwarfs, all costumed in silks and painted like puppets. The dwarfs turned out to be schoolgirls – none older than twelve, if I was not mistaken. One after another he edged them towards the patroness with a little speech; but she pushed him aside rudely before he could finish.

The Patroness drew the girls close and I drew closer as well, pressing through the crowd to hear what she had to say. 'Take,' she was saying, in a throaty voice, 'take all you want,' as she reached into her crocodile bag.

Out came lipsticks, hairbrushes, change purses, and a tangle of bracelets and necklaces. They were pricy items, clearly, not the cheap stuff to be found in our market. There were compact cases – red, heart-shaped, with mirrors that swung open in collapsible tiers. There were candy-coloured hairbrushes, gold and silver handbags and swags of glittering beads.

The little girls lost their shyness as they swapped and grabbed, dropping things in the scuffle, then scooping them off the ground, banging their heads together and not even wincing.

Shameless little grabbers! They'd never amount to anything. What did they know of life beyond their muddy little market? Me, I was a city-girl with Experience. True, I was born in a village not unlike theirs, but I had gone on to ever bigger villages, all the way to the city, the biggest city of all. True too, sadly, that I'd ended up back here in these dismal hills. But not for long. Not if I had my way.

The crowd was slowly thinning; the traders, my companions, began hoisting their packs, shaking their heads and turning away. Two elderly women, bent double under baskets of spinach, exchanged bitter laughs as they shuffled uphill.

The helicopter had lifted off soon after landing, leaving the Patroness behind, but a shiny black van with window curtains was idling by the tea-shop at the edge of the field, waiting. The driver, holding court at one of the tin tables, was handing out cigarettes with showy flicks of the wrist. I saw him stamp out his butt and slide open the van before I realised the Patroness was leaving – and taking four of the scrabbling girls away.

Faces pressed to the window like dolls in a cupboard, the little simpletons pushed aside the curtains to smile and wave. And I smiled and waved back from that dusty field where nothing, but nothing, would happen to take me away.

The sun had collapsed behind the hills and seeped through the gaps in feeble rays. The sounds of people going home – ox-bells rattling, boys laughing and whistling, a farmer shouting to his wife to hurry up with the mule – seemed to come from further and further away. A flock of geese cut across the sky in formation, making an upside-down tick mark on a dark purple page. The traders were gone, leaving me stranded. If I didn't get back soon there would be hell to pay with Daw Daw Seng.

Well, what of it? I thought, with sudden abandon. I could feel my heart banging to a strange new beat as I went up to the Chinaman who was picking his teeth like a man well fed. 'Who was that?' I asked, trying to sound indifferent. 'That woman?'

The Fixer looked up. 'Oh, it's you,' he said, as if he hadn't noticed me till that very moment, when I was sure he had. 'What are you doing here?'

I remembered now why this man made me uneasy: I could never tell what he was looking at exactly. One eye kept wheeling to the corner of its socket. Was he leering at the sky, or at me?

'Going home,' I said. 'But I'd like to know who that person was.'

'Are you stupid?' He tapped his forehead. 'Or just pretending to be?' He spoke Burmese well enough, though with an accent. 'Everyone says you speak fancy English. Don't try to play dumb, you won't fool me.'

Then he took a softer tone. 'Come here,' he said, placing me, I supposed, on the side of stupidity. 'No one's told you about the job brokers?'

Everyone knew about the brokers, of course. They were agents from the big towns, from Kengtung, Tachilek, Taungyi. But brokers, I thought, were scruffy old women – like the loudmouth crones at the weekly grain market, who squatted between their ramparts of rice, fanning themselves calmly while driving hard bargains. No one had told me that brokers were *nat gadaw* with money to burn, dropped down from the sky in gold crocodile heels.

'This time of year is when the brokers come,' he said, 'just before harvest, when money is scarce. They come to find girls to work in the city, for housework. City people need maids, cooks, baby nannies. And they pay good money. That lady was a famous broker, very rich. The girls wait all year for her visit.'

How unfair! I thought. I could read, I could write – and in English especially. I had gone to school in Rangoon; I knew the ways of the city. I was older, too, than those painted little puppets. I was sixteen. And the chance of a lifetime had just slipped past me. Why, oh, why had I not stepped forward boldly?

'Why do you ask? You're not . . .' The Fixer hesitated. 'You're not wanting a job in the city, are you?'

'Ah, I knew it,' he said, baring his gold-capped teeth. 'Your head says no, your eyes say yes. Don't lie to me, there's no need . . . I just wish I had known.' He kept rubbing his chin ruefully. 'I could have presented you to the lady.'

I just wish *I* had known. I looked down at the mismatched rags I was wearing: a man's faded plaid shirt, a tatty green *longyi* with flowers like trumpets, and a shawl wrapped around my head – a pumpkin-coloured towel, really, given to me by a woman from the Pa-O clan who worked at the factory with me. No wonder the Patroness had looked right through me.

'Tell you what,' the Fixer said, with sudden warmth. 'I'll take you to her. I can do that. I know where she'll be stopping next. We'll ride on the bus. I'll buy you a ticket. She'll repay me, no question, if you can't. You can meet her, talk things over. That lady will get you a job in a minute. Then we'll come back and tell your family the good news, pack up your clothes, and take you to your new job, wherever it might be.

'That's it. We'll take the bus, that's what we'll do. You can owe me the bus fare, if you prefer. You'll make enough to pay me back ten times over, even before the end of your first work week.'

He was counting and recounting a stack of grubby money, carefully sorting the notes by colour – blue, red, green – and riffling the edges in a jaunty rhythm, as though playing a little thumb zither.

'Worried about going alone with me?' He grinned, pocketing the cash. Politely he turned aside to spit, then toed the earth primly to cover the stain. His toenails were talons – long, grey, and horny.

I wasn't really worried. This fellow was no stranger. I knew people who knew him; why would he dare try anything funny?

'No need to worry,' he said. 'My wife will come along. Ask her. There she is.'

He thrust his chin at a skinny woman who had kept her back to us, holding herself in a rigid way that told me she was listening to every word he was saying.

'Look, we're running out of time. We have to leave now to catch up with the broker.' His voice was different now, urgent and confiding. 'You have to come as you are. It's right now or wait another year.'

Another year! In another year I would be an old maid! I would be dead, quite probably, killed in the jungle after joining the Shan State Army, the only adventure I could foresee. Or worse: living the very life I was living today. Gathering thatch at dawn. Pounding paddy at sunrise.

Sweeping the yard clear of chicken shit and dead leaves. Toiling at the paper factory all the rest of the day. Then coming home to cook, and clean and fall into bed finally with the ill-tempered Daw Daw Seng.

Once I found real work and was off on my own, Daw Daw Seng wouldn't miss me in the least. Getting rid of me might even be a relief. I'd heard her say as much, and on many occasions. 'Wicked rude' was how she described my sullenness. Things were different now that in her eyes I was no longer a child, a child with a ticket to America. 'What can you expect? You can't teach fish to fly.'

'Knows no gratitude,' was another of her conclusions. 'Not one to count on in your old age.' I couldn't argue with that. If anything was worth escaping, it was the need to be counted on in Daw Daw Seng's old age.

No, she wouldn't miss me, as long as I sent her a note explaining things.

The Fixer had a scrap of paper at the ready. 'Here, hurry up and write. I'll get someone to deliver it to your aunt.'

I wrote in Burmese, just to show Daw Daw Seng I could do it – she belittled me now for forgetting my Burmese in favour of English, when it was she who had once dinned into my head that learning English was more important than anything else. I said simply that I had gone to find work and would return before long. That she mustn't worry about me. That I would be back to repay her for all she had done for me.

A big oily moon showed us the way through the night, turning the footpaths into chalky trails. We walked single file, up one village and down the next – the Fixer in front, I in the middle, his mute wife bringing up the rear. 'Watch where you're going,' he kept warning me. 'Be careful, it's slippery.'

How wrong we can be about other people! What a shifty-eyed scoundrel this fellow had seemed, yet he was going out of his way to lead me through the night, just to get me to the broker in time. And he was looking out for me at every step of the way.

The wife, however, was as hard and dry as a twig. Too high and mighty to speak or even to *look* at me. What did she have to feel so proud about, anyway? I at least was taking chances, going *somewhere*. I was striking out, like a warrior called to battle, at a moment's notice, leaving behind everything save the clothes on my back. I was heading for Lasca.

The teacher in the school I had attended before dropping out to work at the factory was a gloomy young man, a university graduate, who liked to remind us of our sorry fate. 'We are all serfs, we are all slaves,' he would say. He was speaking, I thought at first, of living under the rule of the *sawbwa*. They were lords with life-and-death power over their peasant subjects, who quailed in their presence, dropping to their knees in the royal household, at times slithering across the floor on their bellies. But the teacher was speaking of the world, not the village. 'We are born enslaved. We live on a slave planet,' he insisted.

I didn't believe him for a moment. Somewhere in the world real freedom existed. I knew the call of such freedom, the *sound* of it anyway, from a song on a record that Far used to play.

> *I want free life and I want fresh air,*
> *And I sigh for the canter after the cattle,*

The crack of whips like shots in a battle,
The green below, and the blue above,
And dash, and danger, and life, and love –
And Lasca.

Lasca, I thought I heard Mor say, was all snow and ice, one of the coldest states in America. It was Lasca I believed in, wherever or whatever Lasca might be, not slavery and poverty till the end of my days.

I was headed now somewhere in the direction of Lasca, and the thrill of it made my hair stand on end. The night was alive with danger, but even more so with promise, and I drank in everything – the pull of the moon, the chill of the night – until I fell into a rhythm, a trance. My feet were nimble and wide awake, but my mind was floating, resting . . . at times even dozing.

Early the next morning the bus we boarded had an empty seat all the way at the back. 'Go and sit there,' said the Fixer. 'Get some sleep.'

I stretched out on my side, taking up the whole seat, and slept till the sun was full on my face. The bus was braking on the shoulder of the road, across the street from a row of thatch-front shops.

I followed the Fixer into one of the tea-shops, where three old men in black pyjamas were playing a sombre game of dice. We sat at a table and waited for tea. The wife, I expected, would join us shortly, but then I saw something that puzzled me. She was boarding the bus, which had started up again, and before I could grasp what was happening, the bus had pulled away.

The Fixer had left the table to chat with the shopkeeper

and busy himself with cups of tea. 'The bus!' I called. 'It's gone! And your wife too!'

'She has to get back,' he said, quite calmly, setting down the tea. 'We're not taking the bus from here anyway. We're going by taxi.'

By taxi? Were we that close to our destination? There was no reason to be anxious, then. I realised I was hungry. My tea, I was pleased to see, was thick and milky – unlike the Fixer's, which was clear and pale. I took a sip. It was far too sweet, with an unpleasant kick.

'The tea tastes funny,' I said.

'Well, you've never drunk Thai tea.'

'Thai tea?' It struck me for the first time. 'Are you telling me we're in Thailand?'

He pointed at the lettering on the shop across the street. 'As you see.'

My head was turning soggy. 'But I didn't know we were going to Thailand,' I said. 'You didn't say anything about Thailand. You said we were going to Taungyi.'

'Taungyi?' He laughed. 'What jobs would there be in Taungyi? People are starving there. All the good jobs are in Thailand.'

'But Thailand!' I kept saying. 'I didn't know I was going to Thailand!' In the swamp of my thinking was buried the reason why I should avoid going to Thailand. Blinking hard, trying to correct my blurred vision, I took another sip. The sweetness of the tea was pleasant now – warm and thirst-quenching.

The Fixer was standing. He was gripping me by the elbow to help me to my feet. 'The taxi is here,' he said.

I was dreaming; I should wake. Slow as an invalid, I climbed into the back seat and leaned my head against it to support its huge weight.

Through shut eyes I could see the ladder that had to be scaled, with rungs that led up and up into the ether. The odd thing was that only my head was doing the climbing.

eighteen

I was lying in the middle of an empty field, stiff and shivering, unable to move, to lift an arm or a leg. The cold was making me sick. If I turned my head, I might be able to vomit, but even that small movement was out of the question. The nausea was getting worse by the minute. Then, all at once, my body was no longer on a steady surface, lying still. I was on a raft cut loose from its moorings and being swept out to sea.

Immense black waves were exploding on both sides, but the raft managed to cut a path of its own: underneath and between and right *through* them. The path had the force of an undertow: it was sucking me clean through the great tidal waves, out into a limitless ocean.

The shoreline receded in the distance, at a crazy tilt, a sign that told me I would never see land again.

A man's voice, complaining loudly, dragged me out of the deep, deep sea. Then the door opened – and I saw in that moment I was naked. I tugged at the sheet beneath me to cover myself. That was when I noticed the dark bloodstains. A red-hot pain was burning between my legs, while another kind of ache was gnawing at my ribs.

The man at the door was short and bandy-legged. Bloodshot eyes. A pockmarked face. One look at him and I knew I was finished. '*Phamaa?*' he demanded, unbuckling his belt. He was asking, in Thai, if I was from Burma. But I didn't understand, not then.

I opened my mouth, but the sounds that came out were muzzled and feeble, like a yell in a nightmare that comes out as a squeak.

'*Phamaa!* You no speak!' he said in English. The barrel of his finger was pointed at my eyes. He let his trousers drop to the ground. Then he was on top of me, and something hit my face – bits of metal from a chain around his neck. I batted it away and the metal caught his ear. Cursing, he reared up and clipped *me* on the ear. I felt something buckle and pop inside, then a warm trickle down my jaw.

I could see, on the wall, a poster of a woman in jewels and a turquoise gown. I knew that radiant smile, that flawless face, but I couldn't remember her name.

I don't know what I did next, how I hurt him, but he picked up his pants and ran out of the door. 'Orissa! Orissa!' he was shouting.

A woman's voice answered, loud and harried. More shouting . . . and all at once the room seemed crowded.

They were hoisting a dead weight off the bed. It took the brunt of hard and sharp surfaces as it fell and was dragged across the floor. I was that immovable weight.

'*Phamaa!*' He was back again. A belt hit the wall, and lay coiled at my feet. I noticed the buckle: a large metal square with pointed edges. The first lash came as something of a relief. It's not the buckle, I thought. Just the belt. I can take it. But the lashes went on splitting me down the back, splitting me wide open.

They were ordering me to shut up. But I couldn't shut up: the yowling was coming from more than one place – from inside and outside and all around me. I heard the door open. *Please! Someone! Come in and see what's happening!* I think that's what I was shouting. I didn't care if they saw me as I was: a fright on all fours, naked and bleeding. Maybe that was what it would take to bring help.

Nobody came in; it was only someone leaving. The door swung shut, then opened again. Someone else was leaving.

'*Phamaa!*' The voice was hoarse now, as though from long screaming – although it was I who had been screaming. 'You go!' He pointed to the bed.

This time he got on top of me almost wearily. I turned my head towards the picture on the wall. The Queen of Thailand, that was who she was! The radiant smile, the gleaming hair, the jewelled gown in turquoise silk. Her Majesty, Queen Sirikit.

Now his knuckles were digging deep into my pelvis as he rubbed and rubbed his thing, trying to make it hard, as though impatiently sharpening a weapon.

A taste was gathering in my mouth, a swelling. Soon I wouldn't be able to swallow – or breathe. He stabbed through me finally, a short, hard stab, followed by a slow, spiteful binge of stabbing. He seized up at last, let out a long grunt and fell on me as though slain.

He had barely got up to put on his trousers when I vomited on the bed, then all over the floor, so that he turned, still undressed, and fled.

A woman in a blue batik *muu-muu* came to help me out of bed and show me where to bathe. She waited with a towel on the other side of the curtain while I writhed under the shower's harsh jet. 'Why you bad?' she kept demanding, in English. 'Why you make trouble? Cuthomer, he angry, he tell boss. Boss, he beat you. You stay good, you work good, you fuck good, you be okay.'

The water was running red at my feet, then pink, then red again. I couldn't see how I would ever stop bleeding, or crying, or thinking that the world had come to an end.

The worst of it, the unfairness of it, was that I hadn't been trying to resist. Why on earth would anyone think of resisting? *Look, I'm not resisting!* I kept trying to say. *I'm giving in! Please, just let me give in!*

Once, long ago, I had watched a group of farmers trying to load a mule onto a ferry. The ferry was a raft with a single mast, and the river was swift. At the tip of the mast was an eye, and through this eye ran a cable, each end attached to a tree on either side of the torrent.

The mule had a rope, too, threaded through its lip, by which the farmers were dragging it. Back and forth the beast pranced, caught between fear and pain. The men went on pulling; the mule went on prancing; but the battle was uneven.

Defeated at last, the mule tripped onto the raft, wide-eyed and bleeding.

Such stupidity, I thought then. If only it knew to submit right away, right from the very beginning.

The woman in batik handed me a towel, along with a pink cotton shift. Still snuffling loudly, I hung the towel on the rail, pulled the shift over my head, and followed her down a hallway. We came to a door, which she banged on twice – more a sharp order than a knock for permission – then barged in.

The girls seated on the beds in twos and threes stopped talking to stare. The room might have been a clinic: beds along two walls; patients in pink robes exactly like mine; a hospital smell of stale food and disinfectant. On the ceiling there were tracks for curtains, as in hospital rooms, only here the curtains were absent.

The woman in batik pointed to the far end, to the bed near the corner with the candle-lit shrine where bananas and jasmine were rotting.

'Your bed,' she said. 'But just for sleeping, hah?' She tapped me on the back almost fondly. Then, when I recoiled in pain, she said, 'Sorry, sorry, huh? Sorry.'

'Khun Orissa!' one of the girls called, just as she was leaving. 'What do you want?'

So 'Orissa' was a name, a person. I had thought, when the man in the room was shouting it, that it meant something else entirely. Something like: *The sky is falling!* Or: *The world is ending!* Or: *You are no longer human!*

Number One, they liked to be called.

'Me, Number One,' they would say.

Oh, the Number Ones that kept coming and going, each bearing a red chip that gave him the sovereign right to satisfaction – and by whatever means he saw fit. Who was to offer Number One the box of condoms and politely suggest that he wear one? Who was to *insist* on it when he could pull a gun and say, 'Little bitch! Mind your own business! I'll be the one to decide!'

Number Ones by the dozen, Number Ones by the hundred, twelve hours a day, seven days a week – except for the break during menses. Or for the two days of rest following miscarriages or abortions.

I learned how to do it – to satisfy all of them. Or *almost* all of them. There were those who couldn't be satisfied, of course; who lashed out, swearing, 'You have a torn and dirty cunt!' As indeed I did.

I got up the courage to look at it one day, to take a good long look in one of those handheld mirrors supplied by management – though not for that purpose, I think it's safe to say.

Years later, whenever I came across descriptions of the female sex organ in books and magazines, I could scarcely believe that the thing being described was the selfsame organ I knew. *Moist lips*, they talked of. *Flower petals. Birds' nests. Pussies.*

What I saw in the mirror, spreading my legs wide and peering deep within, was the interior of a cave I had once visited with Daw Daw Seng, not far from the Inle lake. We kept slipping as we trod deeper and deeper into the caverns, past grey and white deformities dripping from the ceiling. Then we came to a wall where we had to squeeze into a narrow passage, and proceed only by crouching. At last the rock opened up overhead and we stood in a chilly abyss.

Daw Daw Seng shone her flashlight at the ceiling, at what looked like artefacts from ancient ruins. I saw sections of skulls, fragments of skeletons, membranes of bat wings spread like kites. I saw colonies of mushrooms sprouting on tree bark. I saw the hull of a wrecked ship, draped with cobwebs as thick as fishnets.

There was a sign at floor level against the wall of the cavern: '*Gu-lan-zon*'.

Underneath was the English translation: 'Terminus of cave'.

'Good God, what are you doing?'

Mo, the Chinese girl with the freckled face, had come in and caught me.

'Looking,' I said, wiping off the fogged mirror and putting it away.

'Looking! At what?'

'At *gu-lan-son*.'

Mo knitted her brows. 'What's that? A rash? Does it burn? Why are you laughing?' Mo seldom laughed, except when speaking of her parents. Then she broke into a bitter chuckle. 'I come from a distinguished family – you may have heard of them. My father is a mother-fucker. My mother is a whore.'

San San was always horrified. 'How can you speak of your own parents like that?' She pressed her palms to her ears, shuddering. San San, like me, had come by way of the Shan state. We spoke to each other in Burmese, though, the common language in our wing, dubbed the Phamaa Block.

Mo smiled. 'How can I speak of them like that? Easy. My parents are pimps.'

San San shook her head and looked away. 'Such hate,' she muttered, and closed her eyes and began to recite the *dhamma*. '"He insulted me, he hurt me, he defeated me, he robbed me. Those who think such thoughts will not be free from hate."'

'Why are you standing like that?' Mo snapped.

San San broke off her chant to glance at her feet. 'Like what?' She was wearing a pair of clunky velvet slippers, the toes pointing in at acute angles.

'Like a cripple.'

San San's hands were covering her ears again. '"Let none wish others harm in resentment or in hate."'

'Look, look!' said Orissa, the eldest of us, making peace-keeper motions with her hands. 'Why talk about hate? Just think of your parents as strangers. A man and a woman Fate put in your path. That's the only way to overcome attachment, because hate is attachment too. Forget you came from *her* womb, from *his* seed. They are just human beings, no better than the rest. Just thieves and liars and pimps, like the rest. Then you won't hate them any more than the rest.'

121

Maybe it was best, then, to treat all Number Ones the same. Like strangers in one's path, nothing more. Like parents, like pimps. Like humans. Humans with the needs of beasts.

To be fair, not all of these Number Ones were out-and-out animals. A few were decent enough to leave a person both grateful and confused. Grateful to the point of thanking them too profusely for their generous tips; confused because it was much simpler to hate.

'Say the *metta sutta,* my friend,' San San kept advising. 'Repeat after me. "Whatever living creatures there be . . . without exception . . . weak or strong . . . big, small or middle-sized . . . short, tall, or bulky . . . whether visible or invisible, whether near or far . . . all those born and all those seeking birth . . . May all beings be happy."'

May all beings be happy, I repeated, mocking.

Oh, I learned all right. When they said, 'Bend over!' I bent. 'Kneel!' they would say, and I knelt. 'Suck!' they ordered, and I did. Why behave like that mule by the river, straining against the rope in a hopeless tug-o'-war, flailing and kicking, struggling to avoid that which can't be avoided? It was not necessary to panic. How much worse could drowning be than the terror of it? Drowning is swift; it ends. Fear is only in the mind, after all. Yes, *only* the mind is the problem. And the mind . . . oh, the mind can be marvellously obedient.

The mind can be trained. The mind can be whipped into submission, taught to sit up and beg. The mind can move mountains, play dead.

When a Number One wanted me to sit on him and ride – 'Ride!' he would say, eager for once to be the beast of burden – the mind knew just how to ride, and at just the right clip, the way I'd seen our shaman, Asita, mount a phantom mare when called to chase away foul spirits.

Sometimes I was a shaman, sometimes a nurse, a helper of the sick. Making beds, changing sheets, sponging off messes, emptying wastes – it was all in a day's treatment. Washing my hands, smearing them with Vaseline, then applying them to body parts that wanted care, that too was my daily obligation.

I, the nursemaid, tending the afflicted, had to take care not to betray the slightest impatience, the faintest boredom, while working the wretched organ – up-down, up-down, fast-fast-fast, slow-slow, slow-slow – trying not to think for even a moment how much longer this one would take, or how long the one after this, before the blessing of a steamed pork dumpling . . . or an ice-cold coffee in a tall thick glass, cloudy with swirls of condensed milk . . . Thank God . . . At last . . . There!

Now all that remained was the mop-up with one of those nubby Good Morning towels, wrapped like spring rolls and kept piping hot under the bamboo dome of a dumpling steamer. Sometimes, unfurling one, I thought I caught a whiff of crabmeat and spring onions.

The trick of it all, I learned in time, was focusing the mind on what mattered. In a book about Siamese twins that someone had left under a bed – another of those customers with freakish tastes – I read about Daisy and Violet, the twins from Texas, and how the one could have sex without the other noticing.

'We quit paying attention,' said Violet (or was it Daisy?). 'Sometimes we read, and sometimes we take a nap. We've learned not to know what the other is doing, unless it is our business to know.'

Well, if they could do it, those Siamese twins from Texas,

there was no reason why I couldn't. No reason I couldn't mind my own business, absent myself from the business before me – the hand-jobs, blow-jobs, sucking and fucking, the grunting and groaning, the coming and not-coming – all taking place under my nose.

It was the girls who hadn't yet mastered these tricks of the mind – the very young kids, or the ones I used to think of as simple – who spoke of pain in such inaccurate ways. *Blinding pain. Passing out with pain.*

The pain, in truth, was never blinding. You could see what was happening, and only too well. You saw the world stop, you saw the world start, over and over, in front of your eyes. You saw it spin in its orbit – only you weren't spinning with it: you were turning and twisting in your own separate little orbit of pain.

As for passing out with pain, it wasn't pain the young girls were passing out with; it was another kind of trick, that was all. Playing dead – isn't that what it's called when a pigeon, stunned by a cat, lies quiescent? Of course, that ordinary pigeon, that rat with wings, is busy turning into a phoenix as it lies there without moving. The phoenix is waiting, saving its breath for that moment of resurrection when it will flap off to freedom, just when the cat least expects it.

We, however, were no phoenixes. Pigeons were all we were.

nineteen

We had a room where we waited in between jobs. The Depot, we called it.

In the Depot we watched television: soap operas, mostly, and Japanese cartoons.

In the Depot we told stories – about how we had come to be there, about the friends and relatives who had acted as agents; their lies and promises of finding us jobs, schools, husbands.

In the Depot we reminded each other of the rules. Never refuse a john. Never leave before he's finished. Never file a complaint. (Complaints led only to arrest, imprisonment and, worst of all, deportation as an illegal immigrant.) And never, but never, hope to escape until your debt was paid. The exact sum of that debt we had no way of knowing.

In the Depot we listened to the new arrivals screaming and being screamed at behind drawn curtains, saw them stagger out bloody and broken – and, worse, no longer sobbing or screaming.

In the Depot we compared the price of soap, shampoo, lipstick and nail polish – of antibiotics and abortions. We estimated the standing of each customer's credit – which ones got the discounts, which ones were bad risks, and what percentage of the takings went to whom. We argued about the value of unbroken hymens, and how many times it was possible to be passed off and sold as a virgin. (Four times, it was decided: for a total of 240 baht, or twelve US dollars, because dollars were always accepted.)

In the Depot we learned it was possible to be fucked fourteen times a day, twenty-eight days a month, with only two days off for our period. To be aborted when pregnant, then fucked a day later. Fucked forwards and backwards, up one side and down the other, by Chinese, Japanese, Indians and, of course, Thais; by Saudis, Singaporeans, Koreans and Swedes; by Germans, Italians and Americans, not least.

In the Depot we counted out our earnings as if raking in chips from a gambling den, when each red chip was only worth four dollars, of which only a third was our share. That share had to go towards paying off our debt, leaving us our tips for extras, emergencies and a midday meal (for the ration was only two meals a day).

We learned what it cost for the endless treatments – birth-control injections; antibiotics for infections; pills to induce abortion; pills following abortion; powders and ointments for cuts and abrasions; tests to keep our health cards current and clean. We compared health cards, and the results of our weekly tests. A pink slip (for negative) was good news of sorts; but a brown slip (for positive) could buy you a most welcome rest. Our health cards were all-important. Being clean and safe was crucial to business.

A-I-D was a disease for which we were sometimes tested, or so it was said. But it was not for us to know when the tests were done, or what the results were. A-I-D was only a rumour then, a superstition. It was a virus, one story went, that appeared under a microscope in the form of an amoeba with horns. You could see the little devils quite clearly. But it was nothing for us to worry about. After so many injections we, of course, were immune.

Whenever I stopped to think, however, every slip, every chip, every banknote was about as meaningful as play money. Numbers, figures, stamps, labels – what did any of these amount to, in terms that actually made a difference? What sum exactly would buy escape? What was the price of a body counted in chips? Or the true value of an intact membrane? A dollar fifty, as netted by one of the oldest girls, or two hundred, as set for an eleven-year-old kid?

Why believe in numbers, then? Why believe keeping accounts would make the slightest difference? Was asking about the repayment of my debt any less laughable than my tribesmen, the Wild Lu, asking if cars were mechanical beasts that ate grass, if headlights were eyes that could see?

What was *my* debt exactly? That, only the owner could know. He would go over the numbers with me eventually. All in good time. He would make everything clear as soon as he had a moment to spare. But the owner was a busy man, very busy, never in one place, pulled apart by the running of five brothels and two gambling dens.

My turn would have to wait.

In the early days I watched with envy the 'take-outs', the girls permitted to accompany their Number Ones into the city for an evening or a day. The men would leave a deposit along with their ID and the girls were all theirs, to take wherever they pleased.

Off they went then, those lucky girls, to strut and preen, dance and drink, and act like free beings. Some came home with souvenirs: cocktail umbrellas and swizzle sticks, thick shot-glasses lifted from restaurants, matches and sweets scooped up from hotel lobbies, and other little trinkets and freebies.

Once someone brought back a slip of paper she was given

by an American woman: a human-rights lawyer, as it said on her business card. On the sheet of paper was a single line: *Debt bondage is prohibited by international law on forced labour and by Section 344 of the Thai Penal Code.*

'Let's call the police,' someone said, and we all laughed. The police were constantly in and out of our rooms, now as clients, now as wardens, armed with their walkie-talkies, side-arms and nightsticks.

After only a few outings of my own, however, I saw that take-out was not all it was cracked up to be. The men often just wanted a warm body to watch them while they drank themselves stupid, to lead them back afterwards to the rented room where they could pass out and begin their loud snoring.

There was a Sikh – blind drunk and unstoppable – who took me for a spin in a sports car and nearly got us killed.

There was the Chinese businessman from Singapore who chose, for unknown reasons, a thorny field way out of the city where the mosquitoes gave him no peace. Attacked from the rear as he squirmed over me, he was obliged to keep reaching round to slap his porky behind.

There was a German who wanted me to shit into a sandwich box so he could deliver it, wrapped, to a business partner who had cheated him. (Why his own shit was inadequate he never bothered explaining, but he thought better of it when I said I couldn't guarantee the neat turd he was describing.)

There was the finicky Japanese who brought his own cleaning kit, packed with disposable cloths, liquids and creams. In the empty office to which he took me, he made haste, glancing at his watch from time to time. Then, picking up speed, he informed me, just before his weak little spasm, that he'd left the engine running – and his wife waiting – in his car outside.

And there was the sick dog – the American, muscular and bald, with a diamond in one ear – who pleaded for punishment of all things. 'Hurt me!' he groaned, kowtowing at my feet, his bald head smiting the ground, his bare behind mooning in circles. 'Oh, hurt me! Whip me!'

What I saw before me was not a man but a mongrel, one of those starving pariahs that lay along the gutters of downtown Rangoon. Every now and then you'd see a half-dead pack of them open their eyes as one of their number started clawing the ground, arching its back, raising its rear in a last grovel of anguish before dragging itself off to die.

This creature before me, neither wholly man nor wholly beast, was begging for a release I couldn't give him. Or *wouldn't* give him – not if I could help it, anyway. It was pain he wanted from me, and it was my triumph to deny it.

Spite was part of my refusal, yes – but the other part was self-respect, dare I call it? That act of refusal was what allowed me to separate myself from the beast; to separate as well the parts of my being that still knew some sensation from the other parts that had ceased to feel. For this refusal I knew what to expect. In the very next instant the *craver* of pain could turn into the *inflicter* of pain. Luckily for me, though, this one just ended up crying like an infant, and asking me whether I loved him.

Of course I loved him, I assured him repeatedly, because he was not like the others – a partly true statement that seemed to comfort him.

Not enough, however, to earn me a tip.

They preferred to believe that we had no feelings, all those men who demanded but mistrusted our affection. And they were right, in a way. It was our business to act without feelings; it was our salvation. There were tricks we invented, stories we told ourselves, games we needed to play to get us through the boredom. Yes, above all the boredom.

Behind their backs, of course, we took our harmless revenge.

'Do that old man, Amala,' we'd say to the girl from Bangladesh, a natural mimic.

'What old man? There are so many of them.'

'The one, you know, with the hyena orgasms.'

'Oh, that one.' Amala would take a long, deep breath, roll her eyes into her head, and bay like some feral beast, till we were wiping our eyes from laughing.

Orissa, our group leader, decided for some reason to take me under her wing. She spoke to me in Burmese now, a sign of friendship, not in the broken English she'd shouted at me in the beginning. Orissa had a room to herself: that was how clever she was, how well she managed things. One day she called me into it to show me the shoes she had bought in a two-for-one sale. 'You can have them if they fit,' she said, offering me the second pair: mules with a cunning mesh that looked from a distance as though the wearer was walking on soles without any covers or straps.

Orissa's room was a warehouse, crammed with boxes and parcels neatly taped and tied for shipping. From a bamboo rod suspended across one wall hung strips of dried meat through which a fat fly was lazily swooping. A quilt of Chinese cotton with flame-red lotus blossoms and shocking-pink dragons lay on the bed. Orissa patted one corner and asked me to sit. 'You are like my own sister,' she said, kicking off her flip-flops to settle down for a chat. 'I understand your suffering. You are suffering the way I suffered. There is no need, believe me. Satisfy the customer, don't make trouble, save every coin, and one day your debt will be paid.'

Orissa, as we all knew, was not to be trusted. She was friendly, she was generous, she was eager to be liked, but she was also the resident snitch. Her plump baby-face was shining with sweat. She wiped the sides of her neck with a paper napkin square, folded it into a small triangle, and pressed the corners into the sides of her nose. She studied the makeup smudges, folded the triangle again, dabbed delicately this time along the edge of her upper lip.

'I want to tell you a story,' she said, stretching out on the bed. 'You see this?' She tucked her chin into her chest to show me the top of her head.

Between tight wads of purplish hair I saw scaly patches of scalp. 'Lice?'

'Be serious,' she said. 'No, I'm showing you this head because of what it has been through. You won't believe the half of it.'

'In the beginning . . .' She was sitting close to me, nudging her flip-flops together with one foot. Her toes were plump and even, like grub worms of uniform size. 'In the beginning, when they first brought me here, I lost my mind . . .' A dreamy look had come over her face, as though she were recounting a childhood memory.

'A good thing I didn't lose my head. I took to banging it against the wall night and day. They slapped me sense-less to get me to stop. They gave me the sharp side of a split bamboo cane so that I couldn't lie on my back, or even sit, for days. It didn't make any difference, I didn't care. I stopped eating, I stopped sleeping. For almost a year I stopped speaking. Dumb, I was dumb. When I was all alone, I talked to myself – just to keep from forgetting the sound of my voice. Yes, I stopped talking, but I couldn't stop the head-banging.

'They thought I'd gone crazy, that I'd injured myself in the head. So they moved me to another house, a two-storey building with barbed-wire fences, and locked me in a room with thin walls – thatch walls, no good for head-banging, they reckoned.

'That was when I first tried to run away. I got as far as the fence, where a guard dog jumped out of the bushes and dragged me across the dirt by the leg. I was bleeding all over when they threw me back into my room. This time it was a whip, not a cane. And you know what? I heard myself begging for mercy. I heard myself speak. I was speaking again.'

Orissa shrugged. 'But why cry? I'm not trying to tell a sad story. I'm trying to tell *you* something important. There is a choice, dear sister, in any situation. A person can choose to speak or not speak, eat or not eat, accept or not accept their fate. Once you see this for yourself, you can always find a choice to save the day.'

'How long has it been?' I dared to ask.

'In this place?' she said. 'A year, year and a half. In this business? Five.'

'Five years! How can you bear it?'

'It's a job.'

I stared at the floor while she went on with her list of consolations. It was a *good* job. Now she stayed because she *chose* to.

Yes, she chose to stay. She could save, she could send home boxes of clothing. The money she donated had built part of a house, even part of a shrine, in her village. Where would she find a better job? Here she had friends, position, police protection. Here she had prospects.

Early on she, too, like the rest of us, could think only of how to pay off her debt. Then one day the boss had made her an offer. She could buy her freedom, if she wanted, just by finding another girl to take her place.

She was happy to accept. But where would she find a replacement?

Well, where else but in a familiar place? the boss suggested. Where else but back home, among people she knew and trusted – where a young friend or relative, say, might be talked into returning with her, lured by the promise of employment.

It was too good to be true, this offer. What was to stop her simply running away?

Reading her mind, the boss went about explaining why nothing would be more pointless than trying to escape. He was the owner of not one brothel but a chain; he had agents everywhere, police connections, the means to track her down without once rising from his seat. Where would she run to, anyway, without papers, without proof? What police would accept her story? And once she was in the clink, who but the same boss would seek her release?

Orissa went home to her village, all gussied up for the mission. She told the right lies, handed out gifts that no one could resist, and when she returned it was with a pretty young girl, a distant relative.

The boss, however, informed her he had miscalculated. He had not added in some of Orissa's expenses: transportation fees, lost income from her absent days . . . She would have to stay on to pay off the balance – maybe until the next year, when she might want to think of another trip home in search of another young relative.

The day did come, however, when Orissa's debt was cleared, when nothing stood in the way of her leaving. But by then she saw no reason to leave – just as she saw no reason to leave now. Why leave? She was good at her job, she was saving money, even earning merit for the next incarnation by contributing to the building of a shrine.

'What I am, I suppose,' Orissa said, jumping up gaily, 'is a *nat*. You know the spirit – what's its name? – the one that guards the temple's treasures?'

I knew that *nat*, all right. Stuck with its guard duties for all eternity, the *nat's* only release comes from seducing a mortal, or from preying on the mortal's greed in other ways. Only then, with a new victim to take its place, can the *nat* roam free – back into the world of human lust and gluttony.

Never, never would I fall into such a trap when my turn came. If ever the day arrived when my debt was paid, I would slither off new into the open spaces, like a snake that had shed its old skin.

Yet when that day came, some four years later – when I held in my hands the pink balance sheet granting me my debt-free status – it turned out to be just like any other. No medals, no ceremony, no singing and dancing in the streets. The only difference I could feel was a whole new fear – a fear of freedom itself. What would I do with my so-called freedom? Where would I go to? A better brothel? A life on the streets as slave to a pimp? The world was no longer any of the places I used to know; the world was the brothel and only the brothel.

Happiness, Mor once said, was like the North Star. Sure, we aspired to that distant light; but it was only a vision, a guide. The North Star, like happiness, was not an actual place to be reached.

The North Star, the North Pole, Lasca, Rangoon – what was the difference now between one and the next when all were equally make-believe? Or was each of those worlds a separate incarnation, all equally behind me, eternities away?

Maybe I'd died and died again, countless times, without knowing or remembering any of it.

Maybe my soul was a butterfly, as the Wild Lu believe, alighting on earth only for an instant, trembling with impatience to be on the wing. If only someone would tell me, though, in which paradise my butterfly soul had been hatched, in order for its wings to be dusted with such minute traces of happiness, freedom, peace.

Cages are not necessary for certain captives. Giraffes, in a zoo, need no fences to stop them straying. A bright white circle painted around their separate space is sufficient. Giraffes never cross a white line, apparently, and nobody knows why.

No, not every prison required bars: in some cases a chalk circle was all it took. Or a curtain. Or a pink balance sheet.

twenty

Minzu, the little receptionist, has taken to dropping in without warning. I can't say I'm averse to her visits: they break up the long afternoons. And she's quieter now, not as silly as she was with the flies. She keeps bringing me things to eat and drink – an iced cake, a ripe mango or papaya, a bottle of sugar-cane juice. Or things to look at – her childish scrapbooks and even more childish collections. Her scrapbooks are filled with pictures of wild animals and movie stars. Her collections consist of Band-aids with Disney characters on them; or doll-sized combs, brushes and hair-clips.

Now and then she brings in a packet of smelly herbs, which she sets about brewing for me with hot water from a Thermos. When I ask what I'm drinking, she rubs different parts of her anatomy, pointing out the connection between symptom and remedy. I suspect it's the same herb she keeps producing. It always tastes the same: bitter and distinctly mouldy.

She obviously thinks I need looking after. But she comes so often I can't imagine how she fits in her other duties. She tries her best to persuade me to join her for a walk – to a noodle shop or a market stall or one of the restaurants by the bridge. But I am firm in my refusal. My early-morning walk to the tea-shop and back is about my limit for the day. She offers to run errands, pick up any odds and ends I might require. She takes away my clothes for washing, then brings them back neatly folded and ironed.

Perhaps what the girl really wants is a chance to practise her English – as well as a chance, of course, to model her teeny-bopper outfits. I don't know how she comes up with those mismatched capris and tank tops, those monkey jackets with the beads, sequins and shiny fabric patches. Or perhaps someone is paying her to keep an eye on me. But now that Jiang is dead, I can't think who that might be.

Unless, of course, it's Yan Ding – the man behind all the arrangements for my border crossing. The man who, as it happens, has come to town, on account of Jiang's death, I'm guessing, and invited me to dinner at the New Prosperity Bridge Hotel.

twenty-one

'No taste!'

No sooner am I shown into the private dining room of the New Prosperity Bridge Hotel than I hear my host shouting, 'No taste, no taste!'

I'm still catching my breath from the confusion that made me late – the lift rides up and down the hotel, first in search of the restaurant, then in search of Yan Ding. It's only after a climb past six levels of balconies (with the tropical atrium below and the steel girders across the glass roof above) that someone points out the dining room at the far end of the rooftop restaurant.

'Look at all this *frou-frou!*' he exclaims, to no one in particular, waving a cigar at the ceiling and drowning my apologies for being late. The ceiling is studded and festooned with imitation jewellery. 'Look at these wall paintings! Dragons! Palm trees! Ethnic minorities in Disney outfits! Look at those girls in saris! Men in turbans! Are we in India? Or China? Water-buffalo! Phoenixes! Any old thing going through the artist's head.'

I'm not sure who his loud remarks are meant for, but he is beaming.

'The Chinese mania for the very big and the very ugly, combined with the absolute lack of taste of the Yunnanese,' he crows. 'Not *bad* taste, *no* taste. None. You have to love the Yunnanese. No one can tell them what to like, how to think . . . Now what will you have to drink?' He looks directly at me for the first time.

'Just water is fine, thank you.'

So this is the famous Yan Ding. I had expected a dandy in a silk suit and gold cuff-links, rather in the style of Mr Wei in Kunming. Not a sixtyish man in a nylon golf-shirt with a splotchy print that resembles mustard stains.

'No beer? No wine? Coca-Cola, then.'

Immediately a waiter's hand, gloved in white, shoots out with a bottle of Coke and fills our glasses. His other arm is pinned behind his back, as rigidly as if someone were twisting it. Three other waiters, all wearing white gloves, hover by the door.

'Poor chaps,' says Yan Ding. 'They're waiters, for God's sake. Servers of food and drink. Why dress them like extras from *The Sound of Music*? But let's have a look at the menu.'

While he goes through it with the head waiter, I try to assemble in my mind everything I've been told about this loud aristocrat who is, according to Will, one of the richest men in the Far East, a kind of negotiator between the big drug lords and the government agents charged with trailing them.

Still studying the menu, he says, 'How do you like your deer penis? Boiled, fried, stewed or sautéed? House speciality. Let's try sautéed for a change.' More discussions with the waiter, who bows over the menu, his white hands clasped in front of his crotch as though desperate for a pee.

'Mr Yan,' I begin, as soon as the waiter disappears, 'I want to—'

'You want to thank me. Not necessary. Will and I are old friends.'

'I am very grateful—'

'Not necessary! No need! Glad to help a young lady from Burma. The Burmese are a charming people. Charming. Not the Burmese *generals*, sadly. The generals are not charming.' He laughs. '*Ahaw ahaw.* They have not been to charm school.'

'Ah! Here comes the tea ceremony,' he roars, as a boy in a bolero and harem pants appears with a copper tea-kettle. It has a three-foot-long spout, which the boy, standing back a good distance from the table, casts like a fishing-rod. The hot stream arcs into our waiting cups with no more than a splash or two on the tablecloth.

'Bravo,' cries Yan Ding, then turns to the boy with a comment that makes him redden and grin before withdrawing. 'I said if he learns to use his spout the way he uses this one, he's going to make a lot of women very happy. But I was talking about the generals in Rangoon. Their problem – quite basic, but no one will say it – is that they think they're ruling a country. Whereas Burma is not a country, never has been. The Brits tried to make out it was a country. Easier to govern a country than a bunch of tribal chieftains always at loggerheads, isn't it? But come on. When was it ever a country? Eh?'

He stares at me accusingly, expecting some sort of response, but I don't know what to say. Will often subjected me to the same sort of challenge, and it always reduced me to muteness.

But Yan Ding is not really waiting for my answer. He keeps chewing his cigar without smoking it, then inspecting the gnawed end as if annoyed by the damage.

'So, of course, the generals are not charming. They're living a big fat lie. Living an illusion. Torturing people left and right to keep up that illusion. Very weird. They seem to know nothing but greed. Yes, money is all that matters, have you noticed? Very sad . . .

'Oh, good! Here comes our famous Yunnan ham! It always makes me think of my old tutor, the one I had as a boy in Kunming. Funny Englishman with an opium habit. He liked taking us out on field trips. *Loved* field trips, because it gave him the chance to slip out for a pipe. I said to him, "I can have someone prepare a pipe for you at home. No problem." We always had opium, always offered it to guests. Three pipes were the norm. More or less was unseemly. A very pleasant habit. Very *beneficial.* But that was before opium became a no-no. Before all the propaganda put out by the missionaries, the tobacco lobby and the Communists. All for their own separate reasons.

'Anyway, this tutor adored ham. "Mmm . . . Yunnanese ham . . . a *Lucullan* treat!" he would say. You know, of course, who Lucullus was? No? A Roman consul, very distinguished, very clever politician. Ended his life as a famous glutton. Famous for his *enormous* meals. Once, when his cook thought no guests would be coming for dinner, he made the mistake of serving a modest meal. Modest for Lucullus, that is. "What?" said the boss man. "Did you not know that today Lucullus dines with Lucullus? Who could be a more worthy guest?" I liked that very much. Yes, dining alone. A rare luxury, these days.'

He finds it a chore, I suppose, to dine with someone like me. Still, he can't help being a good host. 'But you are not eating the eel, my dear. Do you not like eel?'

'I was an eel-catcher once,' I say.

'All the more reason to like eel, I would think. No? Try the bean curd, in that case. You have this same yellowish variety where you come from. Am I right? So many things in common between your people and mine. Not only food. *Characteristics.* The Lu, like the Yunnanese, are stubborn as hell.' I sense he is trying to put me at ease, but it seems a phoney comparison.

'Horrors! A stage show!' he squeals, as a microphone is tested and a band tunes up. 'A *minority* stage show, no doubt. Han Chinese dressed up in minority costumes! What a racket. As a minority myself . . . Yes, my people are the Yi. Why? Did you think I was a Han Chinese? *Ahaw, ahaw!* As a minority I would find this whole industry most offensive if it weren't so *funny*. Don't you think it's funny? Here. I'll ask the waiter to keep the door open so you can see the stage. We wouldn't want to miss the "climbing the knife-blade pole" perform-ance. Or the "jumping-into-the-flames" show.'

All I can see of the stage through the open door are two women. The older one, in a red-brocade cheongsam, is making announcements over the microphone. Beside her, holding a large vase, a girl in a mint-green folk dress flashes a bare midriff and a bare thigh.

'An auction!' Yan Ding shouts. 'What a bore! They're auctioning a hundred-year-old vase! Ludicrous!

'Yes, as I was saying. What was I saying? I forget.'

I wonder if he'll ever get round to the subject of Jiang. 'I'm sorry about Jiang,' I blurt out.

'Yes. Aren't we all, aren't we all? Terrible business. Crying shame.'

Yan Ding is having to raise his voice more and more as the main dining room fills with ever noisier groups. 'Very sad news, very disturbing. Can't say I was entirely surprised. A good man, Jiang. Reliable and honest. But he was going down, down. Downhill. Lost his nerve once he stopped moving and had time to think. I told him to try herbs. Yunnan is the

Mecca of herbal remedies and medicinal spirits. But the poor chap, to be fair, had his share of illness. Became more and more despondent, lost his appetite, lost his way. Depressed that his life had been wasted.

'I heard that one of his favourite videos showed footage of his old battalion commander signing the cease-fire with the Burmese generals. I heard he watched that video over and over again. Crying. Behave like that, whip yourself like those crazy Catholic penitents, and what do you expect? Of course life seems pointless. Life *is* pointless. But why bother to kill yourself? Life will do it for you soon enough. Our Jiang wasn't thinking straight, of course. How could he? A Christian convert as a child, a Communist for most of his life, and he ends up trying to cut his losses by turning to Buddhism. Need I say more?'

Yan Ding goes quiet and examines his cigar. 'Have you met his old comrades?' he asks, licking the ragged tip. 'The ones living in exile here? Did he take you to see them? No? He should have. Crusty old Burmese Communist Party leaders. They were the ones, by the way, who trained your people. The Lu were their fighting force, their military backbone. Until the mutiny, that is. You know about the mutiny, I take it?'

'A little,' I say, regretting that I hadn't listened to Jiang more carefully. 'The battle of Hsi-Hsinwan?' It makes me sound well informed, when the only reason I can mention this battle is that it kept cropping up in Jiang's rapid-fire accounts of events and politics I couldn't help tuning out in my boredom.

'Yes, well, that was a few years before the mutiny. That's where Jiang was wounded.'

'Wounded? Badly?'

'Of course badly. He was not a well man – did you not notice? Can't blame him for wanting to sign out. And I suppose, if one has to do it, his way was as good as any. A certain neatness about it.'

'The receptionist where I'm staying told me he – shot himself?'

'Correct. In hospital.'

'Hospital?'

'Yes. Went in for one of his treatments. They put him in a cubicle to wait. He drew the curtain around it, and – BANG. In the mouth.'

'In the *mouth*?'

I recall, for some reason, a detective programme I once watched. The question was whether the deceased had committed suicide or been murdered: whether the gunshot that had blown his head to pieces was self-inflicted. Without a doubt it was self-inflicted, argued one of the experts, and the evidence was in the scattering of the teeth. Only a shot delivered from that particular angle, by a person putting a gun to his head, could have blown out the teeth in that particular way.

I'm thinking of Jiang's teeth when Yan Ding says, 'Now I've gone and spoiled your appetite. You should be eating. It may be the last decent meal you get in a while.'

I wonder what he would say if he knew I've been feeding like a whale since Jiang's death.

'Try this at least.' He hands me a dish. 'Fried larvae. An explosion of pepper and garlic. The Yunnanese are geniuses, don't you think so? To make a main dish out of maggots? Well, as you are not eating, it is time we drank.'

The waiters begin clearing away platters of food that have scarcely been touched. New plates are brought in, smaller dishes with smaller portions.

'Now this,' says Yan Ding, when the amber liquid has been

poured into our wine cups from a decanter, 'this is the elixir of life. Well, one of the elixirs, anyway. This is *medicinal*.' He holds the cup under his nose, then towards me. 'To a safe journey,' he says.

I take a small sip.

'Oh, not like that!' He pours himself a second cup from the decanter. 'Bottoms up. Like this.'

I empty the cup in one swallow. Choked and blinded by the liquid heat, I grip the table to steady myself. 'Mr Yan . . . Mr Ding . . . Mr Yan Ding,' I am stammering as the words pour out. 'You went to so much trouble on my account. I don't know how to thank you . . .' My tongue seems to have a life of its own. 'But I don't want to go home.'

For a moment he seems confused. 'You don't?' I shake my head.

'Well, that's understandable in a way,' he concedes. 'You are going back to a home that no longer exists. Your village? That area? Gone. Nothing left of your birthplace, by all accounts. A little further south you'll see a village here, a village there, but nothing like before. Another thing you won't see is young men. You'll see old men, you'll see women, yes; children, yes; but you won't see *able* men.'

'Someone's having a birthday out there,' I say, fighting the urge to put my head down on the table. They are singing 'Happy Birthday' in Chinese.

Yan Ding says: 'It's not a birthday. They're singing Happy New Year. For the tourists. It's not our New Year, after all.'

'So you are not going back home, strictly speaking.' Yan Ding is saying. 'You are going back to a world that has changed. Beyond recognition. Your tribesmen are businessmen now. Wheeling and dealing. Buying and selling. Drugs, arms, teak, gems and all the rest. They're past the old "We are just simpletons" act. The old, "We don't know anything because we are the stupid Lu" game. You will scarcely believe your eyes.

'Nonetheless . . .' Yan's eyes are very red, as though he's been crying. 'Nonetheless, you must go.'

'But why?' I say. 'I can't see why I must go.'

'Because Will wants you to.'

'Does it matter now what Will wants?' I say boldly.

For a moment Yan Ding's face softens. He looks as if he is tempted to indulge me. But then he launches into another of his tirades.

'But where else would you go, my dear? Will wants you out of Thailand. I'm sure you can understand why. And you wouldn't want to stay here, in this crazy place. No, no, Will's right. He's always right about these things, alcoholic that he is. You can't see why because you don't want to see. You want to sulk. I know your story. You had a raw deal. A girl with real promise, robbed of her opportunities. Most unfair. But what's fair? I ask. Forget fairness. Take smiling lessons instead.' He bares his long teeth in a parody of a smile.

'That glumness doesn't serve you well, you know. Or that style of dressing. "Hello, what's this?" I said to myself, when you first walked in. "A lesbian Lu?" You're not, though, are you? Of course you aren't. You're hiding. And seething. But look at it this way. Your village no longer exists, but you do. Take what you have and do something with it. You're young, you've got a brain, you're among the living. Your English is an asset. Why not make use of it?

'Will used to tell me that he couldn't get you to study. Couldn't understand why you refused to go to university. I told him, "Leave her alone. What is she going to study?

146

Basket-weaving? Media studies? Literature – most useless of all? Let her be," I said. "She's self-taught". The best kind of education. I myself was a dropout. Sent to Harvard as a young man, complete waste of time. Couldn't concentrate. Couldn't tie my own shoelaces because all my life I'd had servants to tie them. Got sent home – in disgrace, I suppose you could call it. Fortunately my father, a very liberal man though a tyrant, didn't make such a big deal about it.

'As for Will and his ideas of what makes sense . . . I've known Will for donkey's years. Knew him as a crew-cut youngster, an idealist. Too young for Vietnam, but got bitten by the Asian bug in the aftermath. Family money. Never did a lick of work. I'm one to talk. But you can't compare. I grew up in feudal conditions. *Medieval.* My father was a lord, a king. We were not Puritans. Will is a Puritan. The worst kind. Swiss mother, New England father.

'Now he wants to settle down. Wants a wife from his own tribe. An excellent notion, no offence to you. Nice woman, his fiancée. Heart in the right place. Feet on the ground. Dull as dishwater, but you can't have everything. He wants someone like that. He's an American – what can I say? You know Americans. They want wives they can talk to. Why on earth would you want to talk to your wife? I ask.

'It's not that Will did not care for you. Clearly he did, he does. But you were an experiment. He liked being able to say, "Look at me, I'm living with a – with a Wild Lu." Quite a feather in his cap. The experiment was fun while it lasted. But there you were, Exhibit A. What to do with you next?

'It's time you left, dear girl. High time. What sort of life was it for you, holed up like that, not really his mistress but not really his servant either? Neither fish nor fowl, animal nor mineral. Boring as hell for you both, I should think. Time you struck out on your own. What you've got to remember is that Will sees you as something unique, something important. As you should see yourself. Quite apart from the fact that your wretched people are in desperate need of a native daughter like yourself, someone who has seen the wider world, to give them a kick up the backside . . . Quite apart from that, you need to see with your own eyes the world that spawned you. Then you can decide what, if anything, you want to do for your people.'

So Yan Ding is simply a mouthpiece for Will. What a loathsome toady. I should have known better than to appeal to him.

'Anyway, far be it from me to come between you and Will,' he says. 'All I know is what Will has asked of me. And I hope I've done my bit.'

Let's see how smug you feel after two suicides in a week, I think, with sudden spite. But in my heart of hearts I know I've lost the momentum, the strength – not to say the courage – for any such attempt. And the knowledge that even this last resort has been removed from my store of choices leaves me with a profound emptiness. Still, I'm not about to give this heartless old despot the satisfaction of seeing my despair.

'You're right,' I say, with feeling. 'I can't thank you enough. I'm sorry I had the jitters.'

He pats my hand. 'Completely understandable. But don't worry about safety. We wouldn't be sending you back if we didn't have faith that you'll be in good hands. You'll be escorted all the way home, and back, if you wish, by two of my most reliable men in the field.'

'I hope I can walk straight,' I say, standing up. 'What was that wine?'

'Didn't you see it when we came in, on the table at the entrance? The big bottles, the big glass vats, with the lizards and snakes marinating? Very medicinal, very potent. But with no ill-effects, I assure you. Just the opposite. Come, let us leg it out of this appalling place.'

'Have you seen the downstairs?' I ask, still trying to give the impression that I'm over my anxiety. 'The fake palm trees, and all the big parrots flying about in the lobby?'

'Seen it? *Ahaw, ahaw.* Dear lady, I *own* this wretched hotel.'

twenty-two

That snake wine went to my head in more ways than one.
It wiped out the many questions I'd wanted to ask Yan
Ding about Jiang. Where in Burma he was born, for a start.
Jiang told me he came from the Shan state, but the Shan
state is big – the biggest of all seven states – and inhabited
not only by the Shan, not only by mainland Burmans, but
by half a dozen hill people like the Pa-O, the Akha, the
Lahu, the Wa, and, at the borders, by smaller groups like
the Daru and the Lu. Jiang could have belonged to any of
those groups, I thought, except the Burman or the Shan.
A Burman he decidedly wasn't, and no Shan I ever met
bore the slightest resemblance to him. It's possible, of course,
that he did mention his birthplace, and that I wasn't
listening.

If only I'd done Jiang the small courtesy of listening –
especially considering the many courtesies he did me. Waiting
till all my papers were in order before offing himself, for
one. Keeping me occupied, fed, and entertained for close to
a week, for another. Jiang was nothing if not courteous –
and efficient, as Yan Ding said. Who but a courteous and efficient person would think to blow his brains out in a hospital
room? Hospitals are ever-geared to death, ever-prepared for
the clean-up of messes from blood and *what-what* (as Minzu
called it).

I cringe to recall my own half-hearted, half-arsed bid to hang myself. What was I thinking? Nothing, I guess. I wasn't thinking at all. Not about the absurdity of the whole exercise. Not about the improbability of success. Not about the poor girl – about Minzu! – whose misfortune it would have been to discover and dispose of my dangling self. No, courteous and efficient I wasn't. Unlike Jiang, who planned it right, did it right, the genius.

I suppose you could say Orissa at the brothel did right too. Another hospital suicide. Even though she, perhaps, wasn't as clear-headed as Jiang. It was drugs, the story went, that caused her downfall. What else but drugs would have induced her to go to the police for help, when she knew full well, as all of us did, that the police were on the take from the brothel and would be the last people on earth to help?

And when they ordered her back to work under threat of arrest, why would she have tried the hospital next – why, if she were at all sane?

The hospital chief heard her out, according to one version, then asked her to wait while he went into another room – to place a call to the police. By the time he came back the overwrought woman was nowhere to be seen.

They found her hours later in one of the latrines, a black plastic bag tied tight around her neck.

I couldn't believe it. Orissa, the know-it-all, had lost her nerve and done herself in! All that talk about having worked things out – all lies, every bit of it.

San San, the pious, pigeon-toed girl, went on beating her breast and crying for days. 'I want to die!' she kept saying, until Mo lost patience.

'Here!' she said finally, handing her a plastic bag. 'Be my guest.'

Shocked out of her tears, San San looked so startled that we burst out laughing.

Once the papers reported the Orissa case, it was the beginning of the end for us as well. Soon afterwards there was a crackdown by the vice squad of the Crime Suppression Division. The policemen who kept arriving with their notebooks and tape recorders, all that week and the next, were not the regulars who dropped by off-duty, tucking in their shirts and zipping up their trousers as they left the rooms hurriedly, only to return in uniform later in the day for one of their phoney shakedowns. No, these were Special Branch heavies, these plain-clothes men who were seen only rarely, mostly on child-prostitute raids.

But it was left to the old regulars on the police force to close us down. Locking the doors to every room and exit, they ordered the men out. I saw the friendly nods and winks from the boss's assistants, inviting them to come back another day.

Thirty of us were taken to the first lockup: twenty women, eight male attendants, two pimps. The men were released, of course, after a day or two, but we women were held in two separate cells. A jailer walked by every hour on the hour, to remind us that talking was forbidden. He tapped his finger to his lips, then pointed to the walls, where scrawled messages left by previous witnesses described what bad behaviour would bring: deportation, hard labour, or simply being beaten to death.

A week later it was back into the black vans again, for another, longer, wait in another kind of prison. In narrow cells we slept and rose in relays, some two hundred bodies so tightly crammed that turning was possible only when the next person turned, and every movement – standing, sitting, lying down for short stretches – required co-operation.

The cell leader, as usual, had a bed of her own. The rest of us remained on the floor. Standing, sitting, lying down for short stretches, we waited for our numbers to be called, for a turn at the stinking baths and foul latrines, or for a fingerprinting session, where the wardens and clerks were a lot more relaxed, laughing and smoking and idly groping their charges.

Twenty-two days in that holding pen, then it was into more vans again, this time to the Burmese border.

twenty-three

'Almighty God, not Burma. Anything but Burma!'

The voice from the back of the van was a smoker's voice, low and gravelly.

'Are you listening, you all? If you're ever picked up by the Burma Army, the first thing to do is to look for a rope. Then hang yourself as quickly as possible. First they fuck you without mercy. Next they pull you to your feet by the hair, like so, and strap on a load to break your back. *Then* they march you along at gunpoint. So you go and you go and you go, through jungle-hell and heat-hell. Now. *If* you manage to escape getting blown up by a mine, pray they put you out of your misery and shoot you in the head. Pray they don't *spare* you by leaving you alive. Know what it's like to be too crippled to move, too weak to fight off the wild cats, fire ants, maggots closing in before you even shut your eyes?'

'Stop!' someone shouted. 'I don't want to hear any more!'

But the raspy voice went on: 'Say you make it to camp. They'll starve you to death there. And fuck you as you draw your last breath.'

Someone began to cry. 'I just want to go home!'

'But that's the thing, don't you see?' The smoker's voice gave way to a smoker's wet laugh. 'You *will* be home, by that time. The place where they bring you to starve and die, that place will be none other than your very own village.

154

Your birthplace is where you'll be marched back to. And you – *you* – will have carried the guns and bullets brought in to wipe out your kin. As I said, hurry and find yourself a rope.'

'Oh, sister, my friend,' somebody pleaded, 'is there nothing we can do?'

'Are you asking me for my help, or are you just snivelling?'

I twisted round in my seat in the windowless van to see what I could of the tough talker in the rear.

'If you're asking for my help . . .' The voice belonged to a surprisingly delicate young woman, small boned, neatly dressed, with a spray of yellow orchids in her hair. '. . . don't bother asking until you show me how much money you have. But there is a way out – for a price.'

'Who is she?' I asked the woman to my right, the one shaking her head bitterly over the exchange in the back.

'A bloodsucker.' She spun round to confront our informant. 'You're everywhere, aren't you? You're worse than pimps! You'll give away your mothers, sell off your own sisters, to the highest bidder. Then you'll turn round and charge *them* a fee as well. Don't try to scare us. A shelter is where they're taking us – I heard it from the police back there. The higher-ups are in charge now, the border authorities. Not petty pimps like you.'

'Going to a shelter, are we?' The laugh from the back broke up in a coughing fit. 'You'll be all right, then. My mistake, I thought we were going to a cemetery.'

They were right, both of them. The refugee village, our destination at the border, was a shelter with a washed-out graveyard.

The monsoons had broken. The rivers were in spate. The rain roared down for days without respite. The roof over our

155

heads – the blue plastic sheets stretched over the bamboo platforms on which we huddled and waited – kept ballooning and bursting open, drenching us and our capes of thin towels and blankets. The guards strode through the floods in their knee-high gumboots, laughing when our flip-flops were sucked into the mire and we were pitched, face first, into the mud. In the fields behind the centre's office buildings, the latrines and cesspools were steadily overflowing with turds and tin cans, wads of newspaper and scraps of plastic.

The know-it-all in the van with the orchids in her hair – Thaya was her name – returned from a trip to the fields hitching the hem of her *longyi* to calf-height. 'Good God!' She was sighing as she bent over to squeeze out her dripping *longyi* by twisting the ends. 'Between the shit, and the land-mines, and the bones from the flooded graves, you really have to look where you put your foot down in this lovely place.'

As it happened, the mines were not close enough to worry about. They were on the *other* side, behind the Burmese lines, where the guerrillas were still at war with the government. But it was Thaya's way to exaggerate, to scare. She had a gift for theatre, but at least it kept us distracted, if not entertained.

We played cards; we played checkers; we played tic-tac-toe. We busied ourselves with the rain: we stared at the rain; we listened to the rain; we exchanged tricks and tips for out-witting the rain, for keeping our bedding and clothing dry. But the minute we heard the crackle of loudspeakers, we dropped everything to listen.

The Burmese-language broadcasts, picked up from the repa-triation centres on the other side, announced the names of the newly returned, their domiciles and birthdates. Would the relatives of so-and-so from such-and-such region report to the centre to claim their kin? *Parents of Lek Lek, please listen. Your daughter who disappeared three years ago has been found. She is well and wants to go home. Please meet her at the border crossing in Tachilek in three weeks.*

Next came the personal appeals: the choked, shamed voices of the repatriated women whose trafficking days were over – for the time being at least. One by one they pleaded with their families to grant them forgiveness and allow them back into their Burmese villages. And waited.

These voices led me to an idea I kept to myself, the belief that I was not going to be among them. Perhaps it was that no one was waiting for me on the other side, no one who would even know my name – except Daw Daw Seng, of course. And she was not very likely, after all this time, to be waiting with her ear pressed to the radio for news of me. Or perhaps, hearing no mention of anyone from my home state being sent back, I imagined that I, a Wild Lu, was bound for some other place.

'I was a dancer once – did you know?' Thaya said, interrupting my fantasy. 'You've heard of the Mandalay candle-dance troupe?'

No, I said, I hadn't.

'I was part of that troupe when we were sent to Japan. A cultural performance, they called it. It was a general in Rangoon who arranged our trip. Do you know how and where we ended up performing? As bar girls in Tokyo, in a private nightclub. Candle-dance, what a laugh! We never once picked up a candle in Japan, not to dance anyway.

'And you? What about you?' she asked me. 'What promises did they make to get you to the city? Let me guess. A desk job in a hotel? A baby-nanny position with a rich Chinese family?'

My mind was elsewhere. A group of foreigners had just entered the office into which we'd been called for yet another round of reviews and interviews.

'ICR!' somebody whispered. '*God be praised!*'.

We'd all heard of the ICR: the International Committee for Repatriation. They were the ones who negotiated the fate of those waiting to be deported, who bargained on their behalf with officials on both sides of the border.

I noticed him right away, the tall one in the checked shirt who detached himself from the group he'd arrived with and was standing alone, watching me. I'd seen him peering over a relief worker's shoulder at the roll-call list, seen him looking up when someone pointed me out to him. Now I watched him stroll about the room with studied indifference, hands in his pockets, nose in the air. He appeared to be looking down at everyone, but then he would stop to talk to someone with a little bow of courtesy.

Suddenly he was directly in front, bowing slightly and saying something in a language I couldn't understand.

I shrugged. He smiled, apparently satisfied, and went back to join the members of his group. I could tell they were talking about me, nodding in agreement with whatever he was saying.

Later that night Thaya teased me. 'I have only one question about your new boyfriend,' she said.

'What boyfriend?'

'Your *board-certified* boyfriend,' she said.

She had just been telling me the story of a boy she'd once been in love with, whose mother was a snobbish old windbag. 'I have two sons who are *board-certified* doctors,' his mother used to boast. But I still didn't understand what Thaya meant about my board-certified boyfriend.

'That Clint Eastwood character who was trying to chat you up is a board member of the ICR,' she explained. 'I asked one of the relief workers about him. His name is Will something or other.'

'Who are you talking about?' I said,

'You know very well who I'm talking about. The tall American guy. What I want to know is whether he asked your name.'

'No. Why? Should he have done?'

'Well, he was asking you something. But that's good if it wasn't your name. You might get lucky in that case. Only the ones who don't give a damn about you bother to ask your name. They do it out of a sense of duty, to get it over with. The ones who have a real interest in you care about other things. They're your ticket out.'

I looked blankly at her.

'You don't know what I'm talking about,' she said. 'I'll explain. Minami-*san*, for example, didn't ask my name.'

She was waiting for me to ask the obvious question, so I did. 'And who is Minami-*san*?'

'Ah, Minami-*san* . . . Lots of men liked me in Tokyo – I'm not bragging. Some even brought me jewellery. But it was Minami-*san* who actually paid to take me away. He looked at me the way your boyfriend was looking at you in the office. That same determination. He got what he wanted, old Minami-*san*.

'I had a good feeling about Minami, do you know why? His name was Minami, and I was a dancer, a *minthami*. A good omen, I thought. But it didn't work out. You can't make too much of omens. I didn't like the way he teased me by kicking me, like a dog or worse. And the way he shouted as though I was deaf was so rude, so hurtful to my brain.

The worst thing? Once I became his so-called wife, he didn't pay me a penny. I didn't have *any* pocket money of my own, I had to beg for everything, every bloody tampon and packet of peanuts.

'Luckily, Minami-*san* made the mistake of taking me to Bangkok on one of his business trips. One day I made up a story about visiting some relatives down south, across the border from where my home used to be. I don't really have relatives there, but I might have had. I didn't seriously expect Minami-*san* to believe me. But he did. And, even more surprising, he gave me the fare just like that. Maybe he was ready to get rid of me.

'As luck would have it, I met this couple on the train. Agents, can you believe, for a brothel up north, near Kanchanaburi. They offered me a job there and, of course, I took it.

'The work wasn't bad – I'd heard of worse. We even had free lunches and a day off every other week. But I'd been there only a few months when the brothel was raided. They put me in handcuffs. Then, after a week, they sent me back to Burma – to a place not far from my home town, in the south, near Ranong.

'A month in jail there, and I was sentenced to hard labour. Three years. I bought my way out in the usual manner. I slept with the officers, all six of them.

'The first chance I got, I crossed back into Thailand and returned to the same brothel. Why not? They knew me there already. But, such was my luck, I was there hardly a month when there was another raid!

'This time I ended up in a sort of camp – a detention centre, not a jail, the authorities kept saying. Well, whatever. But at least they didn't send me back to Burma. I wangled my way out in the usual manner – it's not that hard. This time I wasn't stupid enough to go back to the old brothel, I found work in a new one.

'But listen to this: what do you think happened there? Yes, that's right. Another police raid. And here we are now. The call of karma. How else to explain it?'

'God in heaven, do you never stop talking?' came a shout from one of the sick beds at the far end of our shack. 'I'm dying here. Can you shut up and give me a little quiet?'

'You want quiet?' Thaya shot back. 'Talk to those big-mouths over there, don't talk to me.'

The camp guards were stamping their feet in the rain, arguing loudly about whose fault it was that the refugee grave-yard, stupidly dug into the slope of a hill, had been washed out in the latest mudslide. They couldn't believe the ungrateful refugees had the nerve to complain! If they hadn't cut down all the trees around them for their firewood, the mudslide would never have happened.

'They're paying for it now, the ingrates,' Thaya said, mocking. She nodded in the direction of the other huts and lean-tos, barely visible through the blur of rain. 'They have nothing more to build with, and they're not allowed to put up anything permanent anyway. All they're permitted now are splintered bamboo for flooring and plastic sheets for roofing.

'Lucky things!' she added, wistful now.

'Lucky? Why lucky?'

'They're light as birds. They've lost everything. They've nothing more to lose. They're free.'

The skies were still grey, but a lighter, brighter grey. Two crows on a washing line, strung from one shelter to the next, sat passive and patient, waiting for the weather to change.

Across the field, in front of the clinic, three small children were playing in the puddles, splashing and annoying an older boy who was missing an arm and a leg.

Later in the afternoon, while I was trying to nap, I heard Thaya yawning and stretching beside me. Snapping her neck from side to side with loud cracks, she said, 'So, what's your name then?'

'I don't know,' I muttered, hoping to sound half asleep.

'Forgotten your own name? What? You're *that* miserable? You've heard the expression, right? "So great is my misery, I've forgotten my own name"?'

'I left home before I could learn my true name,' I said.

'What do you mean?'

'I don't have my name seed. I lost it somewhere.'

Thaya was staring at me. 'You're saying . . . ?'

'It's just a custom where I come from. When a child is born, the mother speaks its name into a seed, a poppy seed, and glues it shut. When the child is old enough, the seed is opened and the child's real name is released.'

Thaya shook her head as if she'd never heard anything so quaint. 'Well, what's your *false* name, then?'

'Na Ga.' I pronounced it in the Burmese way.

I sat up. There was no point in trying to avoid conversation. Thaya put her face directly in front of mine and laughed. 'Na Ga! They're not that bad, your ears.' Then she leaned back once more, and we sat side by side with our hands on our knees, mesmerised by the eternal rain.

'Names!' Thaya yawned. 'I used to think names were important. But if you worry about names in a place like this, you'll end up in a lunatic asylum. The ABC. The CBA. The XYZ. The CIA. The NFD. The CPB. We don't know who the others are – we can't even be sure who we ourselves are

162

supposed to be. Are we DPs, displaced persons? Or are we just common refugees? Or are we IDPs, the internally displaced? Are we IIs, illegal immigrants – or LMWs, legal migrant workers? Or are we, God forbid, TVs – trafficking victims?'

'Well, why don't they just call us what we are?' said another voice from further down the bamboo platform. 'Whore 24681, Whore 24682 and so on?'

The shoulders of two sleeping girls in between began to shake with laughter.

'Look, the rain's stopped,' cried Thaya, grinning. 'Who's coming to the river for a bathe?' She reached between the bamboo slats behind her to retrieve a clear plastic bag tied with a rubber band. 'Ah, here they are,' she said, holding it up to the light. 'My little orchids. The water needs changing, but look how fresh they are still.'

I was about to follow her to the river when my name was called over the loudspeaker, summoning me to the main office.

And there he was again, standing by the entrance to the office, holding out his hand in greeting as I stepped in. Once again he seemed to be speaking a foreign language. Once again I failed to understand him.

'Never mind,' he said in English, laughing awkwardly. 'I was trying to practise the three phrases I have in your language.'

My language? It was only then I realised what he'd been saying all along. He'd been asking me my name – in Lu, of all languages. And now he was telling me his. 'I'm Will. I'm your new – sponsor.'

Sponsor. What could that mean? 'I live in Bangkok,' he added. 'Have you ever been?' I shook my head.

'Want to go there with me?' He was looking down his nose, but his eyes slid shyly from side to side.

Of course I said yes – but with an indifferent shrug, careful not to seem too eager, in case I was being tested, or teased.

A sour smell was circulating in the air-conditioned car – and it was coming from my damp T-shirt and jeans. I couldn't stop my teeth chattering or my eyes streaming. Blindly, I had signed the release papers thrust at me, then followed him out through the camp and into the waiting car, never even stopping to say goodbye to Thaya, or to gather up my few belongings.

It was only when he handed me his handkerchief, saying, 'It's okay, everything's going to be okay,' that I gave up pretending it was the cold that was making my nose run and my eyes stream.

twenty-four

We caught a night flight to Bangkok from Chiang Rai, the nearest airport.

It was my first time on an aeroplane. Looking down through my window, I watched the world below rapidly shrink and expire. One minute the earth was brimming with lights; the next they were distant stars on their way to extinction.

When we landed, after what seemed like half an hour but was actually ninety minutes, it was in a rainstorm the likes of which I hadn't seen since the monsoons in Rangoon.

Nid, Will's driver, was waiting at the airport, and as we drove through the torrent into the heart of the city, I could see the waters rise and rise, beating against walls, ebbing across streets, filling the canals to overflowing. Drenched figures were wading knee-deep, waist-deep in places. Cars were beached along the roadsides, and sandbags barricaded the fronts of shop-houses.

Bangkok was under siege – yet celebrating. Crowds thronged the streets, music blared from the tops of buildings, cars honked to beat the band and lights winked everywhere. Lights on buildings; lights on billboards; lights along walls and branches of trees; lights on the river and along the jetties; blue and red lights on sampans and ferries; lights on the high-rise horizon. And streetlights lit the *klongs*, the filthy canals into which children were leaping, throwing out their arms and legs in jubilation.

'Tired?' Will asked, after we'd driven for a long time in silence. It was practically the first thing he'd said to me since we'd landed. He seemed distracted and irritable, cursing the traffic. I wondered if he was regretting his decision to bring me home with him. 'Not tired, no,' I said. 'Just—'

'Just what?'

Just speechless, I thought, shaking my head, unable even to say that.

'You'll be fine once you get some sleep,' he said. 'But here we are now . . . Home at last.'

Yes, I thought, following him along the stone pathway, through the garden with the large ferns still dripping with rain, under the arch with the flowering blue clematis and into the house with the gleaming teakwood floors and the shutters thrown open. *Yes, home at last.*

Later, much later, I could look back and grasp what it was, then, that made me feel I'd seen that house before. I'd seen it more than once – always at the tail end of a certain kind of dream. I'd be wandering about, in such a dream, in a state of pleasant anticipation. I'd stop here and there to notice little details of no importance along the way: a worm on a leaf, for instance, or the print on a tablecloth. Presently I'd arrive at my destination: a house behind a gate. The gate would be unlocked . . .

No one stops me entering. I'm free to walk through the front door and wander aimlessly from room to room. My excitement builds as I sense what comes next . . . and there it is: the door that opens onto another passageway, another flight of stairs to what I've been looking for – the innermost house of my dreams.

*

Will showed me to the spare room, a kind of annex to his bedroom. 'Feel free to come through any time,' he said. 'I'm not a light sleeper.'

That night, he left the door between us slightly ajar, and I waited till I thought he was settled in bed before coming in quietly from my side. I was starting to undress when he sat up and stopped me, pulling me down to sit beside him.

'Hey, wait a minute, wait just a minute,' he said. 'We don't have to do this. It isn't part of the deal.'

What was the deal, then? He still hadn't told me. This stranger – my sponsor – had bought me my freedom and was giving me shelter. I knew no other form of repayment. 'Look, it's late and I'm beat,' he said. 'But let's get one thing straight. You're not here to be a slave. And it's not your body I'm interested in. Maybe you'll understand that some day.'

Not my body? Why was he mocking me?

'Sleep,' he said, lying down and patting the bed. 'Sleep here, next to me.'

He was mocking me again, I thought almost a month later, when he finally gave in to sex. He had shown me the rash on his back while undressing, saying it had bothered him for days. By morning, the rash had cleared up. Looking in the mirror, he had smiled at me. 'Well, well, it must be true then, what the believers say. Saints can heal lepers just by lying next to the diseased body.

'No, that's not what I meant!' he said, seeing the look on my face. He tried to explain that he'd meant *he* was the leper, not me, but I was *certain* he was mocking me.

He was rich, he was handsome, he inhabited the house of my dreams. And he was taking me in, no questions asked, no services owed in exchange. It was far too good to be true, and I was almost relieved when he took me out one night – I'd been with him hardly a week – to show me another side of Bangkok.

Nid let us out at the head of a narrow street, in a snarl of *tuk-tuks*, mopeds and vendors on wheels. We dashed – it was raining, as usual – into an arcade with T-shirts on tables, watches on trays, *satay* sticks on smoking grills. The ground itself shook in that tunnel of noise, from the din of live bands, boom boxes and the drumming rain. The touts had taken shelter under an awning but continued to call out their greetings anyway.

Will led me by the hand into the first bar – through a barrage of pulsing music, flashing lights and gyrating girls in G-strings. He seemed to know every last person on the scene, pimps, managers, bartenders, go-go girls, and most of the guests as well. Shaking hands, waving, saluting, he made his way through the crowds, leading me along behind him. The girls in the sequined bikinis came down from the stage to greet him between dances. They looked me over, full of curiosity and tease. *Fan*? Was I his *fan*, they wanted to know . . . his girlfriend?

We stayed long enough for Will to make his rounds; and then it was out onto the strip again, with neon signs spelling royalty, victory, and magic. *Cleopatra. Queen's Castle. Napoleon. Winner's Bar. Pussy Alive. Magic Grill.* Every bar we entered, every show on stage, seemed part of the same city-wide celebration: balloons on the ceilings, confetti on the floors, sparklers between the legs of naked girls on trapezes, swinging upside down like gibbons.

'Cunts doing stunts,' I heard a fat *farang* say. Whistles were blown, bottles were opened, spoons were bent, chopsticks were wielded – all by means of the cunt. Cocktails were mixed in upended cunts. Trick scarves without number were pulled out of trick cunts, then turned into flapping doves. Garlands, too, and streamers, and bells on strings, were draped like bunting from cunt to cunt to cunt.

The printed menus, handed out on the street, offered more variations: PUSSY SMOKECIGARETTES. PUSSY OPENBEER BOTTLE. PUSSY PICK THE DESERT WITH CHOPSTICKS. BIGDILDO SHOW. FISH PUSH IN SIDEHER. LONG-EGGPLANT PUSH INTO HER CUNT. BLUE MOVIE FILM SNAKE SEXY DANCE. BOY-GIRL FUCKING SHOW.

In the smoky light below the stages, everything white looked phosphorescent – white shirts, white socks, white teeth. Up on a stage, a long-legged dancer did the splits over a hand-stand, while a bottle of Coke was poured down a funnel planted in her crotch. Back on her feet the girl bowed to applause, then bent to swoop up a roll of toilet paper. She tore off a piece while tiptoeing off the stage and, with a sudden delicacy that made me look away, she held it between her legs to staunch the dripping.

I was beginning to grit my teeth – first in anger, then in fear. I didn't know what was behind Will's eagerness to bring me here, to this all-too-familiar world of flesh for sale. Was he teaching me some sort of lesson, like rubbing a dog's nose in the mess it has made? Or was he trying to say, 'Here it is – the place where sooner or later you'll have to make your way'?

But I had only just arrived in this infamous city, where they had a name for the likes of me – a *kwai* prostitute, one who follows the buffalo and serves the peasantry. I was not cut out for such glamour, such glitz. I would not have a prayer in all that razzle-dazzle.

But maybe Will, my sponsor, was up to something else altogether – something in the shaman's line of business.

I remembered when one of the boys in the Daru village was accidentally shot with a poisoned arrow, and the shaman had to be called in to remove it.

'Watch,' he said, holding up the thin shard he'd pulled out for all to see. 'First you pull out the source of the poison.' The Daru shaman was a different sort of healer from Asita, the shaman in our Lu village: more like a dull teacher than a drunk magician.

'Step one.' He snapped the bamboo in two against his knee. 'Step two. Only when you break the poisoned arrow will the wound close properly. Only now can the flesh begin to heal.'

Was that the sort of healing Will had in mind? Maybe it was his way of saying, 'Look at this great festival of lust and greed. It always has been, and always will be, right here with us. Look it in the eye, face it squarely. See it for what it is.'

His face gave nothing away except mild amusement as he went on greeting his countless friends, leaning into their ears until they shouted with laughter, which I could see but not hear in that din.

'Hungry?' he asked me finally.

I nodded, eager to leave. We wove through the alleys and up along the strip, past Rififi, Blue Hawaii, Memphis Queen, not stopping once to go in.

Down one of these alleys there was a rooftop restaurant, lit with red apples that hung from the boughs of potted trees. The flashing lights on the sign outside spelled Garden of Eatin. There, at a corner table, we sat and ate without speaking, like an old married couple. Or a pair of doomed lovers. Or a whore and her pimp.

It was dawn by the time we drove home, with Nid red-eyed at the wheel. The traffic was light at that hour. We were nearly at the house when we were stopped at an intersection by a procession of Buddhist nuns, out begging on their morning rounds. I envied them suddenly: their sameness, their oneness – yes, even their baldness – as they padded through the dawn without a care in the world, without any need save that of filling up their bowl each day. Especially I envied their safety. *One is one's own refuge*, the *dhamma* tells us.

One is one's own refuge, I repeated to myself – even though the refuge I sought now was with someone else.

I never knew, in the beginning, whether to leave or stay in his bed. Should I lie still, not touching him, but remaining within reach for touching – in case he needed a hip to rest his hand on, a leg to straddle, a breast to cushion him? But would I be able to stifle every cough and sneeze? I was afraid to disturb him, afraid to breathe. Sometimes he caught me holding my breath. Then he shook me. 'Breathe, Na Ga, breathe! For God's sake!' Only when he started snoring could I inhale and exhale deeply.

I was careful to know my place. I bathed in the shower stall outside in the garden, never using the indoor bath if I could help it.

'Christ, you make me sound like Pol Pot!' he said, when I tried to explain my reticence. 'What do I care which john you use?' Then he laughed, and I had to as well, at the different meanings of 'john'.

It wasn't that I thought he cared about such things: I was simply afraid of taking anything for granted. One day I asked him if he had a lot of money.

'None of your beeswax,' he said. 'Why do you want to know? Look, if your allowance is not enough, if you need anything, just say so.'

171

My allowance was more than enough. That wasn't what concerned me. I wanted to know because I was afraid of what money could buy. If he could buy anything he wanted, what was to keep him from buying something else, someone else, to replace me? But money was not a subject Will enjoyed discussing. Neither was the subject of what he did for a living.

'I am an amateur,' he said, when I asked him.

'An amateur is what?'

'Someone who isn't doing what he does in order to make money.'

'For what, then, if not for money?'

'For amusement, for interest, for fun.'

'But what is it you do for real, for money?' I persisted.

'I have my own business.'

'What kind of business?'

Will laughed, but I could tell he didn't like being questioned. 'What is this, a trial? It's not important, my business.'

'Are you a spook?' I asked him. I'd heard some of his friends use that term.

'A spook! First tell me what you think a spook is, and I'll tell you whether I'm one or not.'

'A spy?'

'You don't miss a trick, do you? But, no, I'm not a spook. You speak a few languages, you have a few friends in key positions, and everyone takes you for a spook.

'No, I'm not a spook,' he repeated. 'I'm a student.'

'A student! But what is your subject?'

'The world. I like to look and listen and learn.'

'And you like to collect strange things,' I said, looking around the room at his collection of betel-nut boxes and bamboo back-scratchers, his assortment of iron birds once used for opium weights, his ear-cleaning instruments so dear to the Chinese.

'Why do you think I picked you up?' he teased.

But I was not strange, I was common: a common up-country prostitute now promoted to Will's live-in. Yet even I knew that I wasn't easy to recognise any more – not because I tried to hide it but because I no longer advertised.

By 'advertising' I mean a way of *being*, not *boasting*; a way of thinking, walking, talking, dressing – a way of lying down to sleep. There had been a time when every look, every gesture, every article of clothing was a form of advertising. It had to be. Not any more.

I was dressing now in an altogether different way, in clothes that made me look plainer, sterner and older. It was not deliberate, this sombre change; and catching myself in the mirror, I was sometimes taken aback.

Before long there were other changes. I went with Will everywhere in the early days – to cocktail parties, dinner parties, restaurants, clubs and bars. Then, little by little, I stopped going along on his rounds of the city. For although it would please him to see me all dressed up, ready to go out on the town with him, it pleased him more to have me at home to greet him when he returned at three or four in the morning, and ask if he wanted anything to eat. To bring him the chicken sandwich or pound cake he fancied, and to keep him company while he ate. To lead him to bed afterwards and undress him. To put his clothes away: trousers on the hanger, shirt and underwear in the laundry basket, shoes fitted snugly on shoe trees. To sit at the edge of his bed and ask where he would like me to sleep: in my own bed, or with him.

It pleased him, too, that in the morning I was there at the

table where Samai, the maid, had set out coffee and toast and fresh fruit for his breakfast. Shuffling out of the bedroom in one of his checked sarongs, he would touch me on the head or shoulder before sitting down for his first sip of coffee.

I never asked where he had been or whom he had seen because Will was a truthful person, unlike me. More and more I was afraid of the truth when it might have the wrong consequences. That he might have been with another woman, for instance, was not so worrisome; but if this other woman was likely to replace me, then that was a truth I would want to put off knowing.

I hoped this was one of the qualities Will liked about me: that I was prepared to wait for him to tell me things. I was not impatient, not loud, shrill and excitable, like those women on the Patpong strip, like the one I'd watched annoying the sour-looking European couple in a crowded bar by flirting with the husband long after they had made it clear they wanted to be left in peace. The girl had gone on teasing, hitting the tight-lipped European on the shoulder, ruffling his hair, wiggling on his lap. In the end he had caught her hand and held it, twisted, in a clearly painful grip. With a grimace of effort she had screwed it out of his, but as she turned her back on him to walk away, she had raised a fist, screaming, '*Fuckhead!*'

It wasn't that I was free from such urges – far from it. How many times had I wanted to let loose, to shout and laugh, scream with rage or bawl my head off, instead of always weighing the outcome, telling myself not to laugh so hard, or seem too pleased, or talk too much, because laughing or smiling or talking might not serve me well.

So, keeping my fears to myself and my questions to a minimum, I simply sat and watched Will eat.

I liked the way he could chew with his mouth open and even talk between mouthfuls without being gross, like so many Chinese men – surely the world's loudest chewers and slurpers and the biggest belchers as well. Or like other Europeans – the Swiss photographer, for instance, who once came to stay while Will was away on a trip.

This famous photographer arrived at the table every morning carrying a square piece of linen, which he unwrapped like a bounty. Out of it came a loaf of bread and a jar of jam. The bread was hard, coarse-looking and studded with nuts and seeds. The jam was a brownish slime.

With a Swiss-army knife taken from his pocket, the photographer would saw away at the loaf, then spread on the slice a thick coat of jam. He had the face of a rodent, long and pointed, with teeth that nibbled and eyes that darted. Two slices later he would suck his teeth noisily, close the jam jar, screw on the lid tightly, and wrap it up in the cloth with the bread. He kept the precious bundle on his lap while he finished his coffee, then hugged it to himself on his way back to his room.

When Will returned from his trip, I told him about the man's strange attachment to the bread and jam, and how I had been tempted to steal them from his room while he was gone for the day, just to see what kind of upset it might cause him.

'You should have,' said Will, with a snort. 'And now I know what you're thinking when you sit there watching me eat. Look at that greedy rat, you're thinking, chomping with those long teeth.'

No, watching Will eat was a different thing entirely. I liked the noises he made: the way vegetables sounded crisper when crunched by his teeth, the way he downed his orange juice and sipped his coffee with an *ah* of appreciation. But the important difference was that Will was not a man who would ever sit at a table with another human being without offering to share his meal. Not a meal went by when he didn't offer me a portion or a taste, extending between bites a spoonful, a forkful, in my direction. I could not imagine him hoarding dry bread and jam, or anything else – except, of course, the thoughts and feelings he kept jealously to himself.

Once, when he came home so late that it was already early morning and he didn't want to wake me, he poured himself a glass of juice, found something to eat in the fridge, and was sitting at the dining-table, reading a paper, when I came out and saw him before he saw me. He was bent over the table, engrossed in his paper, the crown of his head a dull gold in the cone of light cast from the hanging lamp above. I drew back and watched him for a long while, overcome with a contentment I couldn't immediately place. Then I remembered those last days in Rangoon, as the dread departure of Mor and Far and Pia drew near – and how I would kneel at my window, spying on the man from Holland in the house next door, watching him attend to his solitary meals as to some sacred rite, his head aglow under lamplight just like this. I prayed then to find a way of attaching myself to the lonely figure across the way. I imagined saving his life through some heroic act, dragging him out of a burning building, perhaps; or nursing him back from a near-fatal illness. What choice would he have then but to take me with him, to a new life in a new country, wherever that happened to be?

Now my prayers had been answered. I had found my

guardian, my protector. There he was, alone at the table; and here I was, in a new life, a new world, with him.

In the days when Daw Daw Seng worried that Mor might be turning me into a Buddhist, she read me stories from the Bible and pointed out the different orders of angels. Gabriel, Uriel, Michael and Raphael were the archangels, mighty and mysterious. Satan and Lucifer were mightier still, hulking warriors with flame-like wings for shields. But the angels that seemed strangest to me were the ones known simply as Watchers. Watchers were not massive, like Lucifer or Satan, or handsome, like Michael and Raphael. They looked like ordinary men: dark-haired, scowling slightly, without a trace of wings.

'That's because they're like us,' explained Daw Daw Seng. 'They're made to look human, so they can show us by example how to be nearer to God, how to become good Christians. Some even take human wives. Watchers are among us, but we can't tell who they are – not until something very big, very unusual, happens. Then we know from their act of charity or sacrifice that we are in the presence of a Watcher.'

Had she ever come across a Watcher? I asked.

No, she hadn't. But Watchers were few and far between, assigned only to those in dire need. 'Someone like you,' said Daw Daw Seng.

'Me?'

'You. Confused and full of pointless questions, without faith, without direction.' Yes, she said. She could see I might end up with a Watcher one day – a Watcher sent to lead me out of my confusion and show me the way.

*

Will was not a Watcher who liked being watched, however – even though I tried to do it only when I thought he wasn't looking.

'Stop that,' he'd say, taking me off guard. 'You're scaring me.'

'Why? What am I doing?'

'Staring. As though I'm some sort of – I don't know – apparition.'

But he was an apparition. A revelation. I studied him as a means of shedding light on the unknowable, unspeakable traits of all men – the way I had learned, from a television programme on crows, to see the business of the brothel as a form of 'anting'.

Many birds, it seems – and not only crows – find relief in crouching or lying flat over an anthill, waiting with wings and tails spread for the ants to crawl all over them. Some birds actually pick up ants with their beaks and rub them into their feathers like a dry shampoo. Nobody really knows whether birds do this because the ants expel an acid that rids them of feather-mites, or whether the acid simply soothes their skin. Whatever the explanation, 'anting' puts birds in a dazed, groggy state, a kind of intoxication.

Perhaps all they wanted, those flocks of men who descended on the brothel, like crows on an anthill, was a temporary soothing of a maddening itch, caused by a species of feather-mite that women can't begin to imagine.

Consider a human being as a form of wildlife, and you are more inclined to overlook his trespasses. You are inclined to curiosity and daring. Watching Will while he slept was the nearest thing I'd known to stalking a creature in the wild. It wasn't the danger that held me rapt. It wasn't the power of unfair advantage: me awake, him unconscious. It was the thrill of touching the untouchable – like having my hand licked by the cow when, as a child, I let my arm hang through the slats in our flooring. Or like shaking hands with the orangutan in the Rangoon zoo. Or like clutching the arm of the nurse in the clinic where we had our abortions. Skinny and severe, her hair cropped to stubble, she looked more like a boy with an opium habit than a woman. I remember the feel of her palm, its papery dryness, as it wiped my brow while I waited for the whirlwind machinery to blast and bore its way through me, wreaking its ruin, then sucking out the debris.

I examined my sleeping Watcher not only through touch but through smell and taste. I sniffed through his hair, licked his skin, and weighed his body parts in the palm of my hand – always prepared at a second's notice to pretend I'd turned on the lamp because I'd seen a mosquito or a bug crawling up his leg.

He, of course, did not have anything like the same interest in my body. As he said from the start, my body was not what was important to him. In time it was not only unimportant, it became uninteresting. In time he ceased finding pleasure in only receiving, never giving, satisfaction. When he failed to coax me into relaxing or enjoying his attempts to soothe or arouse me, he gave up the pretence of trying. Pleasure of that nature, he came to understand, was not pleasurable for me.

I could have feigned satisfaction. If there was one thing I'd learned it was the art of 'faking it'. I could have gone through the motions of heavy-breathing and moaning, yelping like a pup, or letting out cat-calls of encouragement. Screaming *yes!* . . . *yes!* . . . *yes!* . . . *YES!* to exaggerated spasms. But Will was my sponsor, my Watcher: I didn't want to treat him like my client.

And so we entered into an agreement – an unspoken pact – not to pretend to each other, not to lie. He was not going to pretend my body was important to him; and I was not going to pretend it was responsive to him. I'd had my fill of pretence, deception, false promises. I knew it frustrated him not to be able to reach me and heal me in that most basic way, and I was sorry to place that distance between us. Because, when all was said and done, I felt more at home in his bed than in mine, on my own. I knew of no greater comfort than lying by his side, asleep or awake. I liked the solidity of his flesh, its boozy, sour-sweet smells.

Still, the thought of his disappointment nagged at me, and I searched for ways to justify myself. I was doing all I could to make up for my deficiencies. Why couldn't he be content with all my other expressions of gratitude and devotion? Wasn't it enough that I served – dutifully and eagerly – as companion, cook and housekeeper? That I'd got rid of all the servants – except Nid, the driver, and Som, the part-time gardener? That I was running a home-stay for his endless stream of friends, and friends of those friends, who needed a berth while passing through the city? That I not only changed their sheets, and scrubbed their baths and toilets, washed and ironed their laundry, prepared their meals, told them where to find the shops and offices they were seeking, and helped sort out their travel arrangements with phone calls to airports, taxis and bus stations? That, in addition to everything, I sat and *listened*?

How ready they were, these 'odds and sods' as Will called them, to pour out their hearts to a stranger like me, one who no doubt had seen it all, heard it all. I listened to a fat black American, who claimed to be a judge in California, go on and on about his ex-fiancée, a woman he'd thought better of marrying because she *smothered* him. For one thing, she couldn't stop buying him gifts. For another, she had an 'over-eager' vagina. He didn't know how to describe it exactly, but it was scary the way it *vibrated.*

I listened to a Belgian mining engineer worry about whether his girlfriend might have mixed feelings about sex since she tended to vomit on his belly after the act.

I listened to a professor of philosophy from Calgary who described himself as a lover of women. Women were so much more interesting than men, he felt, so much more sensitive and easier to talk to. It made him very sad when he met a woman who had never had an orgasm. He felt a responsibility to 'gift' such a woman an orgasm or two, even though it sometimes required a fair bit of persuasion. And because he loved women, he saw himself as a 'universal donor'. He liked the idea of impregnating women, of making his selfless 'deposits' even in those who would never mean anything to him. He was that sort of person – generous with his seed.

I sat and listened for hours to Nefertiti, a healer from San Francisco with milky skin and the hair of an Egyptian queen: black, polished and blunt above the brow. She herself was not Egyptian, but had studied the wisdom of ancient Egypt. Chem, she said – as in chemistry – meant 'blackness'. It was also the old name for Egypt. Egypt stood for the chemistry of knowledge. Going into the blackness was necessary for salvation.

She advised me to look into my blackness if I wanted to see the light. I had to die to my old life in order to wake to true knowledge. If I went on being nice, being good, I would be disappointed, disappointed, disappointed. She urged me to go down into myself, deep, deep into the darkness. Did I not know the Hymn of the Pearl? We were put on earth to find the pearl, but we drink the drink and eat the food, become drowsy and lazy and forget to go after the pearl.

'"Awake, arise, or be fallen!" Who said that?' she demanded, eyes flashing in challenge. 'Come on, Na Ga, get with it. Don't you know *anything*? Oh don't give me that I'm-just-a-hot-and-cold-running-maid routine. You've got a regular library here, you're surrounded by good books. Why don't you read? Start with the big book, the Bible. It's got everything in it, everything you need to find your way. Lucifer! Lucifer said that: "Awake, arise, or be fallen!"'

She muttered, laughing at a secret joke, 'He knew what he was talking about, Lucifer.' The things that made Nefertiti laugh never ceased to puzzle me.

She made me pick a tarot card from a deck she carried in her purse, then threw her head back and cackled at my choice.

'What do you see? What do you see?' She gathered up the rest of the deck, leaving only my card on the table.

'Lightning?' I said. 'Striking a tower?'

'What else? Come on, what else?'

'The dome knocked off in the fire?'

'And?

'Flames coming out from every window. A man and woman falling head down.'

'If that doesn't say it all!' she crowed. 'Total destruction before salvation.'

twenty-five

It was Nefertiti the healer who put a name to the ailment, the handicap, as she saw it, that kept me homebound. *Agoraphobia*, she said, a Greek word meaning a fear of the market, was what kept me from going into the world and finding things to occupy myself with *outside* the home – from taking an interest, any kind of interest, in the life of the great 'sprawling, brawling' city I lived in.

But why would anyone think I had a fear of the market? I wondered. I went to the nearby Pratunam market at least twice a week: to shop for food, toiletries or plants for the garden. Once in a while, in search of an item that couldn't be found elsewhere, I even went to one of the big department stores – the Central or the Daimaru. It was true that I no longer looked forward to the excitement of the huge Jatujak weekend market the way I used to when Will first took me there.

We'd wend our way through the jostling crowds and the brimming aisles, past acres of piece goods and clothing, shoes and luggage, jewellery and gemstones, wind-chimes and wall-hangings, glass- and copperware, Will striding ahead while I hurried to keep up, hardly ever stopping till we reached the much quieter section of the antiques market.

There he'd take his time looking under tables, peering into dark corners, rummaging through crowded cupboards and shelves in search of some dusty, rusty, broken or damaged object. For a while he tried to interest me in the beauty and value of such relics, especially ones that might have come from Burma: a piece of frayed tapestry, a palm-leaf horoscope that fell apart at the touch, a bowl of blackened silver. But I couldn't see the point of all that fuss – the close scrutiny and hard bargaining over some grimy artefact that seemed only good for gathering dust on a shelf.

He came home once from a trip up-country with something he was excited to show me. 'Know what this is?' Between his thumb and forefinger he held an egg-shaped object, wound tight like a top with string.

'What is it?' I turned it over in my hand, not really curious, but knowing he wanted me to be. He took it from me and shook it next to my ear, to show there was something rattling in it. 'Now do you know?' I didn't.

'It's a name seed! From one of your villages. I found it in a market up near the border. Lying next to some bear claws and tigers' teeth. The sellers didn't even know what it was. "For good luck", was all they said.'

'Then how do you know what it is?'

'I know something about the Lu, remember?'

I wasn't sure whether he was referring to me, or to the fact that he was well read on the subject of the Lu. I rubbed the seed with the tips of my fingers, wondering if it could be the real thing, the name seed Daw Daw Seng had told me about: the seed into which a child's name is whispered, and released when that child comes of age.

I handed it to Will. Suddenly I was afraid to touch it.

'It's for you,' he said, trying to make me take it. 'It belonged to one of your people. I'm fairly certain.'

'It's not mine,' I said.

'What's wrong? What's bothering you, Na Ga?' Unable to get an answer, he tried another tactic. 'Sorry. I thought it might mean something to you. Throw it away if you don't want it.'

So I did.

Naturally I pretended interest when he led me through the antique stalls. Naturally I pretended patience. But I would have much preferred some of the other sections of the market where you could see, for instance, live rabbits dressed in tiger-skin vests; or play a game of tic-tac-toe against a chicken, with corn kernels as board pieces, which the chicken was trained to pick up and drop into the winning squares; or watch Picasso, the 'artist elephant', slap paint on canvases, wielding the brush in its swinging trunk.

I tried to explain to Nefertiti that markets didn't frighten me, they just bored me, but she was having none of it. 'Agoraphobia' really meant fear of the market *as an open space*, she said. That didn't make sense to me, either. I wasn't fright-ened of open spaces, just worried about leaving the house untended.

The number of things that could go wrong even in a short absence! Plants could droop, wither and die. Wet clothes could turn mouldy and stink till the next washing, if they weren't hung out to dry straight away. Meat could go off, and fruit turn rotten, attracting flies and midges. Just a crumb or two on the table or floor would bring the ants marching in. Mosquitoes could make the night miserable. Robbers could break in. The house could burn down.

Will was gone half the time – 'on the road', as he referred to his travels, even the ones by boat and plane. All the more reason for me to remain alert and vigilant, keeping house, keeping track of his comings and goings, looking after the houseguests – many of them strangers even to Will, who felt no further obligation beyond giving them a place to stay.

When I told Will what Nefertiti had said about my so-called agoraphobia, expecting him to snort at such rubbish, he surprised me by saying, 'She may have a point.'

'Think about it,' he said. 'You don't go out any more. You don't do *anything* outside the house any more. You bury yourself in housework, slave over unnecessary things. You've got rid of the maid, the cook. You've saddled yourself with work that no one expects you to do. You don't *need* to do any of this cleaning and scrubbing and . . .'

He stopped himself, realising how heated he was becoming, got up and poured himself another drink. In a calmer voice, he said, 'I have nothing to complain about. The house is spotless, the guests are happy, my shoes are polished, my shirts are ironed. You're waiting for me at whatever hour I come home. It's difficult for guys to say no to such comfort and care. But you're not my housekeeper or caretaker or my slave, Na Ga. Christ sakes, you're not even my wife. What am I doing letting you go on like this? It's not what I want for you. And it can't be what you want for yourself.

'I just wish I knew after all this time what it is you do want. You won't go to school and get yourself an education, you won't read any of the books I suggest, you won't go out and make friends, you won't take trips which I'll gladly pay for. I can't force you to do any of these things. But, really, I'd much rather you devoted your energies to your own well-being than to mine, much as I would stand to lose in the way of comfort.

'Now you're all pissed off,' he said, drawing me to him and putting his arms around me. 'The ungrateful bastard . . . after all I do . . .'

There was a point in his drinking when Will became conciliatory – another point when he spoke in fragments, in a kind of shorthand that I had to struggle to understand. But right now he was still lucid, and expecting some kind of response. All I could think of saying was, 'You know why I don't read? It's because I hate the way you interrogate me afterwards.' He was listening closely, taking me seriously, it seemed. 'You always want to know exactly what I understand and remember and think after I've read something you gave me. It wipes out everything from my head because you're giving me a test that I'm sure to fail.'

'But why sure to fail? Why such defeatist thinking? I'm only trying to discuss ideas with you. It's called conversation.'

No wonder I was afraid of conversation.

'It isn't a test. This whole thing, this life. It's . . . It's . . .' He looked old and tired suddenly. 'Let's go to bed.'

But I knew he'd meant everything he'd said. I'd been put on notice. I would just have to try harder, work better, in order to make myself even more necessary.

How could Will not know what I really wanted? All I wanted was to stay where I was – with him.

I was living in a fool's paradise, of course I knew that. It wouldn't last – it couldn't – for ever. Will was away for increasingly long stretches: in America, in Europe, in other parts of South East Asia. He saw friends on those trips: women friends, even girlfriends, for all I knew.

There had been more than a few before me, of course; even a few live-ins. Like Lana, the model from Hong Kong, who threatened for years to slash her wrists, and finally did – though not fatally: she went on to a successful career in public relations, in charge of a big Saudi account. Like Melinda, a Filipina journalist who had covered the Vietnam War from the age of seventeen, and since then had worn only khaki correspondent's jackets.

One particular friend of Will's enjoyed a special status, however. He'd told me about her from the very beginning: a sort of childhood friend he was expected to marry some day. Maybe he would, maybe he wouldn't. They'd been engaged more than once, but one or the other had not been ready at the last minute.

So I had always known that one day they *might* marry and then I would be sent away. I'd had clear and ample warning. But knowing a thing is not the same as really believing it will ever happen. How serious his plans were it was difficult to tell – except that he made it a point to remind me of them from time to time; and I made it a point to feign acceptance.

'Na Ga, you must see this. Nothing is for ever; no one belongs to another. I am not your owner. I happened by when my help was needed. I did what any decent person would have done. You would have done the same for me. But helping doesn't mean *owning*.'

You only say that, I thought bitterly, because you can own, you are in a position to own and disown as you please.

All over the face of the earth people did own other people. Shaman Asita owned our village; the Daru headman had owned me until his wife released me into Daw Daw Seng's care. I had been owned by the brothel. Now I was owned by Will – even if he didn't want to admit it.

'You don't want to be a slave all your life,' he said, having just insisted I was not a slave. 'Look at me. Don't look away.' Holding my head still, he banged his forehead gently against it. 'I am what I am: a restless *farang* who drinks too much.'

I waited for him to finish the comparison, to say: 'And you are what you are.'

Instead, he said, 'If I don't get down to business, I'll end up with no next of kin. You know what they say: if a man doesn't settle down in his forties, he'll never do it. Time is running out on me. And pretty soon my faithful fiancée will be running out on me too.

'Okay, don't look at me. But listen to me, at least. You have to start living. You're young, you have a future. I want you to start breathing, to quit holding your breath.'

Taking my silence as a rebuke, he said, 'You know I've never lied to you.'

And you are proud of that? I thought. Was lying to a person really the worst thing in the world? How like a judge he could be, for all his easy-going ways: righteous and sure of his position. I once heard, on television, a Japanese man using the word blue to speak of Western ways. A mania for clarity, for right and wrong, a stubbornness – hard-headed and stiff-backed in the extreme: these were 'blue' qualities, he explained.

There were times when Will was blue to a fault: honest, pitiless, true blue.

'I don't want to keep you,' he said firmly. 'You are not mine to keep. We have things to do, you and me both. We have to get on with our lives. You have a past, a home, a family – all stolen from you, taken away. You need to go back and find them, see who you are, who you were before you were . . .' He hesitated. 'Misled.'

Misled. Certain words of kindness could be oh-so-hateful. There was loving-kindness, as the Buddhists called it, and there was the other kind, the kind that made you want to scream. What nonsense could pour out of a man's mouth when it suited him! *Misled! Go back home and see who I was!*

As if I didn't know who I was. I was Na Ga, once a Wild Lu, now a whore in nun's clothing.

Eventually it happened, of course. One day, exactly ten years and three months after he had brought me home, Will asked me to move out. Only for a while, only for ten days, he said, with awkward courtesy but no hint of apology.

Without argument, I agreed. I'd seen the way he beat down prices at the weekend market, hiding his hand, stating his *absolute* limit with the indifference of one prepared to walk away. But I was hardly in a position to bargain with him. So I accepted the deal, if one could call it that, with phoney indifference – the loser's small revenge.

Only for a while, only for ten days, I told myself, fighting panic as I emptied the cupboards and cleared away my things with needless zeal, like a criminal erasing a trail. With a vengeance I went about making myself scarce, packing up almost everything in cardboard boxes for storage, stuffing the rest into two shoulder-bags to take away.

As I cleaned and concealed and rearranged, all for Will's convenience and shifting whim, I noticed that he, too, was hiding things from me. He wasn't telling me everything, no matter how patiently I sat at the breakfast table, no matter how silently I waited. It had to be difficult for him, I didn't think it wasn't. I didn't believe for one minute that it was nothing for him to ask me to leave – even if he did it with seeming ease. Even if he could stand to look me in the eye and say, without further explanation, 'Helen is coming to visit.'

Nid, the driver, took me away. Nobody else was around to witness my going. Will was at work by then, and even the dogs failed to follow me into the car as they were in the habit of doing. They remained on the cement walkway, felled by the heat, their eyes open a slit, if open at all, as though *pretending* not to see.

I was only driving across Bangkok, to another part of the city, but with two full bags beside me I might have been leaving for good. I imagined the nostalgia of leaving for ever; I even imagined the relief. *All of this I will never see again; all of this I will never miss.* Not to want any longer, not to crave: wasn't that a kind of bliss?

Maybe now, at long last, I was on the road to bliss, as I drove through the city of a thousand temptations, with its avenues and alleys of jewels and silks, nylons and plastics, flowers and fruits and vegetables and spices – all beautifully displayed, artfully arranged, in quantities and varieties that defied belief.

But quitting the city was not so simple: it would take a long while – if not a whole incarnation – just to get through the traffic jams.

'Shouldn't we get out and walk?' I once asked Will, when we had been stuck for hours in stalled traffic.

'What for?' he said, turning on the reading lamp in the back seat of the car and searching in the newspaper bin on the floor for something to read. 'We would only trip over the bones of others who have tried.'

Rushing was pointless, I could see in this traffic; why even try when everything on earth – the pace of the traffic, the outcome of our fate – was preordained? Maybe the trick, then, was not to flee in a hurry, but to take it all in through half-closed eyes: the way the dogs watched as I was leaving, the way Nid looked in the rear-view mirror. He sat out this gridlock in a speechless daze, as though asleep at the wheel, asleep to the world, asleep to my misery.

*

When I arrived at Mole's house – for it was he, Will had revealed, who was to be my host – the Englishman seemed depressed. In his glassed-in room with the noisy air-conditioner he sat hunched in his chair, gloomily chain-smoking. It seemed the woman he desired, a Thai princess he'd hoped to marry, had turned her back on him for no reason he could fathom. They had been mad about each other; he had been *serious* about her; even though she was – here he took a ragged breath – *a much married woman.*

'What do you make of her, then?' Mole asked me again and again, in the days that followed. I didn't know what to say. I had never set eyes on this mysterious heartbreaker, although from the stacks of photographs lying around, I could see the fine lines of her figure and face, the jewellery, the silk dresses, the elegant high heels – all the markings that showed her to be every bit as beautiful and rich as he made her out to be.

But I was no better at unravelling the mystery than he. I had as much in common with this heartless beauty as with any of the *farang* women I watched in the lobbies of hotels and clubs, women who moved across the floor, across the earth, with such certainty and purpose, always on their way to someone who waited.

But Mole persisted. 'What do you women want, *really?*' I couldn't help being flattered that he imagined his beloved and me to have similar desires. Weren't we from the same continent, after all, with roughly the same texture and colour of hair and skin? Mole was respectful of me in other ways too, careful to avoid any mention of why his friend Will had sent me to stay with him, or what this might spell for my future.

One morning I found a note on the kitchen table. *Nara – Won't be home tonight, sorry. See you in the morning. Mole.*

Nara? He didn't even know my name. But, then, I had never asked Mole about his real name, either.

How grateful I was to him nevertheless, for asking of me only that I sat late with him night after night while he downed his whisky, filled his ashtray and examined the facets of his loss. I sat at attention hour after hour, nodding and murmuring, wondering all the while where he was now, where *they* were now, Will and Helen.

With Mole gone from the house, I wandered through the empty rooms, picking up things and examining them in a new way, wondering how Will and Helen would furnish the home they would inevitably make together. Then, exhausted, I lay on the sofa and dozed.

I don't know how long I had been sleeping when the phone rang.

'What's up, kiddo?'

'Will! Hello!' I tried not to let on that he'd caught me not only sleeping but in the middle of a dream.

'So! What are you doing? Where's Mole?'

'He's gone,' I said, 'till tomorrow.'

'What? Leaving you alone? I'll have to have a word with him!' A little laugh in his voice – his drinking voice. 'Well, I was just checking in. Listen, I thought I'd come by for a bit, say hello.'

'Now?'

'Now. Well, an hour from now, with this traffic.'

I put the phone down, aware of a nagging dread despite my elation – and remembered what I was dreaming when the phone rang.

It was the book again, and I was searching through it. As usual, I couldn't seem to find what I sought. Then I saw the problem. The book I was looking through had uncut pages. With a forefinger I ripped open the join between two leaves till their insides were revealed – and there it was. The letters were in a strange script, part pictograph, part alphabet, but I could read them all the same. *Na Ga.* My name.

So this is it then, I thought in the dream – my name, finally, in the big *Book of Records*, written by Lu Sa himself. Lu Sa, the god who marks down every one of our names, along with the exact dates for each of our deaths.

Then the phone rang, sparing me the dangerous knowledge I was seeking.

He came through the door and gave me a quick kiss on the head without looking at me, squeezing the back of my neck on his way to the bar in the living room. He poured himself a drink, a double whisky, and took a sip before turning to face me.

We sat in the conservatory, across from each other, while he looked into his glass, shaking it gently as though it was tea he was drinking, with leaves at the bottom he was trying to read. Was my room comfortable, he wanted to know. At least three times he asked me the same question. Then he yawned deeply. 'Come on, let's get a little shut-eye.'

I led him to my room, where he took off his clothes and collapsed onto the bed, not bothering to get under the sheets. I draped his clothes on the chair, tucked his shoes under it, and went to lie with him, my head on his chest. He clasped my arms firmly as though to keep them still.

'I found a dragon today,' he said sleepily. 'A beautiful gold *naga*, lying under your bed. It made me think of you. That's why I came.'

For a moment I was puzzled. Then I understood: he meant

my brass belt with the heavy scales and the dragon-head buckle. How had I missed checking under my bed while clearing up just before leaving? And why had he gone into my room in the first place?

But he had. He'd gone into my room, reached under my bed for who knew what reason, and found something I'd left behind. He had picked it up and examined it. He had thought of me. And, with Helen still in town, he had come to see me.

He was fast asleep now; I could tell from the rise and fall of his chest. But I didn't want him to sleep. I wanted him to wake, to see me for once as I was.

I got up and stripped, then knelt at the foot of the bed. 'Will! Will!' I shook him.

'What is it?' he murmured. Then, seeing I was naked, 'Wow-za!' But pleasure was not what I heard in his voice.

'Tell me what you want me to do! Anything, Will. Just tell me!'

He laughed softly. 'I want to hit you on the head, very hard, so you'll finally go to sleep.'

'Anything!' I said. 'Do whatever you want to me.'

I knelt over him and bent low. First with my hand and then with my mouth I tried, how I tried, to arouse him. But while he stroked my hair, and sighed a little, and lifted his groin slightly to meet my face, he was not to be aroused, not to be seduced – and finally he lay very still.

But I was not about to give up. I took his hand and cupped it over my breast. Then I leaned over and fed my breast to him. And when he turned away I felt the despair of a nursing mother when her infant prefers bawling to the tit. I lay on top him, clinging and rocking.

'Hey, hey, hey,' he said. 'Come on, kiddo. That's not necessary.'

Covered with sweat from all that fruitless effort, I said, 'Tell me what to do, Will! Just tell me what to do!'

Firmly he pushed me away. 'Listen,' he said, 'you'll be back home in three days. Three days is all. What's the hurry?'

'Stay with me,' I begged. 'Please.'

'Na Ga, I can't,' he said, irritated now, getting up to dress. 'You know I can't do that.'

twenty-six

Minzu has given up asking me to teach her English. Instead she has resorted to trying out her Burmese. Not that it's getting any better. Today she informs me that Mr Jiang's bees have been scattered to the winds.

Bees?

Yes, bees, she repeats, seeing my bewilderment. That's what the hospital does for patients without kin.

Ah, I see now what she means. The Burmese word for 'bees' can easily be confused with the word for 'ashes'. That's how I find out he's been cremated.

So there is no . . . *funeral*? I ask, making crude digging motions. To think that a person can vanish off the face of the earth just like that! Body parts incinerated, ashes scattered to the winds, or whatever method is employed by a Chinese crematorium, not even scooped into a plastic bag – for a family member, say, who might want to preserve them.

'Yes,' says Minzu. 'There is no funeral.' At least she has grasped that Burmese speakers always prefer to answer in the affirmative, even if they follow with a negative. Yes, there is no funeral, she says, but there is – here she brings her palms together under her chin, to indicate a blessing – there is a blessing for Mr Jiang, and she will take me to it.

It's at the temple: I should have known. The Buddhist temple Jiang led me to, one of the landmarks famous for escaping destruction. I remember how he lit incense and kowtowed, and prayed with such fervent concentration. And how I waited outside, a little envious of his faith, and hoped to get a rise out of the almond tree. *Speak to me of God!* I had challenged, waiting for it to break out in blossoms, even though I was no St Francis.

I remember turning to face the temple and thinking, No wonder the hooligans left it untouched – who would waste time demolishing such a tacky house of worship? The gilt pinnacle on its brassy seven-tiered roof looked like a paper cut-out that would soon curl at the edges. And the temple was built on stilts, like a common dwelling. Perhaps it had been saved by its very drabness. For wasn't it the ordinary, the plain, that stood a better chance of escaping destruction than the beautiful, the expensive, the sacred?

It's still intact at any rate, this homely, unmolested temple on the outskirts of Wanting: the timber beams supporting the rectangular hall show no sign of termite damage or decay. And the grimacing demons up on the walls and ceilings are vivid and fresh with purple, red, blue and gold paint.

Minzu and I are the first to arrive. We shed our shoes on the landing and step into the empty hall, where incense sticks have been lit along the verges of the shrines. The main shrine is to the left of the stairs; two smaller ones are at the opposite end. Each is equipped with a nest of wooden tables on which offerings of fruit, flowers and bowls of water have been placed. We approach the big shrine, already in semi-darkness because it's nearing noon. The sun has moved away from its path of early illumination and falls in blocks through the open windows onto the floor planks with their dust and grit.

Out of the gloom comes a squat figure with a waddling gait. She is wearing frayed cotton pyjamas, stretched to the limit round her waist. A ring of keys is pinned to one of her breast pockets, and a wreath of blossoms with tough, papery petals encircles her thick, wattled neck. It appears she is the temple-keeper, and wants to be of service. Her hair is white, she is missing two front teeth, and her eyes, when she turns to the light, are milky, but her smile is coy and girlish. The trouble is that she speaks – or rather shouts – a dialect that even Minzu is hard pressed to understand. Mistaking us for tourists, perhaps, she insists on pointing out various features of note: gilt carvings on the lintels, weird *arahats* looking like cartoon man-beasts, winging their way across lurid land-scapes.

Then she draws our attention to the altar and asks if we have brought anything. I've come empty-handed and un-prepared, but Minzu reaches into her shoulder-bag and produces a few tangerines. The girl never fails to astonish me. But the old lady yelps and turns away in disdain. Tangerines! They have plenty of tangerines! Just look at the altars – no shortage of tangerines! She peers into Minzu's shoulder-bag, to see what else it might contain. She searches our faces closely. Have we nothing else to contribute? No chicken, for instance? She flaps her arms for emphasis.

Her mood changes. She wags a finger at us, scolding.

We are saved by voices coming up the stairs. Three people appear: two old men and a middle-aged woman. The small thin man with the horn-rimmed glasses is the first to speak. He looks from me to Minzu and back to me, decides I am the one to address and greets me in a way I haven't heard in ages. 'Daughter?' he asks. In Burma, any woman whose name is unknown can be safely addressed as 'daughter' by someone of an older generation. 'You are Burmese, correct?' Then he introduces himself by name. The only part I can make out is *thakin* – a title reserved for an independence hero.

So these are the former rebels that Yan Ding mentioned: the old leaders of the Burmese Communist Party. I'm trying to think what else he said about them, but all I remember is the phrase, 'They had a price on their heads.' What had he said about them? 'They spent their whole lives in the jungle, they had a price on their heads, and when the Communist Party collapsed in Burma, they were offered exile by the Chinese government.'

'And they live in Wanting?' I had asked.

'No, in Kunming. But they've come here to bury Jiang, who joined them as a young volunteer from the Shan state. They trained him.'

Now something else comes back – a memory, tinged with shadows, from my Rangoon days. I remember Mor and Far going on about the peace talks held by the Rangoon government. The Communist Party leaders were invited, and were offered amnesty. The phrase for 'amnesty' we kept hearing on the radio was 'coming into the light'.

The rebels arrived; the peace talks fell apart; and when they refused to come into the light, many of the leaders were assassinated. It was soon after this that Mor and Far left the country, without taking me as promised. After the talks collapsed, new wars broke out in the provinces, and in the capital of Rangoon people were rounded up in hundreds and jailed, no reasons given. In those days before Daw Daw Seng and I left the city, I kept hearing the phrase 'a reign of terror'.

I heard it as 'rain of terror'. I thought I felt that rain on my skin.

'Yes,' I reply to the thin man with the thick glasses. 'I was born in Burma.' But now I am tongue-tied, uncertain how to address these old warriors. General? Uncle? *Thakin*?

'Glad to see a Burmese relative!' he barks, but ignores my outstretched hand. 'Yes, yes, we heard you were here. The good Yan Ding said one of our countrymen was passing through.' But he is more interested in the ceiling.

'A sad occasion,' he adds, clucking his tongue but still craning his neck to study the *arahats* and demons. 'Very sad for us all, because we are one people, are we not? All sons and daughters of the same land.' I sense he's making an old speech, he's bored and distracted. Then he turns to include his friend in his remarks, and finds that his comrade has lowered himself onto a bench and is having difficulty breathing. 'What's the matter now?' he says. His stout friend is unable to speak, but struggles to rise from his seat. The thin one reaches out to stay him; and with this, the stout one falls sideways onto the floor. There he rolls over and remains without moving, as though thankful to be on his back.

The thin old man gets down on his knees, takes his friend's pulse calmly, as if he does this routinely, then fans him gently with the folded newspaper he's been holding. 'He's okay,' he says, standing up with a frown. His spectacles have slipped down to the end of his nose. He scolds the prostrate man: 'I told you, "Don't come, you're too weak!" Do you listen?'

'You never listen,' the curly-haired woman pipes up all of a sudden – in Burmese, but with a heavy Chinese accent. Now *she* is on her knees.

'He won't even listen to his wife,' the thin one remarks to his glasses, which he is cleaning with the knot tied at the waist of his cotton *longyi*. The Chinese wife is slapping her husband's face. The husband blinks and blinks.

'Awake?' she says cheerfully. 'Then sit up. My knees are killing me.'

We all reach down to help the stout Burman back onto the bench. The Chinese wife sighs, looking through her handbag for something. She brings out a jar of Tiger Balm ointment into which she sticks a large, square thumb. 'He'll be all right,' she says, looking sheepish as she rises to tend her husband. She presses her thumb into his forehead as though squashing a hardy bug. The old man makes a face and tries to turn away – it's hurting him – but she goes on rubbing, assuring him that she knows what to do, she knows what to do.

'Enough! We'll be off now to hospital,' the thin old man interrupts. 'He needs an injection,' he says to me curtly, as though I am somehow to blame. 'We shouldn't have come, but we wanted to pay our respects to a countryman, you see. We have been gone so long from our native land. Homesickness is to be expected. That's the way it is. Let us say farewell, then, for the time being, eh, ladies? Daughters? *Do svidanya*, as the Russians say. Did you know I speak Russian? My nickname in Russian is Sasha. I lived in Moscow once. I went ice-skating – yes, yes, skating! on ice! – in a beautiful park. Gorky. My friend here, however, speaks fluent Chinese . . .'

The Chinese speaker is already hobbling down the stairs on the arm of his curly-haired wife, his face a greyish green. I watch them step into the taxi they apparently came in. Thank God they kept it waiting.

'Who *were* those people?' Minzu wants to know. Before I can answer, the temple-keeper requires our attention. She is making loud kissing noises, as though calling a cat, to bring to our notice an elderly monk – I think he's a monk, but then I don't know much about Chinese Buddhism – who must have come in through the back entrance, and now is chanting in front of the main shrine. *Go on!* her head movements are saying, urging us towards him. *Isn't this what you came for?*

'What is going on?' I whisper. 'What are we supposed to be doing?'

'Don't know.' Minzu puts a finger to her lips and hurries forward in a stealthy shuffle. We take up our positions behind the monk, who is wearing a pointed white hat, white cotton pants and a woven red tunic, coarse and nubby like a horse blanket. He is standing while he chants, but at an angle to the shrine, not facing it squarely, facing instead the open window to the right, so that his blessing – if blessing it is – seems directed to the outdoors, not to the altar with the fruit and flowers and smoking joss-sticks.

We position ourselves accordingly, standing at attention.

I close my eyes and try to let the chant sink in. I try to clear my mind of everything: the odd encounter with the old Communists, their abrupt arrival and departure, the greedy temple-keeper. I won't ask myself why we are here in the first place, or who is behind this 'blessing' for Jiang, or what Minzu has to do with it – what I have to do with it.

Forget everything. Breathe in. Breathe out. Nothing else matters but this very moment. Think only of Mr Jiang. Say goodbye to Mr Jiang. Poor man. Not quite right in the head, evidently. Doomed from the first moment I set eyes on him. A lost soul. Dutiful, nonetheless, till the bitter end. Seeing to my every need until the very last minute. If only I'd bothered to talk to him. I should have asked him more about himself. Told him more about *my*self. Would that have made a difference? Could I have changed his mind, or – perish the thought – saved him? Now I'll never find out who he really was, that stranger who existed less than a week for me. Little did he know I was mired in my own misery even as he was mired in his. And that all the while we were thinking along the same lines, plotting our own nearly identical ends.

But it's hard to stay in the moment.

My thoughts drift to the last day we spent together. He said he would bring the papers round to the hotel in the evening, but would I like to stretch my legs a little? It was hot, I had a headache, and all I wanted to do was lie prostrate in my room. But I thought, I'll humour him one last time.

We had started up the hill to the road ahead – Jiang fanning his face with a folded magazine – when a man in a black turban came riding by, a cage of live chickens on the back of his bike. Jiang stopped him with a question in dialect: something to do with the old cement shed further downhill, I gathered.

The cyclist dismounted to explain, pointed to the shed, then to a spot behind it. The chickens in the cage stopped their squawking for an instant, as though curious about what he had to say.

Jiang turned back to me to translate: the shed was a jail, a holding pen for prisoners awaiting execution, out in that yard with the almond tree. At once I thought of the bulletin board in the market square. *That's where I'll end up!* I was sure of it suddenly. The return of that premonition brought on a kind of thrill. The inevitability felt like the urge that had come over me on the bus from Kunming, when just *thinking* about the drop into the chasm below induced a desire to leap off the precipice.

I longed to return to my room and end it all, right then and there – the pointless wait for papers I would never need; the life I was tired of prolonging. If only I could settle on a foolproof method. Jumping from a window was out of the question. Too many people misjudged the necessary height, ending up for ever maimed and nearly brain-dead, but stubbornly among the living. No, my third floor was not nearly high enough – even if I could get past the bars across it.

I regretted not taking the plunge when I'd still had the chance, back on the Burma Road. I could have leaped off the precipice at one of those spots above the Salween river, where the bus kept stopping to let the timber trucks by. I could still do it, I thought, throw myself in front of a truck or a bus. But nothing moved that fast on the streets of Wanting; and even out on the main highway any vehicle was bound to brake in time. They were used to braking for death-defying pedestrians. What else could I throw myself into, then?

The river! There was always the river – I'd seen a stretch on this side of the frontier, right by the monument for the heroes who'd fought the Japanese in Lungling. A nice peaceful stretch – but not deep enough, unfortunately, to drown in.

There was one other way, of course. A sure-fire way, with no guns or sharp instruments needed.

Minzu is squeezing my elbow and pointing to her Mickey Mouse watch. One thirty almost! We've been standing here for close to an hour, hypnotised by the monk's merciless chanting. Minzu rubs her belly and says in a whisper, 'My stomach is hungry. Yours?'

The monk shows no signs of winding down, has grown louder, in fact, with a second wind. He appears to remain oblivious of our presence.

We signal our agreement with a nod to each other, and turn to leave.

But at the bottom of the stairs, the plump temple-keeper is lying in wait. She leaps out from behind a bush she's been watering. Like a magician in the run-up to his trick, she holds up her can with a flourish – one of those chipped enamel jugs with a stencilled flower design – and sloshes around the water in it. Then she knocks back a mouthful, gargles noisily, and blows it out in a spray over both our faces.

The old witch is delighted. We have made her day. She *must* be a witch. How else would she know of the funeral rite in which our shaman Asita did the selfsame thing? He sprayed the family of the deceased with water from his mouth, beseeching the dead not to come back and haunt the living.

Such a sorry little ceremony, I can't help thinking, as we make our escape.

Far away from home, a lonely man kills himself – and who is there to mourn him but a faceless priest, a loopy temple-keeper, a sixteen-year-old receptionist at a cheap hotel, two old Communist leaders and me. And we, his countrymen, have failed him especially. The old Communists are too decrepit, and I am too impatient, to last through his blessing. Had our fates been reversed, I am certain that Jiang would have stayed to the end for my blessing. As would Minzu, I suspect.

She turns to me gleefully, clapping her hands in anti-cipation of lunch in the market. To think I was prepared to let this happy girl walk into my room and find me hanging.

twenty-seven

Nine nights had gone by at Mole's – nine endless nights without rest, without peace. Just one more to go before my ten-day sentence would end.

Mole chose that evening to bring out his baby pictures and introduce, one by one, reminders of his childhood in England: mother, father, sisters, uncle, a nanny, a pair of shoes, a painting of a church and two horses – reminders of a time when the world was simple and people seemed solid, a time before wisdom and heartache.

Page by page, frame by frame, Mole took me through his past, which had somehow become bittersweet since he, or his loved ones, or perhaps everyone and everything, had 'fallen from grace'.

'And it gets worse with time,' he said. 'Whenever I go home for a visit now, I'm reminded of what a depressive, constipated lot we are. Everyone avoids demonstrative contact. You try to embrace warmly and they all shy away. You feel them tense up and they turn their heads when you try to kiss them. And it's really the same in conversation. A lot of evasions. So very little gets communicated . . .'

I was having trouble breathing with a sudden constriction in my chest. 'Excuse me,' I said, getting up. 'I don't feel well.'

Mole looked up. 'Oh, I *am* sorry.' The concern on his face told me something I hadn't noticed: the endless talk, the filling of every silence, the precious photo album – all of that had been as much an attempt to distract me from my misery as himself from his.

Mole had a tiresome way of speaking, of answering straight-forward questions with roundabout phrases. 'I shouldn't have thought so,' he'd say, when 'no' would suffice, or 'I would have thought' when he most definitely thought. Will once tried to explain that such a way of speaking was called 'the conditional' or 'the subjunctive'. 'The Brits like to talk that way,' he said. But the Englishman was emphatic now in his concern. 'Go to your room,' he said, as though chastising me, 'and get some sleep.'

I went to my room, but only to find my bag and the money I'd need. I hurried past him on my way out, afraid he would try to restrain me. But though he rose from his seat and followed me to the door, saying, 'Where are you going, then? *Must* you do this? Is it wise?' he stood aside to let me by. I glanced at the clock on the wall. It was still early – eight thirty. I knew where to go, where my search had to begin.

In the dark I opened the garden gate and shut it behind me. I broke into a half run along the side-street. Before I reached the main road, a drizzle hit me, but it was too late to return for an umbrella or a rain jacket – too late for anything except ploughing on. Just as I reached the top of the street, the rain lashed down in a fury. By the time a *tuk-tuk* stopped for me I was soaked through and shivering.

'Sukhumvit,' I said to the pedicab driver, and told him the number of the side street. Before he even stated the fare, before we could haggle, he looked away, shaking his head. I thought he was refusing to take me, but then he said, 'Get in.' I climbed into the open cab with its one plastic-covered seat and huddled in a corner as the *tuk-tuk* chugged through the torrent. Even through the sheets of rain I could see the waters spilling and ebbing across the streets, rising and rising as if within a walled city. Cars were stalled and grounded like boats. Hunched figures waded ankle deep, knee deep, thigh deep in puddles. Sandbags barricaded the doorways to houses. At bus stops and taxi stands, queues had formed behind ramparts of plastic and tin.

I could have walked, I could have waded or even swum through the swirling floods, as others were doing; I could have simply waited to be borne away with the refuse and debris. But I needed to get to the house in a hurry.

The *tuk-tuk* left me by the front hedge. I peered through its leaves, to see if it was safe to make my thief's entry. My house! There it stood, solid and tranquil in the pouring rain, but I looked on in panic, as though I could see it sinking.

How quiet it was – how dark and deserted. No lights in the servants' quarters, no lights on the porch, no lights in the living room. Only a faint glow filled the window of one room. My room! Like a trespasser I stole past the *klong* outside, then hugged the wall till I reached the back door where I fumbled with the lock whose secret I knew, and quickly let myself in. I went to my room and switched on the bright overhead light.

The first thing I noticed was the spirit house in the corner, the carved teakwood structure, no bigger than a dovecote, which Will had bought me on our first visit to the weekend market, not long after my arrival in Bangkok. It was my good-luck shrine and I had never left it empty of flowers or candles or knick-knacks that seemed worthy of display. It was now clean and bare. Gone were the jam jars I'd kept filled with hibiscus blossoms and bougainvillaea sprays from the garden; gone were the incense holders; gone were the candles, wax drippings and all.

Gone was my life there, stripped like the spirit house of every trace.

I went into Will's room and turned on the light. I saw the bed made, the space more or less unchanged. But it pained me to see how the contents of his pockets were strewn all over the place. There had been a time when he had handed me everything to keep: business cards and paper napkins, scribbled on with notes and addresses; his comb; the change from bar bills. I used to put it all in the side pocket of my handbag, a sleeve I saved only for his things, and when we got home I emptied them carefully on his bedside table. How long ago it seemed – that simple arrangement I suddenly missed.

I noticed a stain on the floor and bent to study it. It was a length of silk, gauzy and stiff like a dragonfly's wing. I held it to my face. Mor's evening gowns used to smell just like that: cigarette smoke, gardenia and faint sweat.

I took off my wet clothes, and slid the dress over my head. Far too long for me, it floated around my feet. In front of the full-length mirror I turned this way and that, a stunted apparition if ever there was one, until dizziness seized me and I fell across the bed – Will's bed, where it was my duty, my habit, my pleasure, to lie without sleeping. Someone else had come to lie with him now, someone I could smell not only in the dress I was wearing but in the sheets. I closed my eyes for an instant, overcome with fatigue, but quickly opened them again, lest I fall into a sleep from which there would be no waking.

I got up at last, stepped out of Helen's dress, leaving it where I had found it on the floor. I picked up my wet clothes, squeezed them out in the bathroom, and put them on – still wet – again.

Outside, the air was warm and dense. The storm had abated and the rain was slight, but it showed no signs of ceasing. I crept along the wall to keep from being seen, hailed another *tuk-tuk*, and got in without haggling. 'Patpong,' I said this time.

The city was hosting a mammoth celebration. Firecrackers popped and hissed from every direction, and the horns of cars were kazoos. The festive lights were brighter than ever, floating in the sea of rain.

I got out at the head of Patpong 2, where the street was blocked with parked taxis and *tuk-tuks*, mopeds and food vendors. I hurried through the neon-lit arcade of cigarette, newspaper and video stalls, and along the noise-tunnel, where hard rock was thrumming from open windows and doors, competing with the blare of boom boxes for sale.

Under an awning like a wedding tent, the touts took shelter, calling to me in a mix of languages. Where was I going? What was I seeking? But they were asking out of habit and boredom; they knew there was nothing of interest or profit to be gained from this drab, drenched figure charging head down through the noise and the rain.

I hated that place. I'd hated it from the very beginning – from the very first time Will had taken me there. I hated it now more than ever as I plunged into its bowels with no clear plan or motive. I wanted to find Will and Helen. It wasn't the search of a thinking, planning person: it was a mad, hit-or-miss spree. I wanted something more, of course, than just to find them.

At the back of my mind, in the depths of my heart, I wanted to shake them. Explode their smug contentment. Drive her away. Bring him back to me. Or just make a scene for once in my life, a little scene to embarrass him. Show him that I was *somebody*, not just some*thing*. Not just a slave he could own and disown with impunity.

Yes, all over the world people owned other people: this was a slave planet, all right. But even slaves didn't go to their graves without making a fuss or shaking their fists now and then.

All I had to do was show up, stand there in front of them and the poison would spread without a word being said: *Look at what he's done, see how he's left me!*

Even better: I could show up with a baby. Will and his talk of wanting a child, needing to breed, so he was not deprived of next-of-kin. *You want a child? I'll give you a child!*

I remembered the alley behind the pharmacy where Will had pointed out the building to me. 'That's where they rent out babies,' he'd said, nodding towards the second floor.

'Rent out babies? What for?'

'For begging, for photography, for fun, who knows?' he said, shrugging.

It wasn't in the exact place he had said, but the woman upstairs told me where to go next: to the dress shop around the corner.

The one available baby was on the floor, in a swinging rattan basket, right next to the treadle of a sewing-machine. The young woman working the treadle took her foot off the pedal every so often to keep the crib rocking steadily. She made me wait while she finished a long seam, her mouth pointed like a beak. I thought of a gull overseeing a nest in which the eggs have been left by a cuckoo. The child wasn't the woman's, I knew in that instant. It couldn't, simply couldn't have been.

It wasn't a newborn, either, I was relieved to see. Newborns made me nervous – they were hardly human. This one was formed, it was whole, its features were complete. It woke from its sleep long enough to regard me calmly for a moment; then closed its eyes and was still.

The seamstress asked for a deposit and the two-hour minimum. Renting a baby for two hours was cheaper than renting a ball-gown for an evening. She handed me a carrier, a pouch made of corduroy, and showed me how it worked: I could wear it in front, kangaroo-style, or on my back, like a rucksack.

I held the pouch open while she filled it with the still sleeping infant. Then she helped me strap the carrier to my back. Seeing I was without an umbrella or jacket, the seamstress tore off a length of thick black plastic from a rubbish-bag dispenser behind her sewing-machine. This she draped over my shoulders and tied by one end around my neck, like a cape. Bracing myself, I charged back into the rain.

I knew I'd find them somewhere along the strip, where he did most of his entertaining and drinking. *Cleopatra. Winner's Bar. Pussy Alive. Queen's Castle.* I recognised the names from the early days, but no longer remembered which were the bars with the go-go dancers, which the second-storey rooms with the floor shows and special acts.

I hadn't thought through the problem of entrance, either, of how to get past the bouncers, barkers and pimps. How to make them understand that stepping inside for one moment was all I was after. A quick survey of the audience, nothing more. For I could spot him in a single instant. Even below the stages, below the bodies in the spotlight, coupling and writhing, even in that eerie gloom where only the white objects – white shirts, white teeth – looked radioactive, while everything else stayed hidden: even there I would know him right away.

Dashing from door to door, criss-crossing the streets, I scurried like a rat in a maze. In and out of entries, up and down stairs, past bodies and faces, and dancers on stages, and neon signs repeating the same names: *King's Castle, Napoleon, Goldfinger, New Red Door, Mizu, Mango Brutus, Magic Grill* . . .

I was beginning to despair of finding them when I remembered the one place I hadn't yet tried: the Garden of Eatin.

I saw his back the minute I walked in and ducked behind the folding screen that stood between the front door and the kitchen. Steadying myself with a couple of deep breaths, I stepped out for another look.

Under one of those trees with the apple lights for bulbs was the round table where they were all sitting. The friends around him were faceless to me, except the one sitting opposite him, her face turned in my direction.

I had thought of Helen as a girl – a violet-eyed girl with corn-husk hair like the girl in the giant milk advertisement posted all over the city. But she was a woman, this Helen – a pale-skinned older woman with hair like untidy wool framing a troubled face. From the deep crease on her brow and the downturn of her mouth, I could tell she was no stranger to misery.

And she understood mine, I could see. Before I could step back behind the screen, she looked up and straight at me. I stood near the door, trembling in the air-conditioned chill, but there was no turning back any more. Her head tilted; her eyes narrowed and widened. While Will and the others went on laughing and talking, unaware of my presence, she watched me closely as I approached the gathering.

My heart was clapping wildly as I stood at the foot of the table and watched Will's face as it registered surprise, then anger, then a terrible, terrible coldness. He wouldn't – or couldn't – bring himself to get up for what seemed a very long time. The silence at the table was spreading to other tables as well. From the clinking of cutlery and the clearing of throats I was dimly aware of the kind of tension that precedes a public speech. But the only face I could take in was Will's, and the expression on it made me quail.

As though watching a film that had come to a stop and was starting up again, I saw Will rise to his feet. With a mocking courtesy that cut me to the quick, he said, 'Well, if it isn't our favourite fury! Na Ga! What a surprise! Come and have a seat!'

I pushed away his outstretched arm and saw him clench his fist as I worried at the knotted plastic around my neck. The seamstress had tied the ends so tightly that I couldn't get it undone; and in the end I just slid the whole thing back to front, and reached behind to unfasten the pouch with the baby.

'What do we have here?'

I could still hear the ice in his voice as I unhooked the straps from my shoulders and set it on the chair he had offered me. I started to unzip the front of the carrier. 'A baby,' I said flatly. I heard murmurs, clicking tongues, placating noises. *Aw, a baby . . .*

'You want a baby . . .' I couldn't keep my voice flat: it came out like a croak. 'I've brought you a baby.'

I was trying to get the child out of the carrier as quickly as possible – I wanted to thrust it at Will, force it into his arms – but the zipper was sticking, and its limbs were oddly inert and heavy. It was still fast asleep. What an exceptionally placid brat!

My God! It wasn't moving – it hadn't moved! I shook its arm.

I shook its leg. It wasn't moving! I put my ear to its chest. It wasn't breathing! It was dead! The child was dead! Roughly I pulled it out of its pouch and gave it another shake. I slapped it on the back, on its feet, on its face. I held it high, held it low, slapped it again and again.

The child was dead. I'd smothered it under the plastic.

I turned to Will. 'I killed it,' I said, trying to hand him the heavy mass.

The arms that relieved me of the burden were not Will's but Helen's. She took the child from me and gathered it to herself before hoisting it slightly to one side and over her shoulder. Calmly, almost absentmindedly, she rubbed its back.

All of a sudden the baby arched, almost flipping backwards in her arms, but she caught it by the neck and brought its head towards her shoulder again. The baby looked around, confused, its eyes flicking across the room before it let out a shriek.

I saw Helen smile as she went on patting its back, flinching a little as it continued to scream but otherwise unperturbed. The baby worked itself up, yelling its head off. When I reached out to try to comfort it, Helen turned and gave me her back so that the baby was facing me. Seeing me seemed to be the final straw: it flailed about, trying to throw itself out of Helen's arms, while screaming at the top of its lungs. Once more I reached out to take it from Helen. 'Give it to me!' I had to shout to be heard in the din.

A weight fell on my shoulders. Will's hands were crushing – like a yoke or a gibbet. 'That's enough, Na Ga,' he said in his old voice. 'You're coming with me.'

As he led me through the restaurant and out of the door to where Nid was dozing in the car, draped over the steering-wheel, I was aware of the plastic still hanging down my front like a ridiculous black bib. I allowed myself, nevertheless, to be led without protest as though already handcuffed and sentenced.

'Take her home to Mole's,' Will said to the driver, who had started the car and was revving the engine. Nid was used to snapping out of sleep in an instant, at any time of night or day.

'What about the baby?' was the only thing I said.

'Never mind the baby. We'll take care of it.'

I had the presence of mind, I don't know how, to hand Will the receipt from the seamstress, and he slammed the door in my face.

Nid's eyes kept flicking towards me in the rear-view mirror. But he'd learned to be discreet, to mind his own business. His lack of curiosity enraged me. 'I almost killed a child back there,' I announced.

'*Lerh?*' he said, meaning, 'yeah?' in Thai.

Fucking blood-sucking, brothel-owning, baby-renting Thais!

But I knew then that the doors had not only slammed shut behind me; they were now locked and double-bolted for good measure.

Once again this Wild Lu had proven herself unfit for companionship, unfit for slavery. Unfit for child-minding even.

twenty-eight

'It's all here,' Jiang said, on that last day at the hotel, patting his plastic carrier-bag. 'All your papers. Complete.'

We looked around for a place to sit, but a Chinese tour group had just arrived and every seat in the lobby was taken.

'Let's go there.' Jiang nodded towards the room behind the front desk, the glassed-in area reserved for international phone calls where a single telephone sat on a coffee-table between two teakwood chairs. Next to the telephone a desktop calendar showed the month on one side, a snowy Christmas landscape on the other.

I took the seat facing the glass door to the lobby; Jiang faced the large poster on the wall behind me: a colour print of five grinning officials, two in army uniforms, posing in front of a massive dam. 'WANTING – CONSTRUCT OUR BEAUTIFUL HOMELAND,' said the legend across the top.

Jiang brought out of his carrier-bag a sheaf of papers, which he spread on the table, explaining the purpose of each: Chinese exit permit, Burmese entry permit, official permission to enter Special Zones A and B, stamped and signed letters, typed and handwritten, in English, Burmese and Chinese. I squirmed in secret shame that he had gone to so much trouble for these documents that were of no use to me.

'So, that's it,' he said, standing up to leave. 'Everything you need.'

He had gone through the drill step by step of how things would work at various stages: where to go, what to say, how to recognise my contacts on the Burmese side. Now he was expecting me to ask questions, so I went through the motions. 'When do I leave, then?' I asked.

'Any day you like.' He turned the calendar on the table towards him, then turned it back with the month facing me. 'Why not the day after tomorrow? You have everything now. Nothing to stop you.'

I picked up the calendar. The day after tomorrow was the twenty-fifth. Christmas Day.

'Maybe not that day,' I said, in spite of myself.

'Why not?'

'I don't know. Just – superstition.'

'Superstition! Wah! Dirty word in China,' he said, sounding once more like a Hong Kong Chinese. 'Better not mention superstition.' Then he was by the door, impatient to be on his way.

'So I'll see you again?' I asked, prompted by a sudden regret. I wanted to thank him properly, only I didn't know how to without lying to his face.

The phone on the table started ringing. We stared at it while it rang and rang. 'I'll go and tell them a call's coming through,' he said, and shut the door behind him. Through the glass wall I watched him talk to the receptionist. While I waited, I straightened the papers and put them back in the carrier-bag. I needed something to do. When I looked up again the lobby was empty. Jiang had left without saying goodbye.

I knew he was leaving town the next day. He'd told me he had a job to do elsewhere in the province, further south in Xishuangbanna.

'Xishuangbanna! How nice!' I had said insincerely. The tourist pamphlets in my room described this southernmost town in Yunnan as 'a miraculous Utopia where colourful ethnic groups and unrivalled festivities offer climaxes upon climaxes'. 'Business?' I asked. 'Or pleasure?'

He gave me one of his rheumy-eyed smiles that made him seem as if he was smiling through tears. 'Both,' he replied.

But it wasn't like Jiang to disappear without taking proper leave. Perhaps he'd had to rush off on some emergency and would be back later to wish me God speed and all the rest.

The next morning I found myself waiting for him in the lobby as usual, expecting him to appear and take me to a farewell feast at the New Prosperity Bridge Hotel.

The rude young man was on Reception and he watched me with a smirk that said, 'So! You've been stood up!'

I felt a rush of anger towards Jiang. Imagine dumping those papers on me and just taking off like that! What was so pressing that he couldn't at least have seen me to the border, as a courtesy if nothing else? Then again, I had to admit it was a relief to be rid of him. I was free now – free *not* to do as I'd been told; free to decide my own fate.

When it was clear that Jiang wasn't coming, I went back to my room and sat on the bed. The carrier-bag containing my papers was still lying on the sofa where I'd left it last night. It felt like a rebuke – all that work for nothing – and I found myself imagining what it would be like if I decided to go through with it, to arrive at the border as expected.

But I already knew what it would be like. I could see it all happen, step by step, scene by scene, the way things like that happened to women like me.

They'd stop me at the guard-house this side of the bridge while they examined my papers. I'd know something was wrong when they lifted the turnstile and motioned me into the guard-house; when they asked me to wait. More and more guards would appear in due course to pore over my ID. One would disappear into the next room to make a phone call or two. From where I'd be sitting, I'd strain to make out what he might be saying between repetitions of my name.

Yes, this is precisely how it would be. They'd find some wrong to charge me with, some crime to pin on me. They'd come for me finally, to snap on the handcuffs and take me away. They'd lead me to the yard beside the temple, to the execution grounds down there. They'd get me in the end, whatever I did. One way or another they'd get me.

But say, for the sake of argument, they waved me past the guard-house this side of the bridge. Say I made it past the checkpoint on the Burmese side as well and managed from there to keep going. Say I dodged every ambush, avoided every trap, thwarted every other turn of Fate. What then? As so many people had told me, my home no longer existed.

In the end I left my room and spent the day trudging the streets of Wanting.

Weird, how Christmas was observed in the most unlikely places – even here, at the Chinese frontier. Strings of coloured lights were wound round the lampposts at the entrance to the market. The karaoke stalls were belting out raucous versions of 'Jingle Bells' and 'Rudolph the Red-nosed Reindeer', and a hot-air balloon Santa did a bump and grind over the tower of the Yunnan Development Bank.

I remembered my first Christmas, with Mor and Far and Pia. The red, blue and white bulbs strung across the trees in their garden. The muggy air, hot and heavy to me after the cool temperatures in the Lu and Daru hills. The fragrance of tangerines.

By late afternoon I was footsore, but still not ready to return to my room. So I went on wandering aimlessly, up and down side-streets I'd had no reason to frequent, until I came to a shop-front with a flashing sign above the door: 'TINGLE TANGLE SALON'. On an impulse I went in.

Parting a curtain of bamboo and beads, I stepped past the threshold into a pinkish light, a glow I knew only too well. I knew that grimy curtain, the colour of flesh, and behind it the narrow dark stairs. I'd never set foot in this place before, yet how often I had breathed its particular air. An altar was lit in one corner of the room – a shelf with candles, flowers and a porcelain *kwan yin*, the Godess of Mercy. Skimpy sprays of paper roses were tacked onto the walls, side by side with hair-dryers on hooks. A mulch of black hair fertilized the floor.

Three girls were lounging on a daybed with a plastic mattress. They rose reluctantly to greet me. The two younger ones were dressed like schoolgirls, in navy blue pinafores and short-sleeved white blouses. The older girl's shift was red and tight-fitting. A large rip had opened up along the back seam.

I saw how they took in what I was wearing, how much I was worth, how useful I might be. A face can lie, a smile can hide many things – but clothes have a way of revealing more than concealing. My plain T-shirt and jeans didn't fool them for a minute. They knew me immediately. I was one of them.

The older girl in the uniform led me by the hand to a mirror on the wall, where I watched while my hair was played with. Then she ushered me to the bed where the other two girls were already waiting. One took off my sandals before lifting my legs, making me lie on my back with my head hanging over the edge. The girl behind me poured water onto my hair, while her helper held a basin underneath. She soaped and massaged and rinsed with care. Then again the massage, again the rinse, with the same soapy water from the same scummy basin.

Somewhere in the room a tune was playing. I remembered it well, even remembered the name – 'Sakura' – from the music box I'd once shared with Pia: the red lacquer box with the gold cherry blossoms that I broke with over-winding.

But why were they playing this, and only this song? They played it over and over again. The pinging of the strings was both teasing and sad, a dirge with a tinge of mockery. Were they performing some ritual especially for me? Were these repeated rinses, this circular tune, reminders of a cycle I'd been caught in for too long, otherwise known as the cycle of existing?

I startled the hair-washers: first by sitting up abruptly, then by insisting on leaving with my hair still dripping.

The pimpled lout was still on duty at the Friendship Hotel. He sneered at my hair. Rain? he enquired, in sign language, playing an invisible keyboard above his head. The fool knew full well that rain was about as likely as snow in that dry season.

Yes, I replied, with exaggerated gestures of my own. *Pouring!*

He threw my room key onto the counter, in some sort of challenge. I picked it up wearily, without looking at him.

But he wanted the last word. I heard him call, as I headed for the stairs, 'Are you cowed?'

Yes, I thought. Yes, I suppose you could say I am.

Then I went upstairs to hang myself.

twenty-nine

Minzu turns up this afternoon with a rubber mat under one arm, a couple of small cushions in the other. She is dressed in a karate suit of thick beige cotton. 'How you celebrate New Year, Ma Ma?' she asks, chatty as usual, as she sets about unrolling the navy-blue mat with its crinkly surface, and shaking it out onto the floor. She eyes her mat thoughtfully, and for a moment I half expect her to dive onto it with a somersault or a hand-stand. But no, she wants me to sit on it! When I hesitate, she pulls me down – quite forcefully, too – into a sitting position.

Well, at least it's not the carpet: that filthy thing is long overdue for a steam cleaning. It's always slightly soggy, and patterned with stains. I never cross the floor in bare feet if I can help it. Luckily, disposable slippers come with the room. They're ridiculous things, flip-flops that look as if they've been fashioned from twin sanitary pads (one for the sole, one for the cross-strap) and very likely are just that.

I'm struggling to stand up now that I realise what's happening. The girl wants to give me a massage!

No! No massage! I shake my head resolutely. *Absolutely not.*

No! No massage! she reassures me, as if she would never dream of such a thing. She only wants – *no, please*, please *sit down* – she only wants to show me something about my feet.

'The feet,' she says – and before I know it she has mine

pressed together in a grip so unyielding I might dislocate something if I tried to extricate them. I'm sitting with my back against the wall, my legs outstretched and rigid. She lets go of a foot to reach up and tap my forehead. 'The feet are important to the head.' On her knees, facing me, she pulls down on my feet, as though rolling off a pair of tight socks.

'Don't—' I start to protest; but she clicks her tongue to silence me. 'Feet and head . . .' she murmurs '. . . very important, all connected . . .' Then her hands work my feet with patient determination, as though kneading a dough that takes for ever to rise. I'm torn between resisting and submitting.

My thoughts turn to Will, to the time he succeeded in *making* me submit.

I was giving him a back rub, and he was groaning as always, pretending to marvel at my strength. 'How did a runt like you get to be so strong?' he stuttered, between the chopping. 'I wouldn't want to bump into you in a dark alley.'

I told him about Mor's love of massage: how she taught me to press down with the heels of my hands, then with the soles of my feet, up and down her back, as she lay on the floor, face down and sighing contentment.

'But you ladies massaged each other, didn't you?' Will asked, speaking of the brothel. 'To relax, off duty?' It always annoyed me when he referred to us as 'ladies'.

'Some of the *ladies* did,' I said, 'when they had a minute.' I remembered our midday breaks, and how the girls who took turns doing each other's hair and nails would then break into disco dances; how the rest just napped, three or four on a bed.

'And you?'

I said, 'I hate massages.'

'Nonsense!' He spoke into the pillow, so that I had to bend over to hear him. 'You've never had a good one, that's all.'

Flexing his shoulders to shake me off, he sat up abruptly. 'Lie down. I'm going to give you one.' Then his hands were pinning me to the bed, as he held me face-down and knelt to straddle me.

'Will, don't! I can't breathe.'

'Don't breathe, then. You hardly breathe, anyway. But close your eyes for a minute and relax, for God's sake, will you? You're bug-eyed.'

From the corner of my eye I could see his bare chest bearing down on me, I could feel his hairy legs pressing on mine. The roaming of his bare hand on my bare back was making my skin crawl, my stomach clench.

With a firm tug he pulled my shirt off over my head – and began rubbing his palms all over me. Up and out they spread across my back, in a searing butterfly stroke that pushed down on my ribs and shoulder-blades. I was struggling to breathe when he let up; and suddenly, gently, with the tips of his fingers, he began pinching my neck, squeezing my shoulders and running his nails up and down the sides of my spine. I'll never know how it happened: one minute I was fighting for breath, the next I was heaving myself out of sleep.

'Now, that wasn't so bad, was it?' he said.

It was. Being lulled into sleep was bad, very bad.

'I'm sorry, oh, I'm sorry!' says Minzu.

She has pressed on my big toe in such a way that I kicked out in pain.

'I think,' she says, frowning, 'you have bad things in your head. Feet and head are always connected. Do you see?'

I've had all I can take. 'No more massage,' I say, standing up.

But she has caught me off-guard, because when she invites me – for the sixth or seventh time, I reckon – to 'eat rice' with her family the next evening, I say yes without thinking.

thirty

I'm sitting in the lobby, waiting for Minzu's shift to end, when who should come in but the Danish engineer and the Chinese student – my fellow passengers on the bus from Kunming. If they recognise me, they don't show it. They're waiting to make a call in the telephone room. The two are now buddies, from the look of things. They chat about this and that, and once again I find myself eavesdropping.

The engineer is trying to explain why ice beers are dangerous. There is an island, he says, not far from Copenhagen, where he went on a recent vacation. Eighty-nine degrees latitude was the location.

'Eighty-nine degrees!' The student is impressed.

Incredibly, out comes a map from the engineer's bag, the better to pinpoint the location. 'There you must rent a gun,' he says, collapsing the map deftly into its proper folds before putting it away. 'You pay thirty dollars and rent a gun because ice beers can be very dangerous.'

'Ice beers?'

'Maybe you call them polar beers? If you are walking in the snow, you should have a gun because they are aggressive. But the snow is so beautiful for walking. There are many different anamales, many seagawls, for example. The Germans tried to conquer this island during the Second World War, but the Russians, you see, *bomped* the coal mines, so there was no point, really. Now there is a Russian research station, with greenhouses, stables, cows and pigs in the buildings. And also the most northern church in the world. In the church-yard are buried victims of Spanish fever. A very freezing and very beautiful island.'

The student's mouth falls open. 'You went there,' he asks, 'for a *vacation?*'

Out of nowhere I hear a voice in my head. 'You went,' it asks, 'all the way to Wanting? To die?'

'My house is quite far,' Minzu apologises, as we hitch a ride on a minibus packed with traders and farmers returning to their villages for the night. We jump off at a crossroads and follow a footpath through banana orchards and papaya stands, then into a patch of dank, dark wood. Minzu's bare calves – she's in capris, of course – flash ahead of me, white in the leafy gloom. She steps lightly and surely through the brush, sidestepping the thorns, dodging the vines, without a scratch on her calves to show for it.

A girl like Minzu – pretty, healthy, ripe for the picking – incredible that a girl like her has not yet been broken in. Or broken. Or cracked. Or cracked open. It's only a matter of time, of course.

One look at the half-dozen soldiers out by the ditch, and I can see the future that awaits Minzu. There they are, out in the light, where the forest ends: Chinese soldiers – or PRC, as Will calls them – wearing their red armbands. They have their machine-guns, their side arms, their wireless equipment, everything they need, everything on their side, to overwhelm and violate a woman (two women, come to that) crossing their line of sight.

Minzu steps forward. The men turn towards us, shielding their eyes from the sun.

Now here come the catcalls, the shuffling of feet and clanking of equipment, the taunts and heckles as we walk towards them in the confident way of women who are secretly scared to death. That is to say, *I* am scared to death. Minzu isn't. She answers their taunts in a clear, almost cheeky voice. (They sound like taunts to me, but what do I know? I can't even tell what language they're speaking.)

The soldiers ask questions; Minzu answers lightly. I can make out a couple of words. 'Wanting. Kunming.' I guess they're asking who her older friend is, that frump at her side, because she answers '*Mien*' – the Chinese word for Burma – as she takes my hand and squeezes it. Perhaps she senses my fear. But my fear is not for myself, it's for the young girl by my side. It dawns on me, as we walk hand in hand past the men, that for the first time since my days with Pia, I am self-forgetful in my fear.

Now that we're apparently out of danger, with the men's banter dying down behind us, I want to let go of Minzu's hand. Something about its tender, childlike grip feels burden-some, almost repellent. I hate the way she trusts me when she shouldn't. She should be wary of strangers – any and all strangers. She's old enough to know better. She's as old as I was when I was *misled*, as Will puts it. My heart sinks; then tightens and hardens at the thought of trying to warn or guide her. I can't be responsible for her or for anyone else. I shake off her hand. She glances down, as if I might have dropped something without knowing it, but says nothing.

We're almost at her house when Minzu lets fall a surprising fact. The parents I'm about to meet are not her parents but an aunt and uncle who have raised her as their own.

'And where are *your* parents?' I ask.

'Dead,' she says matter-of-factly. Her father – Jiang's friend,

I knew her father and Jiang were friends, didn't I? I didn't?
– her father was killed in battle, when she was still a baby.
Her mother died of malaria when she was three. I *think*
malaria is what Minzu means: she doesn't know the word for
the sickness, she says, but indicates a mosquito bite.

'She cursed my life,' says Minzu, with a puzzling smile,
patting her heart in a gesture of thanks. Once again I've been
thrown off by her accent. What she means is '*saved* my life',
but she's used the tone for 'curse' or 'swear at'.

'Ah, *saved* your life,' I correct her.

'Yes, cursed my life,' she repeats. The girl has a tin ear. I
shouldn't bother.

'So how did your mother save your life?' I ask.

'She gave me away,' she says proudly. 'Poor person, very
poor,' she adds. 'No money to eat. Yes, she gave me away so
I can live.' Her teeth shine in the dusk. 'Then she died.'

We follow a bamboo walkway over a field of green spinach
towards the lone hut at the end.

It's dark inside, with not a window open. Minzu gropes
along the wall, near the door, till she finds a box of
matches. She bends over a stool with a kerosene lamp on it,
removes its glass casing, lights a match and holds it to the
wick.

Parts of the room flare into view – a wooden bench, a
pile of folded bedding, a table with a spirit altar above it –
as she replaces the glass cover, picks up the lantern and leads
the way to the back, where we step down from the bamboo
floor onto the earthen floor of the kitchen.

She sets the lantern on a surface next to a single-burner
gas stove, and right away I see that this is to be an *occasion*.
A round table has been set with enamel plates for four,
complete with soup spoons and chopsticks.

At the centre of the table are the pots and pans. Minzu lifts the covers one by one and fans the fumes into her face. She pours me a cup of hot water from the Thermos on the table, asks me to sit, then rolls up her shirt-sleeves and goes to work at the sink. While she washes the coriander and mustard greens, she explains that the aunt she calls her mother has prepared most of the dishes ahead, so that only the finishing touches remain, and that she and her husband are bringing them home shortly.

Just then the front door creaks open. 'They're here,' she says. 'We can eat.'

The aunt and uncle are small and neat. The aunt looks like Minzu, a plumper version, with a thinner, graver face. The uncle is not much taller than his wife, but broad in the shoulders, with tattooed arms and legs.

'Mother and Father,' Minzu says simply, as introduction. To them she mutters something that includes Jiang's name. They nod and smile sadly. But the aunt is preoccupied. She has a packet of something in her hands, wrapped in thick palm leaves. She sets it on the table and unties the string around it. Threaded on two long bamboo skewers are a dozen baby rice birds – steamed, from the look of it: moist and pale.

Rice birds! I haven't tasted a rice bird in ages!

Minzu dishes out steamed rice onto each of our plates, followed by servings of chicken gizzard, fried mustard greens and stewed pork rind. Then she slides the rice birds off the skewers with her chopsticks, and onto an open palm leaf. There they lie side by side, pale skin gleaming, bald skulls faintly bruised and perfect.

Minzu's father is the first to tuck in. I watch him bite off the beak and suck it clean before setting the bird on the table, beside his plate. Minzu and her mother are starting with what's on their plates, leaving the birds, the treat, for last.

I help myself to a bird and snap off its head with my teeth. The explosion of flavour, grainy and rich, tastes rather like the head of a prawn, only sweeter and more delicate. Ah, but the throat. There is still the throat to come, with its tiny parcel of rice stored in the gullet – the finest bit of a rice bird that has fed only on the finest grain.

We eat in silence, not attempting to speak. It's quiet outside, save for the hum of a distant generator and the *joop, joop, jeeeoop* of a nightjar. Inside: the sounds of four people eating – chewing and slurping, scraping tin spoons against enamel plates, clearing throats, blowing noses. The faces across from me dance in the lantern's glow, darkening and flaring, lengthening and shortening. A family, I think. Mother, father, daughter. Or aunt, uncle, niece. What matter? A family. And I am part of it for the moment.

'She speaks a little Burmese,' Minzu says, with her mouth full, inclining her head towards her aunt.

'No, not speak,' the aunt replies in Burmese.

'We are the Dai people – do you know the Dai?' says Minzu.

'Yes, I know the Bai,' I say.

'Not the Bai, the *Dai*,' says the aunt. '*Dai. Dai.*'

'Dai in China are related to Shan people in Burma,' Minzu explains.

The uncle, who has hardly spoken all evening, suddenly pipes up, saying something about how that makes us all one family. He points to each of us around the table, clasps his hands and taps his heart – as Minzu did that first evening I arrived, to let me know she was a friend of Jiang's. Then he flashes a gap-toothed smile at me.

I could stay with them, I think. They would let me. For a while, at least. Reading my thoughts, Minzu says, 'Sleep here tonight? We have room. We have a bed for you.'

'Are you sure?' I ask, thankful for the offer. I can't face the thought of dragging myself home – even though Minzu has indicated that a neighbour with a pick-up truck will give us a lift back to the hotel. Overcome with drowsiness, I find myself swaying slightly when I stand. But much as I long to lie down, bundle up and go to sleep, I know what to expect the minute I turn in. On the brink of sleep – no, past that brink even – I'll be yanked back rudely, as if by the hair, and put in my rightful place. I'll toss and turn then, sidling my way back to that brink once more till the cycle begins again. I'm used to it now: the craving for sleep and the resistance to it. But tonight I'll need all the help I can get. For the first time in years I'll be sleeping in close quarters with other bodies, and that will not make things easier. So when Minzu offers me a special tea, 'very good for sleep', I can't see the harm in trying it – even though I suspect it's the same old brew she keeps giving me.

Minzu picks up the lantern and we move to the front room: the one with the spirit shrine and the rolled-up mattresses. She spreads out her parents' bedding along one wall, hers at the corner, and positions mine against the adjoining wall. She insists I finish my tea while she straightens the mattresses and smooths the blankets with the happy concentration of a child playing house.

I turn to watch the shadows cast by the kerosene lamp, when the tea starts to take effect. I can feel shoals of tiny ambient fish gliding under my skin. Then they multiply and spread their pulsing warmth deeper and deeper till they're coursing through my blood, my bones, my scalp.

Minzu has receded to the wrong end of a telescope. I watch her suddenly tiny figure light a minuscule match and touch it to the end of a toy mosquito coil. I wait, immobilised, for that distant diminutive creature to signal to me. Then, like a sleepwalker, I move in a trance towards my bed.

thirty-one

Only twice – and only briefly – do I wake in the night: once to the whistle of snores coming from the parents' corner; and once, in the faintest first light of dawn, to a dream about a bird I'm chasing, a cross between a sandpiper and a crow. I watch it disappear into the recesses of a cupboard I can't reach. Later, when I return to the same spot, I wonder where the strange bird has gone and start beating about in the dark cupboard. As soon as it emerges, I try to whack it on the head, but miss. Why is it, I ask myself, in the dream, that my first instinct upon seeing a strange living thing is to kill it?

I wake up, frustrated at not having the answer to my question. Then I drift back to sleep . . . For a while it feels I am picking up where I left off, entering the next instalment of my interrupted dream. A question has been left hanging, and it seems I am approaching an answer.

It's Nefertiti who appears, however. Nefertiti, Will's tarot-card-reading friend, and she is berating me.

Oh, come on, she's saying. *Get* with *it, Na Ga. You know very well why you're so afraid to fall asleep.*

I argue with her. *I don't,* I insist. *I really don't.* The woman is hateful. I loathe her blunt-cut Egyptian hair. She wants to torture me.

Don't give me that, she says.

But I'll be damned if I break down and confess the truth.

The truth is that I *do* know the reason why I'm afraid to fall asleep.

I was asleep that morning when my father picked me up and carried me outside, into the stinging air of dawn. I was six years old, almost seven. I woke as I changed hands, from my father's arms, to the arms of another, who wrapped a blanket around me and lifted me onto the back of a pony. Two men, one on either side, were strapping me in. One was the shaman; the other was the headman from the Daru village.

I recognised the headman because we, my mother and I, had only recently returned from the New Year festival in his village. I had watched this headman bless the pig sacrifice and beat the gong at the festival. I remembered his long face, with the watery brown eyes and the long sparse hairs on his chin.

They're taking me to another festival, I thought, still half asleep. But why had no one said anything about it before? Why was my father turning away now, turning his back on me? And my mother – where was she?

There she was – *there*. Pounding rice in the early-morning fog. Pounding away and not hearing me, not seeing what they were doing to me.

The harshness of the headman's grip alarmed me – a grip prepared for struggle. He was pulling the straps tightly round me. I lunged in the direction of my mother, screaming, but she was not only deaf, she was blind. She was attacking the paddy husks as if smashing to death something live in the seeds. The shaman jerked me back onto the pony. The headman counted out paper bills and handed them to the shaman.

In a flash I understood what was happening. All that talk

among the grown-ups late at night – about bad crops, bad debts, what to grow, what to sell – suddenly came together and made sense. Money was changing hands. Something was being bought and sold. Something was being taken away. I was that something.

The headman pushed a soft lump into my mouth, to stop me crying. Through my tears came a taste, dark and sweet, which distracted me briefly as the headman led the pony downhill. I took the nugget out of my mouth and stared at it as I continued to cry, though less and less noisily. Then I put the sugar lump back in my mouth, where all too soon it melted.

The headman mounted, keeping me in front as he held the reins, his arms like another set of reins around me. We tottered down slopes and clambered up trails, and when we came to an even stretch where the headman's arms were not so rigid, I was seized by a whole new fear.

I had to stay awake. I had to pay attention and note things along the way. *Here is a tree with a lump on its trunk, shaped like a man with a goitre. Here is a path of scented pine needles, with white flowers thick in the bushes. Here are striped orchids like spiders on trees.* Memory was my only hope of returning.

But as we plodded up and down the hillsides, I began to see doubles, then triples, then multiples of every marker: more and more trees with tumours, countless pine-needle beds, poppy fields without number, terraces without end – all impossible to tally or keep straight.

My path was being erased before my eyes. Never, never would I find my way back. But I had to keep trying. I had to keep my eyes open.

I couldn't do it. I couldn't fight the weight pulling down my eyelids. I couldn't prevent my head from rolling onto the headman's arm, from *resting* on it, even, while I slept and slept – like the drugged, like the dead.

Minzu wakes me with a gentle tap on my shoulder. 'It's late, Ma Ma. I must go to work.'

My eyes blink open to brilliant daylight. The parents have disappeared; their beds have been put away. I have been sleeping with the sun beating down on my face.

'You slept well,' says Minzu, with a sly smile.

I'm embarrassed at having overslept, and start to make excuses. 'I was dreaming a lot,' I say. But she doesn't know the word for 'dream', so I try to say it another way. 'I remembered something while sleeping,' I explain.

'Something good?' she asks.

'Something true,' I reply.

thirty-two

It's midday, almost, by the time we get back – and now I feel strangely listless and anxious. This is Minzu's last shift before she takes a few days off for the year-end break, and it's time I made some kind of move myself. I can't go on drifting in this way, putting off any decision about what to do next.

Up in my room, I lay out on the bed the papers from Jiang's carrier-bag. There are the Chinese border passes and the Burmese entry permits. There are letters of introduction and letters of intent. But there is also a small padded envelope I hadn't noticed before, something Jiang left out when he went through the papers with me, and it has my name on it. My heart leaps. Will has come through after all.

He has sent me a letter via Jiang to tell me everything's all right, that he's coming for me!

I have dreamed it might be like this: Will turning up at the last minute, when I least expect it. Appearing at the border checkpoint, as I reach the guard-house gate. Or waiting on the *other* side, even – on the Burmese side. Waving me over. Grinning at my disbelief and joy.

I open the brown envelope, with the slight bulge at the bottom, and tip out an egg-shaped object the size of an unpeeled almond, wound tight like a top with coarse, glued-on string.

A name seed!

I knew it. Will isn't sending me away, after all. It's been a test, a trick, in order to shake things up between us – but only to bring us back together again.

Will, Will! I'm thinking. *Did you really have to put me through all this, just to test me?* The dried-up little thing with its frayed string binding is trembling in the palm of my hand. I close my fingers over it, gently, gently, afraid to crush it – not that I could crush such a hardy relic if I tried – and press it to my heart. Something like a kite is billowing in there, pulling against the wind, straining at its lines, ready to break loose and wheel off into the heavens.

Hands shaking, I reach for the letter. The paper is so thin I almost tear it in my haste.

My heart plummets. The letter is in Burmese.

Na Ga, dear Sister, the first line reads. I turn the page over – both sides have been written on – and glance at the signature. *With* metta. *From Jiang.*

Oh, what a fool I am. What a pitiful idiot. Over the moon one minute, flat on my face the next.

So it's Jiang, damn him, who has written to me. But for what reason? And what is he doing, sending me a name seed? I keep going over the first few lines again and again, before I can put my thoughts in order and read through to the end.

Na Ga, dear Sister:

Please excuse my handwriting. I am in a hurry. I have a favour to ask. I pray you won't refuse me.

The favour is this: when you go home, to Special Zone B, will you take this small thing with you? It's not heavy, not worth anything. You know what it is. Every Lu can recognise a name seed.

But first I should explain.

I told you I am from the Shan state. That is not a lie. I lived there for most of my life. But I must tell you something else now.

Do you remember the saying, 'We know a chicken by its bones, a man by his kin'? Each of us carries marks of our kin wherever we end up in life. I see those marks in you. Maybe you saw those same marks in me? Yes, we have the same marks, you and I. Because I, too, am a Lu. A Wild Lu.

Maybe in your heart you recognised me as your brother. You never told me the name of your village, but it is possible we were once neighbours, even though I left home when I was still a kid and you, of course, are much younger than me.

I left to join the insurgency. There was no food to eat in our villages then. I saw families selling their own children when they had nothing left to sell. You, who somehow became wise and educated, perhaps you were the daughter of a headman and never knew such hunger. I did.

The unit I joined was in the southern Shan state, and at that time we were under the Shan state militia. (We came under the Communist Party only some years later, and that was how I ended up here in Yunnan.) Early on, in the camps, I had to sit and listen to jokes and taunts about the Wild Lu – about our stupidity and savagery. Then I took up arms in a new region, and this gave me the chance to disown my kinsmen, to pretend I was not one of them. Before long I forgot who I was and became as thick-headed and unknowing as we are said to be.

When you showed up in Wanting, when Yan Ding put me in charge of your safe passage, I had no idea where you came from, I knew only that you were from Burma and going home to your birthplace after many years away. When I found out that you were a Lu, I couldn't believe it. It didn't make sense. How could a girl from my province, a member of my ignorant race, go so far in the world, achieve such dignity and knowledge, and still want to return to her homeland? What could she gain from revisiting a home that no longer exists? So many questions. But I could not ask them without having to answer even more in return.

I can admit the truth now, when I don't have to face you. The truth is that I have blood on my hands. Yes. I have killed our own people. I have wiped out an entire Wild Lu stronghold, bombing and burning with a vengeance. Why? Because I was told to by my superiors, because it was my duty as a soldier and because my own people had become strangers to me.

I wanted to tell you all this in person, but I was too cowardly. I wanted to ask your forgiveness, but I was too ashamed.

Now it's too late for forgiveness. What is forgiveness anyway, unless he who is being forgiven can still receive the pardon? Instead I ask this favour. Will you carry my name seed back to my native soil? Will you return it to the earth, any corner of the earth out of which it came? Will you bury it there? If you can do that for me, it will be my homecoming. I am not brave like you, I cannot face our homeland directly, but my longing to return still remains.

It is expecting a lot for someone of your noble character to dirty her hands on behalf of someone like me. But you are a good Buddhist. I know you will have compassion towards me, as towards all beings. When you go to build your shrine, I believe you will take me with you.

May your journey be fruitful and safe. May you live long and find happiness.

With loving kindness,

Jiang

One more thing: My real name is Ai Sha . . . so you know what this seed once whispered.

I am trying to see his face before me: trying to remember his eyes, his nose, his teeth. I can't conjure up a clear image; I can't remember a single distinguishing trait. Yes, grey hair, of course, and dark skin. But was his jaw wide and square, like those of the Lu men I remember? Were his eyes down-turned commas like theirs? Did his gums show above his teeth when he smiled, as theirs did? How can I have failed to see the Wild Lu in him? How can I have been so blind?

There is a Burmese word for a painful comeuppance that Daw Daw Seng used to threaten me with when she thought I was being stubbornly unrepentant. The word is *naungda*, and I understood it to mean an agony of regret followed by an agony of atonement. One day, she predicted, I would get my *naungda* – and, oh, the anguish it would bring!

She was right, I have to admit, as I cry myself to sleep – with my *longyi*-rope serving as both comforter and snot rag. My *naungda* has finally got me.

That's Minzu at the door. I can tell from the feeble but urgent thumping. Maybe if I keep quiet, she'll go away. But no; she lets herself in.

'Ma Ma! What's the matter, Ma Ma?' I hear the alarm in her voice, but I can't get up, I can't look up. I don't want to uncover my bloated face. I've been sitting here, on the floor, on this filthy damp carpet, ever since I stumbled out of bed.

Minzu is on her knees beside me, I can hear the rustle of paper as she glances at the letter, which she cannot read, trying to find an explanation for my sorry state. Her cold little hands are grasping my wrists, not trying to pry them away from my face, just holding them steady. 'Tell me! Tell me what it is! Bad news? Did someone die?'

'Mr Jiang!' I say. My voice comes out raspy and low. I sound like a man with a frog in his throat.

'Oh, Mr Jiang,' she says, not understanding why I am grieving so belatedly for him.

'Mr Jiang . . .' I clear my throat.

'Yes. Poor Mr Jiang.' She doesn't know what else to say.

'Mr Jiang . . . is a Lu!' I howl.

Minzu says, 'A Lu . . . yes, indeed.'

'No! A *Lu*!' I'm shouting to be understood, to emphasise the right tone, not the tone for the same word that means 'human being' in Burmese. 'I mean a Wild *Lu*!'

'A Lu. A Wild Lu.' She is still using the tone for 'human being', but I know it's only her accent now, I know she follows my meaning.

'But I, too . . .' I am beating my chest to make sure she understands – beating it too, to stop myself tearing out my hair. 'I, too, am a Lu! I am a Lu! I am a Wild Lu . . . and I didn't know another Lu in front of my face!'

'Aw!' she says. 'So you are a Lu? And you didn't know your own brother?' Gently she parts my wrists, exposing my face. 'And now you have great regret,' she states, somewhat unnecessarily. 'But don't cry, Ma Ma, please don't cry like that any more,' she says, shaking my knees and starting to cry herself.

After a long while, when I've run out of tears and my eyes are so inflamed I have to squint to see, I watch her stand up and blow her nose vigorously. She arches her back, rolls her shoulders, cracks her neck from side to side and pulls me to my feet.

'Come, I've finished work. Let's go and wash our faces in the river,' she says. 'Let's take our *longyi* so we can bathe.' She picks up a fresh one I'd left at the foot of the bed, folds it into a small square, and hands it to me.

The sun is out, the river is like a mirror in a million shattered pieces. Under the willow where we change into our bathing *longyi*, the light trickles through, warm and inviting. But the first step into the stream tells me we're mistaken. I feel the cold like a clamp around my ankles and shins. Then the clamp loosens and falls away as we wade in, wearing our *longyi* wrapped around our chests and hitched to our knees. When we're waist deep in the current, Minzu half sits on a rock around which the water is gently churning.

'Too cold to swim,' she says, shivering and quickly splashing her face. Then, in a sudden turnaround, she stretches her arms forward and plunges in. 'Aiya!' she yelps. 'Cold, cold, cold, cold, *coooold* . . .'

I strike out on my own, away from the rocks.

Oh, it is good, that swift, cold current – numbing at first, but bracing, then soothing, soothing . . . as it reaches by degrees a comfort close to perfection. I flip over onto my back and float downstream, watching the scudding clouds, the shimmering treetops, the tips of my buoyant toes. Then I head back towards the smooth cluster of rocks in the shallows, where I find a foothold in the turbulence.

I am catching my breath when it takes me by surprise: the collision of currents that wraps me in a swirling embrace. The eddies and surges attend to my body like the old wound it is; they soothe the throbbing boil, the seething heart of my being. It's been there for so long I can't imagine its absence – this wound that is now a part of me. But the water is relentless in its ministrations, and I submit to its balm and tonic.

The wound, after all, is mostly in the mind. And the mind . . .

. . . the mind can be changed, become something different, something bigger and wider – like this stream, for instance, this cold little creek. Nam Long, they call it here, I believe. With its bend into Burma a few miles south, the Nam Long becomes a full-fledged river – the Shweli in Burmese, the Ruili in Chinese – until it finds its way across the border and over the hills, down to the great Mother Irrawaddy.

Yes, just like a river the mind can be changed. Its boundaries are only approximate.

Minzu is kneeling in the water, submerged to the neck. All I can see is her pale, grinning face with its cap of wet black hair. 'I'll show you a lovely spot,' she says, 'so quiet you can hear . . . those things . . .' She waves her fingers, trying to find the right word. 'You can hear them sing.'

'Birds?' I offer.

'No, not birds.' She joins both hands at the thumbs and flaps them. 'What are those things called?'

'Butterflies?'

'Butterflies! Yes! You can hear butterflies sing! You don't believe me,' she says, pretending to take offence with a pout. 'Butterflies can sing.'

'I think you mean birds.'

'Here, follow me, I'll show you,' she says, and swims ahead. When we're side by side, we point at each other and laugh. Our *longyi* have ballooned up around us like buoys.

The *longyi*, as I've said, is a wonderful garment. You can wear it like a skirt or wrapped around your chest, like a towel, after bathing. You can bathe in it, swim in it, float in it, even. A *longyi* can save your life.

thirty-three

Ready at last. The wait is over. Today is the day I leave.

In the dark, by long habit, I check the back of my hand to see if the veins are showing. Yes, there they are, I can see them distinctly – and there goes the morning bell, ever on cue.

It isn't, of course, the old monastery bell – I'm in Wanting, after all, not Rangoon. No, it's the bell on the cart of some noodle-vendor, dragging his way down the pavement. I hear it as my summons, nevertheless. The bell has sounded, calling me to action.

Daylight is staining the window-panes – the ones too high to reach. But I can climb up now, on the stool Minzu has left, for one good look before I leave.

The sky is lightening, the mist is lifting, but the moon is still there, round as the sun and nearly as bright. Far off in the distance is the border itself, a string of firefly lights. Weaker lights, smaller fireflies, swarm on the other side, brightening and dimming, then disappearing into the blackness beyond, the blackness of Burma where my old home lies.

From here to there, from this window to that wilderness, is not a great distance: ten miles as the crow flies, more or less. Not a great distance – but the diversions taken to come this far! From my birthplace in the Lu hills to the village in the Daru hills then down to Rangoon, to the capital city.

Up once more to the northern hills, this time to the Shan state plateau. Back after that to the Thai border and beyond, all the way into northern Thailand. Down from there, once again, way down to Bangkok. Then north in a new direction – to *China* this time . . . and down the length of the Burma Road, from Kunming to Wanting.

All those zigzags and corkscrews, all those hairpin bends of Fate, only to end up within waving distance from where I first began.

The moon is quietly slipping away, riding the dark foam of the treetops. And the trees are coming alive. Just a moment ago they were lumpen black sentries; now they are awake and green. On the slope of a hill where a white pagoda perches, the pennants are up and flying. How they take the breath away, those bright little pennants – just as the flags of a nation, with their stripes and stars snapping, their suns and moons sailing, will make grown men salute and weep. The pennants are announcing a temple fair, and there's nothing like a fair to set the pulse speeding. The crowds. The music. The burning garlic and meat.

Now another temple emerges in stages: a Chinese temple across the way, that I haven't noticed before. (They're sprouting like mung beans all over the place: pagodas, monasteries, temples . . . all cheerfully escaping destruction.) This one looks brand new in the early light. First the brick wall rises, high as a palace; then the red and gold rooftops with their curling eaves; and higher than that, the three satellite dishes, pointed like trumpets at the sky.

When I press myself against the window grille, I can see the shrubbery, and the tops of the fruit trees, marking the temple grounds. I can also see a bald head. A novice from the monastery, most likely.

No, it isn't a boy: it's an old woman, a nun. Impossible to tell her age, but she must be ancient: every step, every turn, is considered with utmost caution.

What can she be doing there so early in the morning, her arms in a feeble reach towards the bushes? She's blind, perhaps – or just confused and unable to find her way. No, she's loitering, taking her time. She's inspecting. Touching the morning dew. Bending to sniff. Stroking the leaves. Pinching off a stem, a twig. Gazing at a patch of bare earth. Plotting a new garden, maybe.

I think of calling to her, just to see what she looks like. She turns at that very instant and straightens in my direction, as though she can hear me think.

My mother! Dear God, it's my mother, here in person – only a stone's throw away. But she can't have aged so, my mother in the flesh, this old woman lost in the garden.

Suppose I shout, '*Mother!*' before she turns and totters away.

Suppose she calls back, squinting up at my window, 'Who's that up there?'

Suppose I call out then, 'Mother, it's your daughter! The one you sold into slavery! The one who's been fucked by a thousand men!'

Naturally I call out no such thing. The old bird is probably deaf, anyway.

'Eh?' she might reply, toothless mouth agape, casting a blind eye at my window. 'What's that you say?'

No, it isn't my mother; of course it isn't.

My mother was a young girl when I knew her last – much younger, it strikes me now, than I am at present. She must have been a child while still carrying me. I've outstripped that child by a good wide margin; I've long since left that girl behind.

But who was she, that child, my mother? What was her name? Who was my father? What has *his* name? Why haven't I tried to find the answers? What is the matter with me?

I am a Wild Lu, maybe that's what's the matter. We're an ignorant lot, we simpletons, the Lu. Ignorant of the world, ignorant of our own history, ignorant of our very names. Even among our neighbours – the Akha, the Miao, the Wa, the Lisu, the Daru – we are known for our stubborn ignorance. We see things only as they are, not as they might possibly be. Nor do we understand the lies known as irony.

'I'm going home to build a shrine,' I said to Jiang, lying through my teeth for the sake of wit. And he took me at my word, seeing me as a builder of merit. What was it he said I possessed? Dignity and knowledge . . . a noble character. What a laugh, what a swindle – and he's gone to his grave deceived.

But how would I know what the Lu are like, these days? How would Jiang know, come to that? Maybe our people have changed beyond all recognition, as Yan Ding put it. They're people of the clock and the calculator now, no longer just wielders of the axe and crossbow. They've leaped across centuries, across worlds, across cultures, while Jiang and I weren't looking – the way Shaman Asita could leap from one world to the next.

Poor old Asita! I see him suddenly, licking his wounds after a failed sacrifice, something to do with a cow and a gun. He's injured his hand, burned by gunpowder from a musket gone wrong. I see myself joining in the laughter as Shaman Asita, that tall, strutting figure, that pleader to the spirits, dances round and round in pain. I see him struggle with a mortar and pestle, pounding with his good hand some herbs for a poultice while delicately wringing the other.

I remember too how he staggered past our hut one night,

cursing and shaking his good fist. 'Asita is tired!' he yelled. '*Tired*, do you hear me? "Oh, Asita, help us, the rain is not falling, the rice is not growing, our children are sick and dying! Oh, Asita, we'll pay you for your magic, here's a bunch of bananas, here's a scrawny chicken!" And Asita must jump for the bananas, kill himself for the chicken. Asita is *sick* of all your problems!'

And the shaman in the Daru village, come to think of it, had just as much, if not more, to answer for: all those pigs to slaughter and chickens to bleed, all the tying and untying of threads and strings – around necks, around wrists – to bring back the dead and send off the dying.

Maybe the shamans we once counted on have all packed up; maybe we're our own shamans now.

There must be something special in this window-pane: some alloy ground into the glass itself. If I stare long enough through the bars, through the pane, I can conjure up all sorts of things. I can wipe out that sky with its reddish-gold tints and call up a mountain range.

Yes, I see mountains now, rising up through the mist. I see limestone columns, and bridges fragile as fish bones strung across the chasms. I see the path I must take, up and down through the valleys, past burning fields and lush terraces, past farmers in their ditches, past women with their heavy loads on the way to their markets, and children harvesting the poppy fields that stain the hills crimson.

And I see the place finally where I must push through a thorn wall.

Now I hear the dogs barking, a baby crying, the friendly shouts greeting me from the other side . . .

But suppose they don't know me – suppose they don't *care*.

Suppose my mother, that stranger, looks at me blankly, asking, 'Who are you? What do you want from me?'

'Mother? It's your daughter,' I shall have to say. 'The one whose life you saved by giving her away. Now, please, will you tell me my name?'

There they are now, the men at my door. They're knocking softly, calling my name.

'Coming!' I shout. I pick up my suitcase and open the door. The two men are in darkness, but they're bowing in greeting. One takes the suitcase from me. These are Jiang's successors, my new minders and bodyguards, sent by the worthy Yan Ding. I called to tell him when I planned to leave, and he promised to send two of his best to accompany me.

Down at the front desk, I hand in my key. Minzu is not on duty: she's coming later, on her own, to see me off. 'I'm leaving now,' I say, to the surly fellow at the desk. With Valuable Body, I think, reading the mysterious sign for the last time.

'Are you cowed?' he sneers, inspecting the key closely as though for any signs of damage.

'Pez,' I reply, with a smile.

Now we're off, my minders and I – stopping, of course, for breakfast at the market. My mouth is watering, my stomach is growling, as I wait for my order of hot tea, warm bread and stewed peas.

I jump up without warning, startling my minders, as I spot a figure crossing the square. I have to catch her, that beggar woman, the one with A-I-D. She's seen me out of the corner of her eye and, wary of my approach, tries to give me the slip. But I corner her in front of the money-changers, and she's forced to look me in the eye. Her face is a fright: her sores are weeping, her eyes are puffy slits. She recoils as I hand her Mr Wei's pen, the expensive pen I forgot to give the bus driver as payment for getting me to the frontier alive.

She's suspicious of the thing I've thrust at her. What is she supposed to do with a pen like that? I shrug. Well, that's her business. She'll find some use for it – sell it if she wishes. Or throw it away, I don't care. It crosses my mind to mention Mr Jiang. I'm still curious to know the truth. Were my ears deceiving me when I heard her say that day, 'Mr Jiang said, "Go home"'? But I don't want her to think of this pen as a bribe. I'm not trying to bribe her, just trying to repay a debt. I was probably just hearing things, anyway.

She accepts the pen finally and, clasping it in her palms, joins them to bestow a prayer on me. Head bowed over her fingertips, she mutters, I swear, '*Sabbasatta bhavantu sukhitatta.*' May all beings find happiness.

I return to our table where breakfast is waiting, and take my first sweet sip of the steaming tea as a band tunes up in the distance. Wisps of sound are floating towards us: a flute, a surge of strings. Then a *whoosh* in the air, like a monsoon storm, from cymbals sounding like rain. Unseen musicians are tuning up somewhere, gearing up for the New Year, the new moon festival of Wanting. I love that coppery hiss of the cymbals' clash, the drums' *bom-pah-pah . . . bom-bam-bom.*

One of my minders is wagging his head in time to the teasing music. He's a big fellow, stocky and dark-skinned, with a nervous giggle and a pockmarked face. His hands are accomplished: they look as if they've snapped an irksome neck or two. The other fellow has poured his tea into a saucer and is sucking it up with a kind of grudging relish. He's thin, with a long jaw, and looks lanky when seated. Standing, he's diminished by surprisingly short legs.

'Where are you from?' I ask them.

'Shan state,' they answer in unison.

'What clan?' I say.

'Shan,' says the thin one, proudly.

'Mizo,' says the black bear.

'Mizo! All the way from Assam! Aren't you very far from home?' I knew a Mizo girl once – that's the only reason I know where the Mizo come from.

'Very far,' he agrees, and goes into a fit of giggles.

'And you, Sayama?' says the Shan. I can't help smiling – *Sayama*, meaning lady teacher, is a respectful term for any woman who bears the marks of higher education.

'Wild Lu,' I reply.

The Mizo whistles; the Shan's eyes widen.

'Wild Lu – very strong,' says the Mizo, in English.

'Brave people – very brave,' says the Shan, in Burmese.

I duck my head modestly.

No sign of Minzu, but a pony caravan passes, hoofs clicking, bells jingling, on its way to the same bridge we'll be crossing shortly: the Prosperity Bridge to Burma. The pack animals here seem wholesome specimens: small and sturdy, with good, healthy coats. The packs on these ponies seem very light, consisting mostly of blankets, bedrolls, baskets and pails. I wonder if they're smuggling anything.

I remember a story about a man and his donkey, and decide to share it with my minders to help pass the time while we wait. I wonder what's keeping Minzu.

A man and his donkey ride back and forth through a toll gate, week after week, month after month. Each time the guards go through his saddle-bags thoroughly, but all they ever find is hay. Each time they search the man from head to toe. Nothing. In a fairly short time the donkey-owner has made a lot of money, but nobody knows how he's done it. One day he is sitting in a tea-shop, chatting to an old friend.

'So, are you going to tell me?' says the friend.

'Tell you what?'

'The secret of your wealth?'

'Smuggling,' says the man with the donkey.

'Yes, but what exactly do you smuggle?'

'Donkeys.'

I don't know what made me launch into such an unfunny joke. The Shan shakes his head and grins politely. But then the Mizo starts to laugh and laugh, his face in a helpless contortion. 'I don't get it,' he sputters.

'Then why are you laughing?' says his friend.

'Because . . . because . . . the *sayama* is laughing.'

The Shan looks at his watch and jumps up. 'We have to go! The van will be waiting.'

Yan Ding has arranged for a mini-van to pick us up in Muse, the nearest town on the Burmese side. 'Until then, you're on foot,' he warned me.

'We can't go yet,' I say. 'I have to wait for my friend. She'll be here any minute.' Then I catch sight of her, thank heavens – a clownish figure in red capris. She is waving apologetically as she rushes towards us, lugging a big blue shoulder-bag, which she hoists like a trophy, trying to tell me something.

'Where were you? We're late,' I say, as Minzu's shoulder bag bumps against me.

Her face is flushed; sweat runs down her cheek and beads her upper lip. 'I'm going with you,' she says, looking straight ahead.

'Yes, I know. That's why I was waiting.'

Without breaking her stride, she says, 'I'm going with you. To Burma.'

'What?'

'I have my things.' She pats her bag. 'Also, a letter from my uncle for those – for your men. To tell them to take me along.'

'Wait a minute. Take you along? But what about your family? What about passes, your papers?'

'My family says it's okay. I have another letter from my uncle, for the border guards. They know my uncle. They'll let me through.'

'Minzu, no!' I pull her back by the strap of her bag. 'You can't just . . . They won't just . . .' Insane! The girl is insane. How can I possibly take her with me? She has no idea what it's like on the other side. *I* have no idea. I have enough to worry about.

She trots ahead, pulling me along. 'Come,' she says. 'Don't say anything. It's all okay.'

Suddenly we're at the bridge, and the traffic is in a queue. Lorries, mini-vans, sedan cars, and motorcycles are spewing jets of exhaust in their wake. Bicycle racks are loaded front and back with chickens and infants. Horse carts, bullock carts and pony trains follow their leaders over shit, old and new. The border guards in their grasshopper-green uniforms are striding in and out of their boxes, checking and stamping passes.

At the pedestrian footbridge, too, people are waiting, but the queue is moving faster and our turn is coming up soon. I can see across the bridge to the big hand-painted sign marking the Burmese border: 'NO FURTHER ADVANCE FOR FOREIGN FRIENDS.'

Minzu is already having it out with the Mizo and the Shan. They study the letter she produces, confused and unnerved by this sudden request. In Yunnanese – I assume it's Yunnanese, but I still can't tell – they carry on heatedly, Minzu by turns explaining, insisting and threatening. I keep trying to interrupt, but it's no good, they're in the thick of the argument.

What has possessed the girl? Why is she doing this? I don't want her with me. I can't be responsible for another person. What is she going to do with herself once we reach our destination? The last thing I need is a child to care for, to worry about, to protect. On the other hand . . . would it make such a difference to have another body on the trip? It might even be useful at times. She is, after all, a good-natured girl, and helpful.

'Sayama!' says the Shan. I'm being summoned to the front of the queue. It's our turn already!

I hand over my papers. The guard glances through them without undue interest. He asks me a question, which the Shan answers for me in Chinese. The guard's appraisal of me is wry but not unfriendly. He says something to my minders – they clearly know one another – making them laugh and return some pleasantries. Then he stamps my pass, two quick double-bangs in succession, hands it to me and waves me through.

Minzu is next – the men have hung back reluctantly, letting her go ahead. Immediately I can see there's going to be trouble. The guard takes one look at the pass she's handed him and throws it back at her with a contemptuous flick of the wrist.

Minzu spreads her uncle's letter in front of him and points to the writing. The guard calls one of his colleagues, who reads over his shoulder. Both men shake their heads. No good, they appear to be saying. But Minzu is standing her ground, pointing to the box with the emergency telephone, insisting they make a call.

The guards fold their arms, resolute. The first bites his lip, as though controlling an urge to become violent. The minders weigh in at this point, trying to persuade the men that they can vouch for Minzu.

All at once the second guard loses his temper. He starts yelling and pointing his finger at Minzu. He crosses his wrists to indicate handcuffs. He's threatening arrest if she keeps this up.

Minzu turns towards me, stricken. 'Ma Ma!' she cries, reaching out in panic as though she's being dragged away, though no one has yet laid a hand on her. I signal to the guards my request for permission to step back through the turnstile, to have a word with my distraught friend. They wave me through brusquely, muttering as they resume their checks.

'Minzu, what are you doing?' We're pressed against the wall of the guard-house, hidden from the curious stares of those waiting in line. 'This is not the time for games.'

'I'm not playing games, Ma Ma! I want to come with you because . . . because . . .' She can barely choke out the words.

'Because *what*, Minzu?' The Mizo has poked his head around the corner twice already. Now the Shan appears long enough to tap his watch.

'Because . . . I don't want you to die like Mr Jiang.'

'Oh, Minzu.' How should I comfort her? Pat her shoulder? Take her hand as she took mine to still my fears? I put both arms around her and hug her tightly. 'I'm not going to die like Mr Jiang.'

'I don't know, I don't know. I just had a bad feeling in my mind. You were so sad.'

'But I'm not sad now,' I say, wiping the tears from my cheeks, which makes us both laugh while crying.

'But who will look after you?' she says, sounding quietly practical now. I point in the direction of the Mizo and the Shan. 'They will.'

'No, I mean like a . . . like a . . . sister.'

'You will,' I say. 'But first you have to learn English, or better Burmese, so we can write to each other. Or I have to learn Chinese. What do you think is best?'

She considers this seriously, then says, 'Anguish.'

'Minzu, I have to go now. I *have* to go.'

'But you'll come back, Ma Ma?'

I mustn't lie to her, I mustn't make any promises I can't keep.

'I need to come back, don't I? You still haven't shown me a singing butterfly.'

She's crossed over the footbridge and is on the other side by the time I turn and wave. She waves back with both hands, in a curious way. No, she's showing me something, linking her thumbs and flapping her hands. Ah, I see what it is — butterflies.

I raise my hands high to wave likewise.

She doesn't know what's making me laugh all of a sudden, so I point to the sign behind her. It has two big arrows shooting in opposite directions.

'WANTING', it says under one arrow; 'NOT WANTING' under the other.

She looks up at it but sees nothing unusual. 'What?' she enquires with her palms upturned.

Never mind . . . I am trying to mouth the words and semaphore at the same time. *I'll tell you later!*

Then I turn and cross the line.

acknowledgements

For their help in realising this book, I thank:

My daughter Jocelyn Seagrave Fundoukos, for her one-thousand-and-one readings and uncountable contributions;
David T. K. Wong, generous benefactor and even more generous friend;
Will Schwalbe ('Where there is a Will . . .')
Susanna Lea, agent extraordinaire;
Kerry Glencorse, my London light;
Clara Farmer, for her grace and vision;
Rebecca Carter, whose feather-touch can bend iron.

And special thanks to my husband John. But for his abiding love of books, this one might never have come into being.